KT-459-512

MOONDUST
GEMMA FOWLER

2 PALMER STREET, FROME, SOMERSET BA11 1DS

Text © Lumite Ltd 2017

First published in Great Britain in 2017
Chicken House
2 Palmer Street
Frome, Somerset BA11 1DS
United Kingdom
www.chickenhousebooks.com

Gemma Fowler has asserted her right under the Copyright, Designs and
Patents Act 1988 to be identified as the author of this work.

All rights reserved.
No part of this publication may be reproduced or transmitted or utilized in
any form or by any means, electronic, mechanical, photocopying or
otherwise, without the prior permission of the publisher.

Cover and interior design by Steve Wells
Cover illustration by David Wardle
Typeset by Dorchester Typesetting Group Ltd
Printed and bound in Great Britain by CPI Group (UK) Ltd, Croydon CR0 4YY

The paper used in this Chicken House book is made
from wood grown in sustainable forests.

1 3 5 7 9 10 8 6 4 2

British Library Cataloguing in Publication data available.

PB ISBN 978-1-910655-42-9
eISBN 978-1-911077-33-6

DISCARDED

014163951 X

A MESSAGE FROM CHICKEN HOUSE

On a Moon colony, years in the future, Aggie gazes upon an Earth whose new infinite energy source has a secret and terrible cost. Our funny, clumsy heroine has stumbled across a life-changing, world-changing truth . . . But who is to be trusted? In Gemma Fowler's shadowy, intricate and thrilling debut, we discover a world – and a Moon – torn by the cost of peace.

BARRY CUNNINGHAM
Publisher
Chicken House

To Mum and Dad,
For keeping my feet on the ground,
and my head in the clouds.

Lunar Inc. Base, Civilian Sector
Day-Cycle 02

The Moon has quakes. They were everyday. Part of the routine. Most Lunar Inc. personnel didn't flinch at the sound of the alarm any more. But then, most personnel hadn't been through what Aggie had.

She clung to the edge of her bed as the quake took hold, and listened to the rhythm of her belongings smashing to the floor. Her blinds clattered against the walls, slivers of pale lunar sunlight escaped into the darkness.

She concentrated on pushing her breath into slow ins and outs. But the quake had shaken her memories loose.

They rose up around her in the darkness of her pod like ghosts.

Aggie would relive Adrianne tonight, or not sleep at all. The reactor room started to materialize around her. The phantom smell of smoke and burning metal stung her nose – she pushed it away. Too painful. Too real.

Her heart beat in time with the drone of the alarm. Not the alarm in her pod, but an alarm from a different place, in a different time . . .

The great lumite reactor pulsed – its spinning saltwater jets cooling the violet crystal at its core. Her father was at his desk, his hands a blur as he worked the shaking control panel. Something was wrong. There was too much dust, too much heat—

In her pod, the screen beside her bed flicked on, casting grey light into the room. 'No, no, no,' Aggie moaned.

When he saw her, his eyes grew as wild as his red hair. His grip tight and feverish on her arms as he threw her into the clear plastic booth and pulled the hatch. 'Daddy?' He was getting in with her, wasn't he? He wasn't going back to the reactor, was he?

Outside, in the corridor, the other Lunar Inc. personnel whooped and hollered as they made their way to their shifts, the quake providing nothing more than entertainment for their commute. But Adrianne refused to let Aggie go. Not yet. Not until the part that hurt the most . . .

Her breath fogged the wet glass inside the booth; the hot, thick air sticking like glue in her lungs; the rush of water, the shudder of the reactor room rattling her bones away from her skin—

'Hey Agatha.' A strangely detached voice shook from the ceiling, but to Aggie it was distant, underwater, far away—

There was a click, then a popping noise that sucked up all the sound. Suddenly, she was flying . . . She squeezed her eyes shut as a blinding light washed into her small, dark space.

'Hey Agatha,' the voice echoed again, 'your heart rate is currently out of the healthy spectrum.' This time, Aggie clung to the sound, using it to pull her foggy brain back to reality.

'*No!*'

Aggie opened her eyes. She was standing in the centre of her room, covered in sweat, panting. She took a deep, shuddering breath and fell back onto the damp sheets.

It's not happening again. You're safe. You're safe.

Above her head, the small red light of the Eye camera danced in the rumbling darkness.

'Hey Agatha,' the voice rang out once more, 'we're experiencing a routine moonquake in this sector.'

It was Celeste, the base's computer system, speaking from the swirling Ether panel beside her bed. The billion electrified atoms that made up the computer's shifting 3D interface swirled back at her creepily. It always looked to Aggie as if someone had trapped a black hole in a tiny picture frame – a really annoying black hole.

Celeste was the AI system that ran the entire Lunar Base, from operating the giant, gravity-producing domes that kept their feet on the ground, right down to assessing whether you'd had the right amount of vegetables in your lunch. Celeste's eerie, spinning Ethers and black and red Eye cameras were everywhere on the base. Wherever you looked, Celeste was there looking back. The AI was designed to be a happy, positive and supportive influence on the personnel; Aggie just found her a bit creepy.

'For your information, Agatha, the time is currently 6.15 a.m., Lunar East. Your shift begins in fifteen minutes.'

'Thanks,' Aggie muttered, as the mattress went from a shake to a dull simmer and finally became still. The quake was over, but despite her best efforts, Aggie's heart continued to flap pathetically inside her like a frightened bird.

'How about we try some calming breathing exercises?'

'I know how to breathe, Celeste,' she said to the ceiling.

Aggie leant up on her elbows and surveyed the damage to her room; pillows and blankets lay in jumbled heaps around her bed, the old paper books and rocks she'd smuggled up to the Moon from Earth had sprung from her shelves and lay in heaps on the white plastic floor. To her left, a bottle of something that was probably noxious had spilt and was slowly oozing into a puddle under her bed. She silently hoped it wasn't one of the botched toilet water samples she'd hidden under there a few weeks ago. Though it smelt as if it might be.

Aggie sighed. To be honest, her room didn't look that much different from the way it usually did.

She rubbed the sleep from her eyes and pulled herself up.

At the first sign of movement the blinds on her round pod window began to lift, allowing crisp, cold sunlight to flood into the room. Aggie lifted her arm to her eyes.

'No, Celeste! Earth's sake, I'm awake!' she grumbled.

The surface was at the start of its day-cycle – days and nights lasted two Earth weeks on the Moon. The light was faded after the wane, but still stronger than the soft, atmosphere-filtered sun on Earth, and it was just too much at this time in the morning.

Outside, the lunar surface lay like a great tan and grey desert, broken up by a cluster of squat buildings that made up the Lunar Base's Civilian Sector. Not a great view, but if she pressed her cheek right against the glass, Aggie could just make out the glittering cathedral of the Whole Earth Complex, its great rainbow-coloured windows pointing towards the patch of space where the whole distant Earth hung like a marble.

Aggie's pod was part of the messy sprawl of science blocks and dorms which housed all the civilian personnel: surface analysts, astro-geologists, lunar chemists, security guards, management and lifestyle staff, medics, mining operatives, tech engineers, mechanical engineers, admin personnel and all the others Aggie couldn't remember.

Beyond the Lunar Base and spreading out to the horizon were the vast white mining domes and low red buildings of the Prison Sector, where prisoners mined and processed the lumite crystal that powered the Earth. No one from Civilian ever went there, unless you were a guard, or a mine op, or an engineer, or just mental.

'OK, Agatha,' said Celeste, 'please run your diagnostics. I've noticed that your sleeping patterns are currently out of the healthy spectrum. My psychological analysis systems would suggest this is the result of the upcoming tenth anniversary of the Adrianne—'

'Not now, Celeste.'

'Disrupted sleep encourages disease, Agatha.'

Aggie looked at the Ether uneasily and walked to the mirror.

What she saw made her want to get back in bed. Thick red curls stuck up on one side of her head and lay flat on the other. She pulled her StraightBrush from the wall and ran it through them quickly.

'Hey Agatha, I must remind you to—'

'In a minute,' she spat, hairpins sticking in her mouth as she tried to pull her newly straightened hair into the standard Lunar Inc. bun – not easy with trembling hands. 'Just one minute.'

Why did the moonquakes have to do this to her every time? Adrianne was ten years ago. Ten years – and her flashbacks had only got worse. She cursed herself for being so weak.

Her hair roughly bunned, Aggie popped two tiny blue plastic circles from the container beside her bed. She sighed and placed the blue contact lenses over her violet eyes. She blinked away the water and took a step back. She was finally starting to look like herself – or the version of herself she had become after the disaster.

The thick geometric panelling on her canary-yellow Lunar Inc. overalls emphasized any unwanted lumps and bumps beneath, and the colour clashed horribly with her red hair. It wasn't a great look, but it was safe. She looked just like everyone else. Anonymous.

Still, Aggie pulled the sleeves self-consciously, covering up the shiny skin showing through at her wrists. Not scars exactly, but the side effects of the nano-healers that had saved her after the explosion.

Her identification lamp shone in the centre of her chest, pulsing a soft, yellow light with the beat of her heart. Silver, semi-opaque comms panels were located on her forearms, their flexible screens glowing in sleep mode.

'Hey Agatha—'

'I'm here, I'm here!' Aggie stepped back to the side of her bed, flipped her forearm over Celeste's Ether screen and sat back to wait. A tiny 3D graph appeared out of the black-grey swirl as Celeste inputted her data.

'Great, diagnostics completed. I have updated your health alerts to level six, a priority level.'

With a familiar hiss, the locks on the pod door released. Aggie was free to leave.

'Stay bright, Agatha.'

'You stay bright too, Celeste,' she muttered as she made her way into the corridor, the quake still rumbling away in the back of her mind.

The bustle of personnel in the corridor only renewed the fluttering in Aggie's chest and she had to stop and take a few deep breaths. She'd never liked crowds, but she'd got used to the familiar multicoloured, dead-eyed commuter traffic on the base. Not this morning though, apparently. She leant against the curved wall and checked for the ridge of her contact lenses under her eyelids. She hated getting flustered – it drew people's attention.

Pull yourself together, she told herself harshly. No need to panic. No one knew who she was.

She began to weave her way through the busy corridor. Now if someone could just tell her heart that everything was normal, that would be cosmic.

'Hey, watch it!' a green-overalled geologist cried as she accidentally whacked him with her shoulder.

'Sorry! It's busy in here,' she said, looking down, avoiding his eyes.

As she turned the corner she spied the white LED outline of a security scrambler ahead – one of the fat-wheeled, dual-gravity scooters that looked like the love child of a three-wheeled trike and a golf cart. A familiar figure was in the driving seat.

Aggie's heart skipped. Instantly, the tight feeling the quake had given her melted away into the crowds. She grinned and rushed forwards. Creeping up behind the scrambler, she jabbed the figure sharply in the back of his black overalls.

'Oh, hey there Earthling!'

The guard let out a noise like a boiling kettle and jumped a mile into the air. The coffee in his hand leapt out of the cup and cascaded down his overall.

'Ow, ow, it's hot! Oh, it's burning. It burns,' he spluttered.

'Ooh no, Seb!' Aggie cried. 'I didn't see. Here, let me help.'

'It's on my skin. It's burning my skin!'

'Ah! Hold still.'

Aggie swung herself up into the passenger seat and

began to flick the coffee off his overall and out of his frizzy brown curls. The globs flew towards the control panel, fizzing and sputtering onto the swirling black of the Ether.

'Hey Sebastian,' Celeste's voice drifted up from the controls, 'there seems to be liquid contamination on this scrambler. Please wait a moment while I reconfigure the system.'

'Aw, man, look what you've done, Aggs!' Seb wailed. 'Third-degree burns and a system reconfigure, all in less than five minutes!'

'I'm sorry! I was trying to help. Who holds a coffee when they're driving a scrambler anyway? You know what I'm like!'

Seb's eyes widened. 'I got it for you! I hate this SimStim stuff. I just wanted to have a proper conversation without you being all grumpy. Wish I hadn't now, though – look at me!'

Aggie looked at Seb fondly. 'Aw, did you really? Thank you,' she said, leaning forwards to give her friend a squeeze. Suddenly her horrible morning didn't seem so bad any more. Seb's easy Californian aura always had that effect on her. He was like a human happy pill.

Aggie grabbed the SimStim and sipped on what was left. It tasted a bit like soil, but it was better than nothing.

'So, how was it?'

'What?'

'Your leave, you black hole. Earth! How was it? Tell me.'

Seb put the scrambler in gear, 'Oh, OK.'

Aggie raised her eyebrows. 'Aaand?'

'Aggie, it was forced leave, I wasn't having fun. I didn't even want to be there.'

Aggie let her mouth fall open theatrically.

Seb glanced at her, smiling. 'I dunno, what do you want me to say? There was some lovely clean air.'

'Wow, so insightful.'

'Aggs, it was boring. I dunno, they brought back this animal called a tiger from extinction. That looked cool, but I only saw it on the news so, not really news or anything . . . They've finally finished the Hyperloop between the New South American state . . .'

Aggie shook her head. She loved the Earth. She'd give anything to be able to go back, feel the wind in her hair and the smell of plants and trees – the Lunar Base had been her home for two years now, but she missed the nature of Earth almost as much as she'd missed Seb these past two weeks. She guessed you always wanted what you could never have.

'C'mon,' Seb said, grinning, 'you know I'd rather be here. I'm not like you. I'm built for space.'

Aggie laughed. Seb was allergic to everything on Earth: flowers, trees, certain types of wood, gluten. If it was natural, it was out to get him. The manufactured world of Lunar Inc. suited him perfectly.

'Stupid rock,' he added sulkily.

Aggie smiled. 'Hey, you can't blame the rock. The rock didn't put the base into level one shutdown, did it?'

Seb put his head in his hands and groaned. 'Ugh, no I guess not.'

'And we all know aliens don't exist.'

Seb half smiled, 'Hey, that rock looked a lot like an alien, in my defence. I swear it moved.'

Aggie shot Seb a look.

'OK, OK, also in my defence, and this is what I told the disciplinary dudes too, you've not even seen the Border-lands, man. It's not like the Near Side at all. There are rocks everywhere, they're all crazy shapes and all these creepy shadows and you're all on your own. There are noises, Aggs, I swear, like creaking, wooing . . .'

'You don't get noises like that on the Moon . . .'

'Well, I'm telling you: that place, it does weird things to your head.'

Aggie nudged Seb playfully. 'How long was the base in shutdown again – seventeen hours? Or was it eighteen?'

'Enough!' Seb laughed and kicked the scrambler up a gear as it came back online.

They left the white corridors of the dorms and entered the migraine-inducing yellow of the Analysis Department.

'Sorry about the coffee,' Aggie said, putting her head on Seb's shoulder as they drove. 'It's been boring without you.'

Seb patted her head. 'Aw, I know.'

A bleeping noise high overhead signalled the start of the morning shift, and the yellow corridor started to fill with personnel. Aggie looked at them nervously, but the best friend and coffee mix had been like a medicine and she felt a bit better. Seb stopped the scrambler right outside the doors to Aggie's department.

'Lunch, tomorrow?' he called from the driving seat. 'By the custard?'

Aggie nodded and waved as Seb disappeared into the throng.

She fumbled with her fringe in front of the retina scanner. It buzzed negative three times. Aggie blinked her contacts into the right place and was finally allowed through into the cold rush of her quiet, sterile world: Domestic Analysis 1.

2

Day-Cycle 02

Aggie passed through the two small airlock doors and into the Domestic labs. They were some of the oldest on the base and were part subterranean, which meant that the only daylight came in through tiny Plexiglas panels in the ceilings. The yellow walls were scratched and peeling at the edges.

As one of the least respected sciences on the base, Domestic Analysis was also constantly losing its equipment to the other departments. Aggie rolled her eyes as she noticed an empty spot against the wall where their main sampling booth had stood when she left on Friday. No doubt Professor Spooner had had it shipped off to the fancy new Surface Analysis suite in Sector B.

She wasn't exactly surprised; Domestic Analysis had a soulless, zombie-like workforce of Lunar Academy dropouts and flunked trainees, sentenced to a life of air-quality checks and toilet water sampling. Most personnel on the base didn't even know that her department existed, which was exactly why Aggie had decided to work here. Well, and the fact that she was completely useless at everything else.

As she made her usual beeline for the breakfast vending machine, Aggie noticed that something was different in the labs today. It was only after she'd swiped her Blipcard on the reader and the machine had spat out her freeze-dried peanut-mallow protein bar that she'd figured it out. It was quiet. Funeral home quiet. Aggie could actually hear the shuffle of her bulky surface boots as she made her way along the row of desks to her own.

She checked her contacts again nervously. No, it wasn't that. But what?

She noticed a group of girls whispering and glancing at her from behind their screens, and a familiar feeling of dread swept over her. What had she done wrong this time? She winced at the memory of a previous incident with over-acidic toilet water. Aggie had never really tried to make friends with the other Domestic personnel, but she'd made herself even more unpopular that day. Some of the staff in E Sector still couldn't sit down.

She walked up to her desk uneasily, placed her breakfast

down amid her bombsite of paper printouts and sampling tubes, and slowly began to unearth her Ether screen. Her desk was an abomination, a state of organized chaos that opened a small window into the way Aggie lived her life. Basically, like a mess.

As she moved a pile of sodium readouts, something slipped off the side and clattered loudly to the floor. The sound was deafening in the unusual silence. Aggie looked around at her colleagues and mouthed a theatrical, 'Oooops!' in their direction. Mo, who sat next to her, just rolled his eyes and slunk back down behind his screen. Not even a 'tut' of disapproval from Mo? What on Earth was going on?

She bent down and picked up the offending item. It was the broken mineral depositor she'd hidden under there on Friday. The magnetic cap was stuck in 'on' mode, making it impossible to get the tiny air con filter sample out of it. Not wanting to go and see Professor Spooner about another breakage, Aggie stuffed it into her overall pocket so she could stash it under her bed later. Out of sight, out of mind.

'Agatha?'

Aggie jumped. Astrid was calling to her from behind a nearby sample booth. Aggie instantly turned her attention to an evacuation poster on the opposite wall and pretended not to hear her.

'Agatha? Hellloooo, base to Agatha? Are you reading me?'

Aggie took a bite of her bar and made a show of pretending to notice her.

Astrid giggled, 'Aah, Agatha! Houston, I think we have a problem.'

'Oh, hey Astrid. It's early. What's going on?'

Astrid was fresh from the Lunar Academy, and Aggie had been assigned as her mentor. All of the younger personnel had mentees, and despite her protests, it had been decided Aggie should have one too – it would draw more attention to her if she didn't.

Astrid was a proper Lunar Inc. geek and hung on Aggie's every word. The intern made Aggie nervous. The last thing she needed was someone following her around, asking an endless stream of questions. But Astrid's enthusiasm was proving to be stronger than nano-fibre. Aggie often thought that if Astrid ever found out who she really was, the shock might kill her.

Astrid pointed to the corridor. 'Look. Look!'

Aggie followed her gaze to the glass doors that separated Spooner's office from the labs and saw two sky-blue-overalled guards flanking the entrance. Guards wearing sky blue instead of black could mean only one thing.

Astrid took an excited breath, confirming Aggie's suspicions. 'Aggie, it's *him.*'

The doors swished open and a skinny, hook-nosed man skittered out into the labs. He looked around for a second before spotting Aggie. As his beady eyes focused on her, her heart stopped.

'Ah! Agatha, there you are,' Professor Spooner snarled. 'Only thity minutes late today, quite the achievement. Thank the Earth that today was the day the *commander* decided to pay us a visit, Earth knows why.' He gestured with a gnarled hand for her to follow him. 'Maybe the shuttle is finally ready for you; Earth knows how often I've suggested it.'

Beside her, Astrid made a noise like the emergency warning siren. The shuttle the professor was referring too was the Shuttle of Shame, the transit shuttle that took misbehaving members of Lunar Inc. staff on a one-way trip back to Earth. Aggie forced a smile and followed the professor, her heart pounding in her chest for the second time this morning, and it wasn't even 7 a.m.

Giant portraits of the god-like Founding Five stared down at Aggie from the walls of the corridor leading to the professor's office. These were the legendary men and women who discovered lumite power. The people that had united the Earth.

She couldn't look at the painting obscured by shadows at the end of the row. Her father's youthful face gazed out against the backdrop of the colossal lumite reactor he had invented. She pushed away the familiar urge to rip the painting down, and turned to the largest of the five, the one that hung over the doorway to Spooner's office.

Adam Faulkner, the newly retired CEO of Lunar Inc. and the man who'd brought her up as his own. His grey eyes sparkled, even in paint. He held the tiny lumite cell – his invention that had single-handedly saved the world from the energy crisis. Aggie felt a sudden flush of pride. She straightened her shoulders and walked past Spooner and the guards into the office.

The doors snapped closed behind her, cutting the professor off. But it didn't stop Aggie picking up his whining voice through the glass. 'A liability, that girl. I've always said it. I'm surprised it's taken this long.'

A man was standing on the far side of the glass-walled room, staring out at the base. He was dressed in a sky-blue Tranquillity overall. The only indication of his high rank were the lumite violet badges on the arms and shoulders – this man's rank was the highest of them all.

Aggie's breath caught. She found it hard to believe that he'd come all the way to Domestic just to pay her a visit.

Roger Rix was an important man.

Slowly, Rix turned and smiled.

'How are you doing, Aggie?' he said brightly and gestured for her to join him by the window.

Aggie shuffled her feet. She'd known the commander for most of her life; he was the man her godfather had charged with engineering her disappearance. The only person on the base who knew. But despite that, Aggie always felt as if Rix was behind glass. Distant.

As Aggie approached him she instantly felt huge. Rix had the slouched, fidgety energy of a first-year from the Academy. The faded geometric tattoo on his cheek was the only indication of his past in the gangs of the Dark Days: a past her godfather had saved him from, a past that, despite Rix's small frame, had earnt him a fierce reputation on the base.

'So,' Rix continued, 'are you going to tell me? Or shall I start guessing?'

Aggie was confused, 'I, er . . .' She could feel the broken mineral depositor in her pocket.

'About how you're doing?' Rix prompted with a smile.

'Oh right. Yeah. That should be easy,' Aggie said, laughing nervously.

Rix had the usual mixed-up accent of the United Earth, but with the clipped tones of the African territories. His words came out with sharp edges.

She took a deep breath; she hated questions about work. She'd always been so bad at science. It was a constant embarrassment, especially after her godfather and Rix had done so much to hide her away. Adam Faulkner had expected her to have at least some of her father's head for physics, but all she had showed so far was a fantastic ability to break stuff. Expensive stuff, mainly.

'I, er . . . we stopped a CO leak in one of the Medical Centre vents last month. I, well, I mean, the maintenance team stopped it, really, but we noticed a spike in the—'

'Well, that's great, Aggie, really great.'

'Well, it's not usually that exciting down in Dom—'

'Thing is, Aggie,' the commander said, cutting her off. 'The thing is, we're still fighting, that's the truth. Until the next generation, there will always be a fight.'

Aggie didn't have a clue what he was talking about. But instead of letting on and looking stupid, she nodded knowingly, following his gaze out of the windows and onto the sprawling base beyond.

'These are difficult times for that fight, and it's important that we're doing everything we can to put an end to the possibility that we might lose.'

Now Aggie was really confused. Had she missed something? Were they at war again? Surely not, there hadn't been a war on Earth in her lifetime, not since the discovery of lumite twenty years ago; when the countries of the Earth signed the United Earth Treaty and became a peaceful planet.

Rix waved a hand at her dismissively, 'Oh, you wouldn't remember, you were too young. But I'm telling you, the days after Adrianne were almost as dark as the ones before it.'

Aggie froze.

Rix was talking about Adrianne, the disaster that had given her her lumite violet eyes and her fame. The disaster that killed her father and changed her life forever. The disaster that her treacherous brain refused to let her forget.

'A society without hope isn't a society at all,' Rix continued, taking a bright blue protein pack out of his overall and tearing it open with his teeth.

Aggie still couldn't move. The last thing she wanted or needed was to reminisce about that day. In all the years she'd known him, Rix had never even mentioned it before now.

The commander stared at her, scrutinizing her face while sucking on his drink loudly. It made the pale lines of his tattoo pull and sag.

'See, you can't have that many people die and ignore it.

But we never tried to hide it, did we? We faced it, your godfather and I. We stood up and we took it head on.'

He flicked his hair from his eyes. When he looked back, they were on fire.

'There will always be opposition ready to poison people to think another way. Terrorists. Non-believers inside the United Government . . .' He shook his head. 'Whatever we do, Aggie, there'll always be someone out there who would risk going back to how it was before. Going back to the dark and the violence, all for some crazy twisted moral. You heard about Tokyo, right?'

Aggie shook her head.

'Oh well, get ready, the whole base will be talking about it by tomorrow. People are finding it too easy to forget what lumite has brought to our planet: cheap power, fresh air, regenerated climate, no war . . .' Rix paused. 'Ten years of progress. And still FALL are intent on destroying it. Destroying us. The tenth anniversary of Adrianne has lit the touchpaper. Now it's only a matter of time before they hit us hard.'

Aggie reeled. FALL stood for the First Anti-Lumite League, though no one ever cared what the letters stood for any more, thanks to the group's love of violence. Aggie hated FALL: they were extremists, they didn't care who got hurt or what damage they did, as long as they destroyed something Adam Faulkner and Lunar Inc. had created. FALL pretended to be political, that their goal was to sit beside the ministers in the United Forum, but everyone knew they were just another gang left over from the Dark Days.

Rix looked back out of the windows. 'The timing is terrible, with the cell recall in India, the problems with the quotas on B Face – we're losing control . . .'

He turned back to Aggie and gestured to the chairs, jumping into the nearest one. 'So,' he said, his tone suddenly brighter, 'how about it?'

Aggie sat down opposite him. 'Wh-what?'

Rix leant forwards. Aggie could smell the protein pack on his breath. Blueberry.

'How about we fight back? Fight the terrorist propaganda with some propaganda of our own. Show the people of the United Earth that lumite is strong.'

'I don't understand . . .'

'Ah c'mon, Aggie. Did you really think you could spend your whole life hiding behind a new last name and a pair of blue contact lenses?'

Aggie's heart stopped. Rix grinned.

'When FALL feed the people their poison, you are our only antidote. The world can't listen to terrorists. It just cannot. It needs its Angel back.'

Aggie felt as if the world was starting to collapse around her. She couldn't go back. She couldn't be the Angel again.

Camera flashes, crowds of people chanting her name, hot studio lights, strangers reaching out, touching her with desperate, clammy hands . . .

'You need save them again, Aggie,' Rix continued. 'Just like you did after the explosion, that's all.'

It was crazy.

'Roger— Sorry, Commander, I can't—'

'It's a lot to take in.' Rix nodded. 'I get that, but what did you think would happen? Really? Your whole life is a lie, Aggie. The truth is going to slip out sooner or later . . . You can't work in Domestic Analysis forever.'

Aggie tried to control her breathing. 'But, it's been so long . . .'

Rix rubbed his temples. He was losing his patience. 'G Face opens next month,' he said sharply, 'It's going to be the biggest face in the mine. The new, shining diamond in Lunar Inc.'s crown.' He bent further towards her, fidgeting in his chair. 'We're going to launch it with a show like nothing the United Earth has ever seen. Show the non-believers that – anniversary of Adrianne or not – the future of lumite is bright.'

Rix's eyes flicked over Aggie's face.

'See, Aggie, your daddy—'

There it was. Aggie felt as if someone was scrunching her stomach into a ball.

'He was a good man,' Rix went on, getting more animated with each word. 'A good scientist. I owe him. Adam owes him. Hell, everyone on that big ball of blue down there owes him. But they just don't want to know it.'

Aggie squirmed in her seat, fighting the urge to run out of the room.

'He brought all this into being. His brain. His science. If it weren't for your daddy we'd all still be fighting in the dark like animals. Now, I know that, but there's no point saying that to anyone on terra firma. He made a mistake, he rushed through the safety tests to make the Switch On deadline. He took a risk, yes he did, and when that reactor exploded he paid for it with his life, and the lives of thousands of others.'

Aggie winced.

'Down there,' Rix continued, 'there's a lot of hate, and FALL are using it to destroy us.'

Rix clenched his teeth as he talked, his knees bounced up and down. Aggie just felt sick.

'But what those people down there need isn't a reminder of his mistake. They need reassurance. We need to remind them that Adrianne was a one off. And it will never, ever, happen again. We need to let them know that every one of their precious sons and daughters out there on our base is protected, and that they're protected down there, in their little lumite-powered lives.

'We'll never forget that day, for sure, but we've learnt from your daddy's mistake – no more reactors, just the cells. Production here, away from the Earth – and we've used what we learnt to make lumite power stronger.'

It was all getting too much for Aggie now, 'Please, Roger, I just—'

Rix moved closer, so he was almost crouching at her feet. He tilted her chin, forcing her to look at him. 'You got to get used to talking again, little Angel. The tenth anniversary of Adrianne is only a few weeks away. I know you haven't forgotten. Celeste shows me your sleep records. It's a tough time for all of us, but I've got to show everyone that everything is good. Only the Angel can distract them from whatever FALL have planned. You get that, right?'

Aggie nodded.

'And what that means?'

Aggie stared at Rix, terror whirling inside her. 'I'm sorry.'

The commander bounced back to his feet and pulled another pack from his overall. 'Hey, I don't need you to be sorry,' he said, checking himself in the mirror. Aggie caught Rix's pale eye in his reflection.

'I need you to make up for it,' he said, 'for what your daddy did.'

Aggie looked away.

'For ten years we've hidden you. I've given you everything you ever wanted. I've kept you safe, haven't I? Now, all I'm asking for is a little payment. You understand?'

Aggie didn't respond.

'I'll take that as a yes,' he said, stepping towards the door. 'So, it's time to get you out there. Get a bit of moondust on your overall. The G Face opening party is the show, but as long as FALL are gunning for us, Lunar Inc. is gonna need its Angel.'

He made his way to the door, where Professor Spooner still lingered. 'A team from Earth Relations will contact you.' He pointed to Aggie's eyes. 'Keep them blue, for now. Until the party we act as if nothing's changed. Don't want our little secret getting out before the big day, hey?'

Aggie nodded.

'Stay bright, Angel.' Rix smiled and disappeared down the corridor, followed by his security.

Only the faint sickly smell of protein packs indicated

that Rix had ever been in the office.

Aggie sat for a moment and tried to calm her breathing. *Bring back the Angel? Be the Angel of Adrianne again after ten years?*

Aggie almost laughed. During her two years on the base she'd grown more confident, more assured that her disguise was working. But there was always that fear in the back of her mind. That all it would take was one slip of a lens, or one over-curious friend to blow it all apart.

Now she guessed that Rix had been planning to blow it apart all along.

Over the years Aggie had stupidly believed that Rix had had her best interests at heart, that he was following her godfather's orders, nothing else. But really, Aggie wasn't a Lunar Inc. employee, she was company property.

She took a deep, shuddering breath and looked out of the window – at the great rainbow-hued Whole Earth Complex which shone in the centre of the base. Aggie loved this place. The Moon was her home, her sanctuary, her whole life. And with a few words, Rix had just destroyed it all.

3

Day-Cycle 03

Aggie pressed her forehead against the cool shuttle window. The commuter shuttles were super-fast maglev trains that sped across the base through a raised network of clear Plexiglas tunnels. They had some of the best views on the surface, but today Aggie didn't care.

After Rix had dropped the Angel bombshell in Spooner's office, Aggie had been escorted to her pod and told to wait for her orders. The orders had arrived the next morning in the form of an incredibly early wake-up call from Celeste.

Rix's plan, as Aggie understood it, was simple: her

colleagues in Domestic had been told that she'd been transferred to the new Surface Analysis suite in Sector B. It was an insane cover story – Aggie was by far the most incompetent person ever to grace the underground hovel of Domestic – but it meant she got to keep her yellow overall and her anonymity . . . for now.

She sighed and closed her eyes. Last night her Adrianne nightmares had been worse than ever and the nervous energy that was currently fizzing through her body was just exhausting. She felt as if she needed a week of sleep, not the 'Exciting Tour of G Face' that had just been put into her personal schedule by someone called Mir-from-Earth-Relations.

Aggie checked the schedule on the comms unit on her forearm again.

Mir-from-Earth-Relations.

Aggie wondered if she was named after the old space station. Her file listed her father as a cosmonaut in New Russia, so it sort of made sense. The thought of asking her that, of engaging the girl in some sort of normal conversation, made sweat erupt on her palms.

Mir-from-Earth-Relations knew.

Someone else knew.

It was exciting and terrifying in equal measure.

The shuttle shuddered, making Aggie's forehead bounce off the glass. She looked around and caught the understanding eyebrows of a blue-clad tech head in the opposite seat. She turned away quickly, scrunching herself deeper into the corner.

Out of the window, the bright colours of the Civilian Sector started to slip away and were replaced by dusty white mining domes, dirty red tunnels and huge tangles of evil-looking mining equipment.

The Prison Sector.

Not just the Prison Sector, but the furthest reaches of the Lunar Base itself. The new G Face was built right at the end of the shuttle line, where the Earth-facing Near Side disappeared into first the Borderlands and then the restricted Far Side.

Aggie had never been into the Prison Sector before, let alone this lonely, dusty outpost. She'd always wanted to explore the Moon, to get out and see this strange alien world where they lived, but Lunar Inc. was usually strict about its borders. For obvious reasons, really, given that the place was crawling with prisoners.

'Last stop, lady,' a gruff voice boomed above her, 'If ya don't move you'll wake up in the depot. Gotta be quick.'

Aggie glanced up and saw a squat engineer in a dusty orange overall grinning at her as he held the shuttle doors open.

'Good job you're so yellow, otherwise I wouldn't a seen ya there.'

The shuttle doors whined as he held them. Aggie got up from her seat and stumbled past him out onto the platform.

The engineer laughed at her face. 'Not what you was expecting, ay? That makes two of us, then.'

A temporary roof had been inflated over the magnetic

track, and the curve of clear plastic bubbles was their only protection from the Moon's atmosphere beyond. The ground beneath her surface boots was rocky and littered with bits of discarded machinery and materials.

'Analysis?' The man asked from beneath his dust-crusted helmet.

Aggie nodded and looked away.

'Lucky you. This face is gonna be the easiest ride of your whole shift. Been here eighteen days already, ain't seen nothing but moon rock.'

Aggie followed the engineer along the platform to where a gaggle of black-overalled guards, mine ops in white and engineers in orange were queuing at a set of huge airlocks that led into the half-built dome of G Face.

The prisoners didn't use the airlocks, she remembered from some distant training session. They were housed in inflatable habitats – habs – tucked inside the domes themselves. No one wearing a red overall had any reason to leave their face during their lunar rehabilitation. Aggie had never even seen a Lunar Inc. prisoner up close, and she hoped to keep it that way.

Aggie tucked into the back of the queue and looked up at the giant Eye that hung from the top of the gate. Its red iris flickered this way and that, scanning every set of eyes that passed under it and entered the airlocks.

When the red light paused over her, Aggie shivered; there was something horribly human about the way it looked at her.

'Next.' The clipped tone of the guard at the gate

made her jump.

She hurried forwards into the nearest airlock and felt her overall click. The dual-gravity suits automatically re-adjusted to surface conditions as you stepped through any gate, the thin mesh exoskeleton hidden in the fabric becoming rigid and the helmet and visor unfolding from their casing inside the collar.

As the first set of airlock doors closed behind her with a soft thud, Aggie peered out at the face, trying to get a better look at what lay beyond. It was a distraction technique she'd learnt during her countless counselling sessions. Ever since Adrianne, Aggie had never been comfortable in small, confined spaces, especially see-through ones.

'Hey Agatha,' Celeste said from the Ether on the wall. 'Did you know that due to our increased construction schedule, the G Face now has a fully stable Earth environment?'

Aggie shook her head. The computer loved to tell her pointless facts.

'That means you are no longer required to wear a helmet and visor on the face.'

'That's cosmic, Celeste.'

'OK, Agatha.'

A rush of air erupted from below her feet. Then stopped. The lights in the airlock flicked to red.

'One moment, please.'

Aggie looked around; she couldn't see anything that looked wrong. Panic crept over her skin. 'Celeste?'

The computer didn't reply.

The thick Plexiglas walls of the airlock started to constrict around Aggie. The air coming into the airlock suddenly felt thick and syrupy.

'Celeste!' She choked.

There was dust. Heat. Her father's face pressed against the glass, tears behind his glasses, red lights, the drone of the alarm—

'Hey Agatha.' The Ether swirled. 'The G Face systems are experiencing some operational problems this morning.'

The red light went out. There was a rush of cool air, and Aggie felt the floor vibrate as the airlock doors began to open.

'Lunar Incorporated apologizes for any inconvenience.'

Aggie shook herself and stepped shakily out of the airlock.

'Stay bright, Agatha,' Celeste said, before the doors whipped shut.

The air on the other side of the airlock was thick with dust. Aggie stopped and sucked great mouthfuls of it, trying to calm herself down. She was just being a black hole. It was an airlock, the safest place in the world.

A stream of orange- and black-dressed personnel were starting to make their way through the airlock now with no problem, smiling and chatting to the Ether as they passed. Why couldn't she be like them? Some Angel of Adrianne she was going to be. She couldn't stay cool if she tried.

Aggie re-joined the queue of personnel who were walking down the rocky trail towards the mine. She fanned her face and took long dusty breaths. The last thing she wanted was for Mir-from-Earth-Relations to think she was weak.

'Agatha?' a voice suddenly permeated the dust beside

her. A female voice, with an accent that sounded New Russian. Aggie cast around her and spotted a sky-blue outline a few metres away.

'Yes?' she shouted to the figure, tripping over a rock and coming skidding to a halt by a pair of perfectly shiny blue surface boots. She straightened up and found herself face to face with a pretty girl who must have been Mir-from-Earth-Relations.

Mir-from-Earth-Relations blinked, twice.

Not one hair was out of place on Mir's head, not one scrap of dust was visible on her overall. Aggie had been on the face for five minutes and already her overall was caked with grime.

'Agatha?' Mir asked again, looking her up and down.

'Reporting for duty,' Aggie said with a nervous laugh, patting her overall down self-consciously. She realized the trip had made her hair come loose, her bun was now dangling somewhere behind her left ear. With the dust and hair and panicky red face from the airlock, she must have looked like a clown.

Mir's green eyes shone against her dark skin as Aggie struggled to pull her unruly hair back into its tie.

'Agatha Sommers?' Mir repeated, glancing down at her forearm to check her notes.

Aggie smiled. 'The one and only.'

Mir continued to look puzzled. The silence had started to get awkward.

'I can take my contacts out if you like.'

Mir jumped. 'Earth, no!'

'Oh no, it was a joke. I was joking! I couldn't take them out here, anyway, with all the dust and grit. And, you know, gloves. It'd—' Aggie stopped when she saw Mir's face.

'OK,' Mir said with a quick glance at the top of Aggie's head. 'Let's go, shall we?'

Without saying anything else, the girl strode away into the depths of the mine. Aggie grimaced. That had not gone well. She'd never really tried it before, but making new friends clearly wasn't her thing.

Eventually Mir led Aggie onto the face and suddenly Aggie forgot about everything else. She had never seen the inside of a mining dome before. It knocked all the breath out of her.

The face that spread out before her was a dirty, clanging maelstrom of machinery, sweat and noise. Under the glowing white of the gravity dome, it stretched for miles in every direction, the edges fading away into a flurry of dust and activity.

Everywhere she looked, white, black, red and orange specks crawled over lumps of rock and machinery. Dust plumed from machines as they ground the moon rock with giant metal teeth, sending chunks cascading down into some unseen tunnel network that connected the faces to the underground lumite-processing plant. Spider-like builder machines crawled on the inside of the white dome, slowly stretching nano-fabric panels over the complex valves and ducts of the gravity generators that pumped and whirred, busily keeping the personnel's feet on the ground as they worked.

Aggie stood still for a long while, just taking it all in. She was amazed by G Face, by the scale of it, by the productivity inside it. Lumite was literally keeping the world running. A rush of pride washed over her with such force that she felt giddy. This was her godfather's achievement.

'Follow me, please, Agatha,' Mir shouted and Aggie quickly stumbled after her before she lost her again. Mir didn't walk, she marched.

'We'll see the staging area first, it's in the centre of the face, quite a walk, better if we go quickly.'

Mir led Aggie to where a great stage was being erected. A towering black column, surrounded by three huge vid screens, was flanked on one side by a colossal drill that made all the others on the face look minute and insignificant. The shining serrated teeth of its rotating drill discs hung just metres above the stage.

'Now we're away from the other personnel – I'm Mir,' the girl said, offering Aggie a petite hand.

Aggie dragged her eyes away from the face. Mir had stopped and was now standing beside her, looking up at the giant drill that framed the stage.

'And I'm Aggie. I promise,' Aggie said, concentrating on not crushing the girl's tiny hand in her fist.

Mir smiled in a polite way that suggested she still wasn't completely sure.

'That's Daisy,' she said, pointing to the massive drill. 'The mine ops named it. It's for luck, apparently.' She'd started the march again and gestured for Aggie to follow. Aggie had to speed up to stay with her. 'It's box-fresh, actually. It's the biggest drill on the whole mine. We should mention that, I think . . .'

Mir typed something into the comms unit in her forearm. 'You don't remember me, do you?' she asked when she'd finished.

Aggie's stomach dropped. *Oh no.* She did not recognize Mir. Not at all. Aggie squinted. *From Analysis?* Surely not, she wasn't over sixty.

'We had Astro-Geology class together, at the Academy.' Mir smiled. 'With Seb? But he said you might not remember. You did keep to yourself a lot. I know why now, of course, but we did the assignment on the properties of silicon in lunar impact craters.'

Aggie winced. 'I'm sorry that I put you through that.'

Mir laughed. 'Ah no, you weren't too bad. Seb was worse, I remember. If I'd known who you were, though, well –' Mir mimed fainting and laughed. She looked down at the comms panel again, her face suddenly solemn. 'My mom, she was a First Responder at Adrianne. She was there when they found you. She thought you were so brave, we all did.'

Aggie felt as if she'd been kicked in the guts. When they'd found Aggie alive and digging desperately in the rubble, the First Responders had refused medical help so that they could join her, to look for survivors. They'd worked for days in the toxic air – they didn't find anyone else.

'I'm sorry Mir, my memories aren't—'

Mir waved her hand dismissively.

'She was blinded, obviously,' she continued tightly. 'Of course she has implants, but still, she doesn't see well.'

Aggie felt the guilt of her survival bearing down on her shoulders. Mir's mum had lost her sight because of her. The First Responders had sacrificed just as much as Aggie had – more, even – but United Earth only cared about its precious Angel.

Aggie kicked a rock with her boot. For the first time in years she had someone her own age to confide in, and already the Angel's legacy was ruining it.

'Mir, I'm—'

'So!' Mir smiled, pulling herself together. She held her comms unit out in front of Aggie. 'Please, I can't tell her about you yet, obviously, but . . . it would mean a lot, to all of us.'

Aggie hesitated, looking at the comms unit then back at Mir.

Mir's eyes went wide. 'For you to sign, obviously!'

'Oh, right. OK.' Aggie quickly scrawled her name onto it and shoved it back.

'Hmm,' Mir said looking at the signature with a frown. 'This won't do. I'll put, "Practise Angel signature" on your to-do list. No one knows you as "Aggie".'

Aggie's mouth fell open.

Mir caught her eye. 'Oh, don't worry, the next weeks are all about learning to deal with the public. Though you should teach me something about interview technique. I've been watching the archives. So competent for a child.'

'I've repressed most of it,' Aggie said to herself.

Mir laughed this time. But it wasn't a joke.

Mir continued with her unnatural, supersonic speed as she led Aggie past the front of the stage, and through a tented seating area. 'Backstage,' she muttered as she inputted still more stuff into her comms. Mir was so neat, so efficient. It was a running joke that Tranquillity personnel never mixed with the other sciences in the Whole Earth Complex. Aggie understood why now – it was as if they were a different species.

As Mir guided her through the tented 'backstage' area, Aggie started to feel eyes on her. She glanced around and saw gangs of red-overalled inmates looking back at her from the shadows.

Prisoners' inmate numbers glowed on the chests of their dusty overalls as they worked. Their faces were half hidden, underlit by the strings of LEDs around the edge of their visors. Aggie's breath caught. *The prisoners were here? They were allowed this close?* She picked up her pace.

They climbed up a narrow set of black steps, ducked under two more sets of curtains and finally emerged onto the stage itself.

'So,' Mir began matter-of-factly, 'the seating area will be out there, obviously; the VIP's will be in the raised section there . . .'

The stage was massive. Bigger than Aggie had ever imagined it could be from the ground. The huge screens hung above her head and on either side of her; they looked easily as tall as the Domestic Analysis building. Aggie imagined her face beamed up there, as big as a planet . . .

A bright flash blinded her from Mir's comms unit.

And suddenly she was seven again, wearing a violet dress and sitting quietly on a small chair, its rough fabric itching the backs of her legs.

'Off you go, little one,' her godfather said with a warm smile, gesturing towards the line of cameras with blinking red lights.

In the tiny, hot studio; people with clipboards and phones lurked in the shadows. She took a deep breath and spoke the words she'd rehearsed . . .

Another bright white flash brought Aggie crashing back to reality.

'Aggie? Hello? Are you still with me?' Mir was standing in front of her, holding the comms unit in her forearm up in Aggie's face. 'You don't mind me taking a vid, do you?' she asked quickly. 'But, maybe . . .'

Aggie blinked hard and the world came back into focus. Mir was gesturing to her hair, which had now completely broken free of its tie and was flapping around her shoulders. She felt as if she'd been electrocuted. 'Frag!' she shouted, pulling it back and tying it so tightly it gave her an instant headache. If anyone saw—

Aggie stopped.

The ground shuddered beneath her boots.

'What was that?'

'Oh, just another quake, probably,' Mir said, still staring into the crook of her arm, 'nothing to concern us. If you're higher, you feel them more.'

Aggie looked down at her boots. The ground was

making them vibrate visibly, the screens above them groaned and started to sway. She could feel her heart starting to race.

'Let me show you the platform,' Mir shouted, beckoning Aggie forwards as if she was a loyal old dog.

Aggie staggered after her, glancing up worriedly at the shaking dome above.

At the centre back of the stage a raised platform was being constructed by a group of prisoners and mine ops. As the girls approached, Aggie heard a few whoops and hollers and she looked away, though she imagined most were directed at Mir.

'The prisoners—' she began.

'They're helping with the construction, yes,' Mir snapped. 'So, at the party the commander wants you appearing here. A lighting rig will be installed behind the platform, which means you'll be in silhouette – that's my idea, very dramatic, yes?'

Mir nudged Aggie with her elbow, but Aggie wasn't listening. Now she was looking up at the quivering masonry above their heads. It was really starting to jump about now.

'I don't like quakes . . .' she muttered, trying to hold it together in front of Mir.

'The vid screens will be playing a mixture of footage from the disaster,' Mir continued, unaware that she'd lost Aggie's attention again, 'and obviously *the* footage of you in the wreckage. There'll be a pause, and then as you come on there'll be the company logo. I think a . . .'

Aggie watched the mine ops throwing equipment up to the red-overalled inmates. They shouted to each other through their helmet comms. They chatted and laughed. They seemed just like the engineers and mine ops that worked around them.

'What did they do?' Aggie asked, interrupting Mir's speech about lighting or something.

Mir wrinkled her nose in disgust. 'Them? Oh, you don't want to know.'

The ground lurched, sending a drill flying out of one of the prisoner's hands and crashing to the stage a few metres away. Mir didn't even flinch. Aggie wondered if she was actually a robot, a very convincing humanoid.

'I do want to know,' Aggie said, peering at Mir's face, looking for an 'on' button or something. No, she was definitely human. Aggie was almost disappointed.

Mir frowned up at the red overalls. 'They're FALL. Terrorist scum.'

The change in her tone took Aggie aback.

'They should never be allowed here,' Mir snarled. 'Let them rot in a real prison like the Pacific Pen with all the murderers. You can't rehabilitate terrorists.' She took a breath, then looked back at Aggie. 'Sorry. Only, this is the intake from Tokyo. When you see the Forecast . . .'

Aggie nodded. 'Rix mentioned it, yeah.'

'It's OK, we're safe. Celeste has special monitors on them, and the mine ops keep them too busy to think about anything but work. That's why the lunar mines are such an effective method of rehabilitation.'

Mir looked back down at her comms panel. The screen was jumping about so much that reading anything on it must have been impossible. 'Now, yes, in fact, we're having the stage repainted in midnight blue—'

The ground lurched again, sending Mir sprawling to the floor.

When Aggie pulled her up, her green eyes were wide. She grabbed Aggie's arm. 'What . . .' she began, then the lights inside the giant dome flashed red then violet.

'All personnel. High magnitude lunar quake in Mining Sector G,' Celeste's voice wobbled overhead. 'All personnel brace, brace.'

Mir cried out as the ground below them started to jump. The rickety half-finished stage heaved and swayed around them. It felt as if it was all going to come crashing down any second.

Aggie stood rooted to the spot. G Face moved around her in slow motion, the foggy air turned red by the alarm light. As debris started to fall around them, she forced the images of the smoking reactor room out of her mind. Then Aggie's survival instincts kicked in. She grabbed Mir's hand and dragged her back in the direction of the steps. She'd never experienced a quake like this before, and it felt bad. The way the stage was shuddering, Aggie knew the first thing they had to do was get as far away from it as they could.

Around them, the white-overalled mine ops were shouting at the prisoners to move as masonry and equipment started to rain down.

'All personnel, please evacuate the G Face construction

area,' Celeste's voice rattled. 'Please evacuate G Face.'

Aggie and Mir raced down the stairs, through the back-stage area and out onto the face. They emerged just in time.

With a long slow creak, the half-built black platform started to tilt and then collapse in on itself, sending a dense cloud of dust and debris pluming into the red air.

'Visors!' Aggie cried as a cliff of grey dust enveloped them. Just as Aggie's visor snapped down, the cloud hit. She stumbled blindly forwards. Mir's hand slipped out of her grip. 'Hey!' she shouted, 'Mir!' But when she looked back, all she saw were red and black ghosts running in the dust.

'Mir!' she yelled, 'MIR!' She flailed around in the smoky air, desperately looking for a blue overall. Her head was spinning, her blood hammering in her ears.

Footsteps beat against the ground, voices shouted back and forth over the comms, the overload made the comms system distort and feedback. It all added to Aggie's disorientation. She turned on the spot, blind and deafened, desperately trying to find a way out of the dust cloud.

Which way was out? It was impossible to tell. 'Celeste?' she shouted into her helmet.

'Please evacuate the face,' the computer replied uselessly.

'I'm trying!' Aggie cried, stumbling forwards and tripping over a boulder. The visibility was so bad, Aggie felt completely alone. She could sense the panic rising deep in her chest. A pure, potent kind of panic, one she hadn't experienced for a long time.

'Hey!' a voice shook over her comms. A male voice. Close. A guard.

'Over here!' Aggie cried, then felt something launch into her back, knocking her to the floor. An instant later, a great crashing noise ripped through her ears as a lighting rig smashed into the ground beside her head.

Aggie lay on the ground, panting. The bouncing stopped, and finally, she felt the rock beneath her start to go still.

'What are you doing?' the voice said.

Aggie stared at the ruined rig on the ground beside her. She couldn't find any words. She'd be nothing but mush if she hadn't been pushed out of the way.

A figure crouched in the dust beside her.

'You need to get out of here,' he panted, his number, 209, lighting him up in the dust.

His inmate number.

Aggie gasped and pulled back. A prisoner.

'Hey, wait. Here.' To Aggie's surprise, the prisoner held out his arm.

Aggie hesitated, then took his arm and stood.

She winced. Despite the exo in her overall, her shoulder pulsed with pain from her impact with the ground.

'You OK?'

Aggie looked up into his face.

'Thank—' she began, then stopped.

The prisoner was staring at her.

The way he looked at her made a shiver run through her whole body. She knew that look – it was the look people had given her before she'd gone into hiding. Before she'd transformed back into Aggie.

The prisoner stood as still as if he were made of rock.

'A—' he started to say, then hesitated.

Red dust swirled between them.

'Are you OK?' he asked again, his voice wavering.

'I'm . . .' Aggie started to speak, but the words dried up. She couldn't take her eyes away from his. It was impossible. It had to be, but the air around them hummed with it.

He knew who she was. Oh frag, oh frag, he knew who she was. And now he was about to walk away.

'Wait!' Aggie cried, struggling to run after him on the still-shivering ground. 'How did you know? Wait!'

'AGGIE!' a shrill voice pierced the cloud.

Mir staggered into view, her visor glowing red with pressure alarms. 'Earth below, Aggie! Are you hurt? Are you OK?' She stopped when she saw the red overall. 'Who are you?'

The prisoner turned and ran.

Mir pulled on Aggie's arm, her eyes were wide behind her visor. 'Aggie? It's OK, he's gone. Did he hurt you?'

Aggie shook her head, watching the prisoner's red overall fade away into the dust.

Her head felt like it was going to explode.

A prisoner knew she was the Angel.

A prisoner from FALL.

4

Day-Cycle 04

Aggie sat in her pod quietly, a used lumite cell in her hands. She peeled back the rubbery connective casing and held the crystal up to the window. It sparkled in the sunlight like treasure.

It was a kind of treasure, really. The most expensive commodity in the United Earth. Where would the Earth be without it? *Dark*, the voice inside her head answered. *Dark and dead*.

Aggie was too young to remember the age before the discovery. A time when a world built on technology was pulled into a new dark age by a lack of power, and countries fought a constant war from behind giant invisible walls. Before Lunar Inc.'s scientists had found lumite hidden deep beneath the Moon's surface.

Aggie was a child of the Lumite Age, too young to remember the dark, but she did remember the stories, the films from the archives at the Academy that were so hard to watch, the pictures of poor people driven to desperation while the rich cowered inside their illuminated compounds. In the darkness of the blackouts nobody was safe. A shiver ran down Aggie's spine.

'Saviour of the world,' she muttered, turning the crystal slowly, making spots of light dance over her face. She pressed the cool, polished mineral to her forehead and let out a long sigh.

In the last few days the base that had become her home had started to contract in on her, suffocating her so much that just the idea walking down a corridor was terrifying. The accident on G Face hadn't helped. Her mind drifted to the prisoner who had saved her. Mir had written down his number as soon as they'd escaped the dust cloud. Aggie had mixed feelings about him – terrified and intrigued in equal measure. He'd saved her life, after all. Was she in danger? Probably. But the one thing she was sure of was that she didn't want to tell Rix. Not yet.

Aggie sighed. It was as if the surface itself didn't want the Angel there, and was throwing everything it could at her to make her go away.

Aggie dropped the lumite to the floor with a thud. The quake on G Face was the last straw. She'd tried to accept the idea of being the Angel again, she really had, but she just couldn't do it. She wanted out, and there was only one way she could make that happen.

'Celeste?' Aggie said.

'Hey Agatha.'

'Could you call him again, please?'

'OK Agatha. One moment please … the Earth channels are very busy this evening.'

Aggie breathed out loudly. 'OK.'

There was a moment of silence, then the Ether screen beside her bed buzzed to life.

'Moon to Earth connection established.'

Aggie sat up and watched as the Ether particles spun and settled to show a shaking view of the grand, perfectly maintained roof gardens of the United Government head-quarters in Tokyo. Blurry, grey-suited figures moved in and out of the video as the camera bounced up and down.

'Adam?' she said, tilting her head to try and make out where her godfather's comms feed was coming from.

'What was that?' Adam Faulkner's voice drifted over the noise. 'What did you say, Massimo?'

'Nothing, sir.'

'Adam. It's Aggie.'

The camera spun around wildly.

'I'm on your sleeve!' She groaned loudly. Then to herself, 'You've had the comms unit for months and you still do this every time!'

'I can hear something!' she heard her godfather say again. 'Hello?'

'On your sleeve!'

'Steve? Do I know a Steve?'

'No, sir.'

'IT'S AGGIE!'

'Oh! Aggie!'

Aggie laughed and slammed her head into her hands. When she looked up, Adam Faulkner's smiling face was staring back at her. The bodyguard, who must have been Massimo, was standing guard over his shoulder.

'Finally!' Aggie smiled. 'I think that was a record.'

Her godfather rolled his eyes. Deep grey, like the surface beyond Aggie's window.

'Ahh, ridiculous place to put a comms unit. Whoever thought it was natural to talk to your elbow?'

'I think you did, when you designed the overall.'

'Well, no one should have listened to me.'

'Everyone listens to you.'

Her godfather took a step back, revealing a sliver of bright blue sky. Aggie's breath caught in her throat. It was so beautiful. She instantly felt sick of the dull black of space.

'Well, they're all just black holes, then.'

'Adam, you can't call the whole of the United Government a black hole.'

Her godfather huffed, and then said hello to someone Aggie couldn't see. It might be the United Leader himself, for all she knew. After Rix had forced him into taking retirement from his position as CEO of Lunar Inc., Adam Faulkner had become a space resource consultant for the United Government. Aggie couldn't really imagine it, but her godfather was more powerful now than he'd ever been, only he was now based on Earth, not on the Moon. She missed him on the base.

'Speaking of black holes –' her godfather grinned – 'how's our old friend Roger?'

'Terrifying,' she said, nervously running a hand through her hair, then took a deep breath. She hated asking Adam for anything, he'd done so much for her already, but, well, she was desperate.

'He told you, then?'

Aggie's head snapped up, 'You knew?'

'Well, yes. I had to know, really. He neglected to tell me when he was telling you, though.'

'Oh.' Aggie had had no idea that her godfather and Rix still spoke at all. She guessed they had to: although Adam Faulkner had very little to do with the base these days, he was the world's foremost expert on lumite power. Rix just knew how to smile at the right times, or so her godfather said.

'I'm so sorry, Aggie.'

'It's OK.'

'Well, it doesn't sound OK to me.'

Her godfather shuffled to the side and sat down. A manicured flowerbed appeared over his shoulders, broad leaves and bright flowers swaying in the breeze. Aggie could almost smell the pollen in the air. She wished she could be there, in that garden, under that perfect blue sky.

'How do you feel?'

Aggie hesitated. She hated talking about feelings, even

to the man who'd brought her up as a daughter. 'I don't want it,' she said in a small voice. 'Adam, I don't want that again. I can't . . .'

Adam pulled the camera nearer, so close that Aggie could make out the wrinkles at the sides of his eyes.

'Aggie,' he sighed, 'you're made of graphene. I've always said it. You might look fragile but no one can break you. And Earth forbid the people who try.'

Aggie shook her head. She was made of jelly right now, not graphene.

'I . . .' she faltered.

'Aggie, darling. Adrianne might have taken our families away, but we have each other, and each other is all we have, remember? I will do anything to protect you, you know that don't you?'

Aggie nodded, blinking away tears.

'But the Angel of Adrianne stopped a war all those years ago. When darkness threatened the edges of our United Earth, the Angel was their light. A tiny, broken little girl trying so desperately to save the lives of others, when her own life hung in the balance. What you did, it gave the people a reason to keep going, to believe. Now, isn't that a wonderful, powerful thing?'

'I was scared. I was looking for my dad. I wasn't trying to save anyone else.'

Her godfather looked away, gathering his words. Talking about Aggie's father made them both hurt.

'The Earth will believe what it wants.'

Aggie sighed. The Earth believed what they were told,

more accurately. Her godfather had always had a gift for spin.

'I'm not ready, Adam. I can't,' she continued stiffly. 'Maybe Rix can find someone, someone that looks like me—'

'Oh Aggie!' Adam Faulkner gave a sad smile. 'The Angel isn't just about a pair of violet eyes. She's an icon! You did that, Aggie, with that glittering grit you have. You inspired people. You brought out the good in people, made them believe in something.'

Aggie clenched her teeth. 'I don't want all that – the people and the staring and the speeches and the vids.'

'I know you don't.' Pain crept into his voice. 'I know you don't, little one.'

He shook his head and looked up to the sky. 'I hate asking you, Aggie, really I do. But we can't go back, no matter what it takes. You and I, I'm afraid, have as much choice in what we do as those prisoners up there with you. Only difference is we didn't do anything to deserve our sentences.'

A sombre expression passed over her godfather's usually happy face. Aggie suddenly felt terrible. She wasn't the only one who'd lost everything at Adrianne. Her godfather had lost his whole family. His wife and son had been in the crowds at Switch On Day – out in the open they never stood a chance. Adam hadn't been the same since they'd died. There was a sadness in him that showed itself sometimes, when he was tired or stressed. It made Aggie's skin crawl; her own father had killed them. She closed her eyes tight and fought the spread of guilt she felt for just being alive.

'Aggie?'

Tears had started to roll down her face. She hadn't noticed.

She'd hoped her powerful godfather would help her, tell her Rix was wrong and he'd sort it out. That she could kiss goodbye to the cameras and perfect Mir and everything. Now she suddenly felt like the most selfish human being in the world.

In the Ether screen, Adam Faulkner's grey eyes stared out at her. He was right. They were in this together. They were what they were, and nothing could change that. Plus, how could Aggie live with herself if FALL kept killing people while she could prevent it by bringing back the Angel, with her buzzwords and infectious positivity and unyielding commitment to lumite? She couldn't.

'OK,' she said, sniffing the tears back. 'I get it. OK.'

'I'm so sorry. If there was any other way . . .'

'I know.'

Massimo stepped forwards and tapped her godfather on the shoulder. He shrugged him off angrily. 'Tell the AstroExpo executives they can wait.'

'Adam, It's all right. You can go. I'm OK now. I feel better.'

'See,' he said after a while, 'just like graphene.'

Aggie smiled. 'I love you.'

Faulkner grinned. 'I love you too, little one.'

He got up to leave, the sky flashing bright blue again for

- 53 -

a second. 'Stay bright, Aggie.'

'Stay bright, Adam.'

'Oh, and call me if Rix starts being a clagger's ass.'

With that, the Ether went blank.

'End of transmission,' Celeste reported.

Aggie leant back against the bed and stared at nothing. A deep uncomfortable feeling was growing in the pit of her stomach. She'd exhausted all her options. It was real. This was actually happening.

Her happy, quiet, insignificant life would soon be over. Soon enough, she would be presented back to the world. The Angel of Adrianne, older, and presumed wiser.

The look on Mir's face when they had first met flashed before her. Mir was disappointed in Aggie – it was so obvious. How could the Earth believe in her again if she was just one huge disappointment?

Aggie shook herself. She couldn't think about that right now. She just couldn't. Agatha Sommers only had a few days of freedom left, and she wasn't going to let Rix and Mir ruin them completely.

Lunchtime couldn't come around quick enough. Aggie was meeting Seb in their usual spot; the frozen custard cart by the All-You-Can-Eat Bumper Buffet, on the first-floor balcony of the Whole Earth Complex.

There were two types of cuisine available on the Lunar Base – wet food and Spacefood. Wet food wasn't as bad as it sounded; in fact, most personnel would fight for a bowl of wet, normal-looking chilli con carne over the square, freeze-dried alternative. Personally, Aggie loved the weird, papery, smoky texture of Spacefood bars, but that was an opinion only she and Seb shared. The food outlets in Whole Earth's great mall-like atrium specialized in wet food, which was why it was so popular.

The Bumper Buffet outlet's, sticky trestle tables and cross-contaminated buffet trays tended to put off most personnel. This meant that it was the sole haunt of tech and the guards. Always half empty, and never a yellow overall in sight. Just the way Aggie had always liked it.

The frozen custard cart was at the far side of the balcony, tucked in the corner by an emergency escape hatch. Weeks ago she and Seb had dragged a table in behind the dispenser, out of the way of the crowds. Aggie was sure they were breaking a million safety codes by obstructing the door, but it was worth it to create their own private frozen custard heaven.

As Aggie ascended the steps up to the cart, she checked her eyelids. She'd checked them for the ridges of her lenses fifty times today already, as if some freak in the gravity system had meant they'd sprung out of her eyes and floated away unnoticed. They hadn't, obviously.

She took a long, shuddering breath. She hadn't felt this paranoid since Rix had allowed her to join the cadets in the Lunar Academy.

In the distance, Aggie could just make out the skinny silhouette of Seb on the other side of the custard cart, filling up a huge bucket with something pink and glittery – Seb loved frozen custard for lunch, even when the other option was burritos.

Aggie looked around the atrium and, for once, noticed how beautiful it all was: the swirling colours in the Whole Earth's towering glass windows, the comforting murmur of personnel as they gossiped at their tables, the smell of coffee and sugar and the sizzle of synthetic meat drifting on the air. It was sad to think this could be one of the last times she came here as Domestic Analysis Aggie.

When she finally reached the Bumper Buffet, she grabbed herself a burrito from the stack, heaped it with some beige cheese, sloppy beige guacamole, added a worryingly beige salad leaf and made her way over to her friend.

'Hey, Seb. Been probed lately?' she heard a guard shout to him.

'If you see any of them little green ladies out on your next patrol, don't forget to send them our way.' another added with an explosion of laughter.

Seb smiled tightly. 'Hilarious, dudes.'

Aggie placed her heaving burrito plate down on the table.

'You OK?'

'Cosmic, Aggs, yeah. Totally cosmic.' Seb sighed. 'Also, how long does it take to get a shuttle from Analysis these days? My next shift starts in fourteen hours, I was worried you wouldn't get here in time.'

Aggie felt a twinge of guilt and sat down.

'Commuter shuttles were crowded,' she lied. 'Sorry.'

She couldn't tell Seb that she'd actually been in her pod,

chatting to Adam Faulkner, the man who was like a living god to anyone who wore the Lunar Inc. overall, anyone on Earth, really.

Seb nodded and brought his frozen custard pot to the table triumphantly. The thing was huge – interstellar toffee with extra chocolate stardust sprinkles and some glittering silver ball things that Aggie guessed were supposed to be planets. It was excessive, even for Seb.

'Well, that's quite something,' Aggie said, taking a big bite of her burrito. It almost tasted like real beef. Almost.

Seb slammed his spoon into the pot, sending silver planets spinning across the table. 'It's therapy food, man. I need it.'

Aggie nodded. 'Join the club.'

Seb shook his head. 'The Rock-Aliens are ruining my life.'

Aggie glanced back to where the guards had disappeared, 'Oh, Seb, they're just a bunch of black holes. Ignore them.'

'Oh no, those denks don't have enough brain cells to bother me.'

Aggie frowned, 'What is it, then?'

'They've put me back on border patrol. For like, a whole cycle.'

He took a huge bite of custard and chewed it angrily. The chocolate planets crunched loudly.

'I mean,' Seb continued with his mouth full. 'I thought the forced leave was the punishment, man. Two weeks with my parents? C'mon, and they say torture is supposed to be illegal.'

Aggie laughed. Seb could be so melodramatic. How bad could a border patrol be, really? Right now, Aggie would kill for the chance to fly out into the lunar landscape alone for a few hours, leaving the busy, noisy, base behind her. Exploring the craters and mares, getting a glimpse of the restricted area on the Far Side. A place where there was no one around to care who she was. It sounded totally cosmic.

Seb was still shovelling custard into his face. 'That place is so creepy, man. And, the last thing I need is that bunch of clagger's asses reminding me what I did every time I start a shift— Oh! Argh!'

Seb's hands flew up to his temples, his face twisted in agony.

Aggie jumped up.

'Seb!' she shouted, grabbing at his arms. It was as if he was having seizure.

'Medic! Help!' she cried. But no one heard her.

Seb battered her away. 'Dude! What are you doing?'

Aggie staggered back, her heart was jumping against her ribs. 'What?'

'Brain freeze, man.' Seb groaned, rubbing his temples. 'I got a brain freeze.'

'Oh.' Aggie fell back into her seat.

Seb frowned at her. 'Aggs, I get brain freeze every time I have custard. You know that. Why are you so jumpy?'

She was still panting. 'Sorry, I just—'

'Hey.' Seb's hand touched the top of hers. 'You OK?

You've gone the same colour as your burrito.'

Aggie twisted Seb's fingers in hers, then realized what she was doing and pulled her hand away. Seb was her friend, her only real friend, she wasn't going to ruin it by making it anything more.

But she was jumpy – a massive quake on a Face surrounded by prisoners would do that to anyone – but she couldn't tell Seb that. The look on the prisoner's face flashed before her momentarily. She pushed her burrito away. There were too many nerves in her stomach to be properly hungry.

'I'm fine, sorry. I've just . . . been busy lately, that's all.'

Seb raised an eyebrow. 'Uh oh, not another toilet emergency?' he said, winking theatrically. 'I can see it now, a whole department covered in— Oh! Hello, Astrid.'

Aggie turned and saw the intern hovering awkwardly behind her, her tray piled with soggy-looking nachos. When she saw Aggie, Astrid let out a little cry and slammed her tray down on the table.

Seb was grinning so much Aggie could see all his teeth. He thought Astrid and her Lunar Inc. loving ways were hilarious. Aggie felt her whole body tighten up.

'Hello, Sebastian!' Astrid beamed and sat down in the seat beside Aggie. 'Hey, Agatha. Oh wow, you know, I was going to get the burrito too!'

'Spooky.' Seb grinned.

Aggie smiled nervously. Astrid had probably travelled all the way from Analysis just in case she bumped into her.

The intern flicked her white-blonde hair over her

shoulder and picked at her plate. The array of 'society' badges on Astrid's overall sparkled in the light from the atrium windows; Aggie was sure Astrid had added a few more since she'd seen her. How did the girl have enough time to be part of that many extracurricular societies?

Astrid sighed, sticking out her bottom lip directly at Aggie. 'Oh, Agatha, it has been so *desperate* in the labs without you. Mo has been driving me c–r–azy.' She twirled her finger beside her ear and rolled her eyes.

Aggie picked at her burrito as Seb stifled a laugh in his custard pot.

Astrid was oblivious. She took a sip of her bright green juice and leant forwards, eyebrows waggling, 'So, tell me. How's the "secret mission"?' She said the words 'secret mission' as if she was holding in a burp. Aggie didn't find it funny. The way she was feeling right now, Astrid might as well have leant across the table and slapped her.

The Domestic personnel had been told she'd been transferred to Surface Analysis, but thanks to Aggie's general ability to mess everything up, rumours were rife. Obviously, Astrid's enthusiastic mind had gone into overdrive.

Aggie laughed nervously. Seb was now staring at her with a look of amused bewilderment.

'What "secret mission"?' he said slowly.

Seb was teasing her, Aggie knew, but still, even the slightest hint that something was wrong was too risky. She couldn't have Seb finding out the truth, not without her telling him first.

'Nothing!' Aggie said, sweat breaking out on her palms. 'Just Analysis stuff.'

'Don't be so modest, Agatha!' Astrid exclaimed. 'It certainly didn't *sound* like "just Analysis stuff"! I mean, Commander Rix doesn't come into the Civilian Sector for nothing, does he?'

Seb's eyebrows had disappeared right up into his curly hair. 'He certainly doesn't, Astrid. He certainly doesn't.'

'It's been the talk of the Cadets,' Astrid continued proudly, 'and the G-Ball club, the Young Miners, even the Erms—'

'Erm . . . the erms?'

Astrid stopped and looked at Seb as if he was the crazy one. 'The Emergency Rescue and Miners' Society,' she replied matter-of-factly. 'ERMs.'

'Cosmic.' Seb was containing so much laughter now he'd started to go shiny. Aggie kicked him under the table.

A high-pitched alarm echoed around the atrium. Everyone stopped what they were doing and stared up at the Ether screens that littered the walls.

Aggie threw her fork down on her plate. Saved by the bell. Lunar Inc. personnel knew better than to miss the Lunar Forecast – the official vid roundup of life on the Lunar Inc. mine that was also beamed down to Earth.

The Ether in the wall beside them fizzed, and the Lunar Inc. logo – a violet lightning bolt cutting across a grey moon – spun hypnotically in a flickering star-speckled spacescape.

Aggie could feel Seb's eyes boring into her. He knew something was up. The only thing in Aggie's favour was that he'd never guess the truth. Not in a billion years.

The electronic jingle floated happily through the air and the logo was replaced by the shining face of Roger Rix. A shiver ran up Aggie's spine.

'Citizens of the United Earth,' he said, flashing his white teeth enthusiastically, 'it is my personal pleasure to introduce you to the 545th Lunar Forecast, live from the Sea of Tranquillity.'

There was another trumpet, and Celeste appeared to the right of the screen, an androgynous, plastic-looking avatar with dead eyes.

'Thank you, Commander Rix.' She beamed as a montage of images of happy life on the base streamed behind her. 'This is a Lunar Forecast for the First Quarter.'

Aggie sighed. Her godfather had dreamt up the Forecasts after Adrianne as a way of promoting the company, of keeping the citizens of the United Earth in appropriate awe of what was being done in the pursuit of lumite. Aggie wondered how long it would be before she was the subject. The idea of it felt unreal as she sat staring at the screens with her friends.

On the Ether, Celeste's fake face had grown solemn. 'The original programmed Forecast has been replaced by this special message from the Government of the United Earth in Tokyo.'

Aggie's heart started to flutter. This was the Forecast Rix and Mir had mentioned. FALL had done something terrible in Tokyo, and she was about to see what.

Behind Celeste's avatar, the happy images of Lunar Inc. were replaced by images of fighting. Men and women with covered faces sacking a white marble concourse. The camera swivelled and shook erratically as projectiles bombarded the line of United Government guards that protected the building.

'FALL, the terrorist organization, are continuing their enduring campaign of violence on the United Earth. Their aim is not certain, other than to destroy as much as they can. Destructive and mindless violence that will damage their political attempts within the United Forum.'

Everyone in the atrium was silent. Only the muffled sounds of screaming and crashing from the vid echoed off the walls. Seb wasn't staring at Aggie any more – his mouth was hanging open, looking at the screens.

'I've never seen anything like it,' Astrid muttered as they watched the protestors break through the line of guards and race up the steps into the government building.

Aggie was mesmerized. This was what Rix had talked about. FALL was getting stronger, more confident. This was why Lunar Inc. needed her.

'Last night,' Celeste continued, as the footage intensified, close-ups of fires and people screaming, 'the United Government headquarters was attacked. Over a hundred dead, including Sanya Moya, the United Government's Minister for Energy, who many believe was the gang's original target. This attack is the latest in the terror group's prolonged reaction to the upcoming anniversary of the

Adrianne Disaster. Our thoughts go out to the minister's family.

'Hundreds have been injured, thousands are locked inside their homes, too scared to go outside. FALL are determined to bring back the Dark Days in their fight against the clean, enduring light of lumite. And they will stop at nothing.'

From the screen a sound like a drill backfiring resonated around the giant atrium. Screams erupted from the balconies as a fireball swallowed up the crowds outside the facility. Aggie felt Seb's hand on hers, squeezing it hard. She gripped it back. It didn't feel so weird this time.

A bomb? Was that a bomb?

How could they? All those people?

'This atrocity was unprovoked and unexpected. We urge citizens to be vigilant. We shall fight back against this extremism. We shall have peace again.'

Aggie let out a long breath. She couldn't believe what she'd just seen.

'It's like the Dark Days,' Seb said, turning back to the table. 'I've seen vids like that from the Dark Days.' He sounded terrified.

'How could that happen, Aggie?' Astrid stammered, looking up at Aggie as if she had all the answers.

Aggie opened her mouth to reassure them but then the screens flicked from the riots to a flurry of lights and colour.

'What the—?'

'Lunar Inc. personnel,' Celeste's voice rang out, her tone

had changed, she was back to her usual fake, happy self, 'ready your dress uniforms and dust off your dance moves. Commander Rix and all on the Lunar Inc. board would like to invite you to celebrate the launch of our magnificent G Face. Our largest and most majestic mining face to date, a true feat of engineering and scale. Come enjoy a drink and celebrate the birth of lumite, and of course, on this tenth anniversary year, pay respects to the victims of Adrianne, who are never far from our hearts.'

The personnel in the atrium started to clap and cheer. Aggie looked around at them all. It was as if the horror of the Forecast had never happened. All that pain and violence, forgotten in seconds at the promise of party and some free food.

But those pictures had settled deep inside Aggie's bones. The ball of nerves in her stomach grew.

'EARTH BELOW!' Astrid cried.

'No way,' Seb breathed. 'Are they for real?'

Aggie looked back up. The screens had changed again. A silhouette of a woman now stood in front of the Lunar Inc. logo. Her face and overall were obscured by the shadows, but no one watching could miss her shock of bright red curls, blowing over the backdrop of the dusty mining face.

Aggie froze. *No.*

The air in the atrium buzzed. Aggie winced as the word 'Angel' drifted up from the seating area below.

'We hope you are looking forward to the party –' Celeste smiled, now into her end piece – 'and all the surprises it may bring! Interact with your screens right now and see how you can become a shining light for the United Earth.'

Aggie looked at Seb. He was still staring at the screen.

Astrid's head was down, already texting her friends on her comms panel. Excited chatter rose up from the balconies.

The room started to sway around Aggie. She remembered the face, her hair slipping, the flash from Mir's comms. That sneaky Earth Relations girl had posted the vid she'd taken of her.

Anger started to pulse in waves through her. Rix hadn't said anything about this. How could he and Mir do this without telling her? She felt her eyelids nervously; the ridge was still there. She was still just Aggie – for now.

'Stay bright, United Earth,' Celeste concluded with a smile.

5

Day-Cycle 06

Aggie squinted through the haze of dust on G Face and distracted herself with the 'tint' function on her visor, making the face go from orange to red to pink to yellow.

'...and while we're here,' Mir said, gesturing to the huge black Eyes that hung from the ceiling of the vast G Dome. 'At the party, Celeste will be recording the footage at higher angles mostly, but there'll also be close-ups from some of the Eyes on the daisy drill as you walk around, and some vid from your visor feed, maybe. So be sure you smile as much as you can. OK?'

Aggie flipped the tint again.

'Aggie?'

She went with pink. The face seemed a lot friendlier in pink.

'Aggie?' Mir said again.

Aggie nodded. Mir had been giving Aggie a 'walk-through' of the face all morning. It wasn't exactly going well. Aggie was easily distracted at the best of times, but today there was one thing playing on her mind. One huge, terrifying, prisoner-shaped thing.

A week ago, only one person on the base knew the truth of her identity. Just one. The commander. A man she trusted. Aggie glanced around the face and shivered. Now there were three.

One of them was Mir.

And one of them was FALL.

She couldn't just ignore it. She just couldn't.

Mir sighed loudly. 'What's the point?'

Aggie snapped the visor back. 'What?'

'You're not listening to me.'

Aggie squinted out at the face again. 'Yes I am.'

'OK. Well, look, there's a whale in the top of the dome, he'll be the main cameraman, filming you with his flippers.'

Aggie nodded, peering at the mass of red dots working in the distance. 'Great.'

Mir gave a cry of frustration and stepped into Aggie's path.

Aggie refocused quickly. Mir's cheeks were flushed. 'Whoa, what's backfiring your drill, Mir?'

'You are, Aggie! It's you!' Mir threw her arms above her head in frustration. 'This is a big opportunity for me, you have to understand, the entire Earth will be watching and if you don't know where the cameras are . . .' She sighed. 'Look, I know this is hard for you, so I see why you're being difficult, but this is important . . . Aggie!'

Aggie had turned back to the face and was following one red dot as it moved deeper into the mine, a number blinked on her comms display: 209. Her heart started to race inside her overall. The prisoner.

Aggie started to back up towards the scrambler they'd been using to tour the face. 'Mir, It's cosmic. Really. I'm OK. Everything will be great. I'm sorry, but I have to . . .'

'Where are you going? Aggie, you need to see the camera angles!'

Aggie swung her leg over the seat. 'I need to . . . Look, we'll do it another time.'

'The party is in four days!' Mir cried in frustration. Aggie felt bad, but she needed to get away – this was more important. Mir would get that, if she ever found out.

'I'm sorry!' Aggie shouted over her shoulder as she drove the scrambler away in a cloud of dust.

Aggie glanced back. Mir's pale-blue overall was disappearing into the dust. She breathed out. She felt bad, running away like that. But the last thing she needed was Mir finding out what she was up to. The girl would just run straight to Rix and then she'd never have a chance to speak to the prisoner.

When Aggie finally took her hands off the scrambler's controls, they were shaking. What was she even doing? She must have gone mad. She'd be seeing Seb's Rock-Aliens next.

But as the red smudge of the prisoner got closer, Aggie knew that, deep down, she had to do this. She had to see him again. Ever since he'd pushed her out of the way of the debris, Aggie couldn't get the prisoner out of her head.

She tried to calm down, to think rationally, but it was as if her limbs had a faulty connection to her brain. They didn't move when she told them to. Her body was just reluctantly going along with what her heart was telling it – her head had nothing to do with it.

'Get a grip on yourself, Aggie,' she muttered through gritted teeth as she accelerated the scrambler back up to full speed. Its fat inflated wheels bounced along the trail towards the prisoner's team, taking her around to a new, unexcavated area filled with rocks and boulders and other non-mineable 'surface materials'. The group of prisoners were busy clearing the way for the lumite seam that must lie somewhere underneath.

Aggie parked up on the edge of the trail and watched the prisoner as he heaved rock after rock into the waiting loader truck below. The exo in his suit was taut, helping him lift the massive boulders, but still Aggie couldn't help but notice how broad his shoulders looked.

She saw him look up, and a cold sweat erupted over her body. She pretended not to notice. Instead, she sucked her stomach in as far as she could and leant back on the scrambler. Trying to act casual.

As soon as her weight hit the trike, it made a screeching noise and fell over, sending Aggie crashing to the mine floor in a plume of choking grey dust.

A cheer sounded from somewhere. Aggie lay back and wished the ground would swallow her up.

'For frag's sake,' she moaned, spitting bits of moon rock out of her mouth.

'You should keep your visor shut if you're going to kick up the dust,' said a voice.

The prisoner was standing over her, the great white dome reflecting in his visor.

Aggie went cold.

'Oh! I . . . hmm,' she stammered, casting her arms about wildly, trying to get a grip on something solid so she could stand up.

'Here.' The prisoner stepped forwards and flicked her visor down. Aggie sucked in the fresh air gratefully. He offered her a hand and pulled her up.

'You OK?'

Aggie looked up. The reflection of the dome had disappeared and for the first time, she saw his face properly. He was young, no older than nineteen. His eyes were the exact colour of the surface. They flashed in the shadows of his helmet like lumite in the seams. A thin half-moon scar traced its way down his right cheek. The soft push and pull of his breath fogged the Plexiglas on his visor as she watched – deep and steady.

Suddenly the contents of her head slipped out of Aggie

like dust through her fingers. She stared up at the prisoner, empty of everything. *Your name is Aggie,* she reminded herself, *You are standing in front of someone who probably wants to kill you – pull yourself together.*

The prisoner was still staring at her.

It was now that Aggie began to panic properly. Why had she come here? Why had she ever thought this would be a good idea? She glanced to left and right, there was no one around. No one within close comms anyway. She looked at the panic button inside the palm of her glove. No. Celeste would report to Rix. That had to be a last resort.

'Are you OK?' Her comms crackled again. Aggie whipped her head back so fast her neck jarred.

'What?'

'I said, are you OK?' The prisoner sounded younger than she remembered.

'I . . . yeah. I am.'

'Good.'

The prisoner began to walk away down the slope that led back to his team. *That was it?* No, it couldn't be.

'Wait!' she cried, stumbling down the slippery hill. 'Hey! You, wait!'

The prisoner turned sharply and Aggie came skidding to a halt in front of him.

'What do you want?' he said, his grey eyes flicking over her overall.

'I . . .' Aggie began, 'I . . .'

The words dissolved.

The prisoner looked around them, then pointed to the

black ants on the distant guard post.

'Do they know who you really are?'

Aggie gaped up at him in horror. Was he threatening her?

He smiled at her response. 'Just me, then.'

Aggie felt as if she was going to collapse. 'What are you going to do?'

The prisoner frowned at her again. 'I'm going to get my drill,' he said, and walked off.

This time Aggie didn't follow. Was he going to come back? Or was that it? She watched the prisoner haul the rock he was carrying onto the loader and say something to the white-overalled foreman who stood by it. Aggie shakily pulled the scrambler back up onto its wheels. This time she remembered to flick the stabilizer down so the stupid thing stayed upright.

When she looked up again the prisoner was already walking back up to her, an evil-looking corer drill strapped to his shoulder. What was he planning to do with that?

'I'm helping you,' he grunted as he pushed past her towards a boulder at the back of the trail.

'I don't need any—'

'You want to talk to me, right?'

Aggie nodded and watched mutely as the prisoner set the drill to the edge of the rock.

For a long time Aggie just shifted from foot to foot. Every muscle in her body was so tense, it felt as if she'd activated her very own internal exoskeleton. She had to keep reminding herself to breathe. *Think of something to say. Anything.*

'They don't let FALL on the base,' she blurted, her heart beating along with the pulse of the drill. 'You usually get the Earth prisons.'

The prisoner didn't look away from the rock, 'Lucky me.'

Aggie picked up a rock and started to toss it between her hands, trying to figure out the right words. 'Thank you, for what you did. I didn't say that before.'

'Saving your life?' the prisoner muttered to the rock. 'I didn't know who I was saving.'

Aggie's stomach turned.

That was exactly what she'd thought. The Angel of Adrianne was a mascot for everything FALL stood against. Killing her would have made the prisoner a hero. Aggie should have been terrified – and in some ways she was – but there was something about the prisoner. That look he kept giving her was intriguing, in a life-threatening sort of way.

'This an interrogation?'

Aggie straightened up. 'No.'

'You're alone?'

Aggie took a step back. 'No,' she said, unconvincingly.

The prisoner shook his head and went back to his drilling. 'No one's alone here,' he muttered to himself, jabbing the drill back into the seam. 'There's always someone watching.'

Aggie shuffled her boots in the dust.

'Why FALL?' she said, peering at the prisoner, trying to read the look on his face.

'I believe in FALL,' he said flatly.

'FALL believes killing people is OK.'

'So does Lunar Inc.,' the prisoner replied, pushing the drill deeper into the rock, 'only FALL can't afford the PR.'

Aggie felt as if she'd been punched. He was talking about the people who died in Adrianne. 'That was an accident,' she hissed.

'If that's what you want to call it.'

Suddenly anger was building up in waves inside her. How could he think like that? How could he even compare what FALL did to what Lunar Inc. had done for the world? And how could he look so assured? So comfortable? Did he not know where he was? What he'd done?

'FALL use *bombs*,' she said through gritted teeth. 'On *purpose*. Usually in places where innocent people can get hurt – like Tokyo.'

The prisoner scoffed. 'No one in the United Government is innocent.'

'What's that supposed to mean?'

He didn't answer for a long time.

'Do you ever ask why?' he said. 'Do you know anything about us?'

Aggie was struck dumb.

She knew FALL had become politicized after Adrianne, and were linked to Lara Komori, a member of the Founding Five. She also knew the Komori family had ties to the gangs of the Dark Days, and that they had a history with Rix and possibly her own father. The thought made Aggie shiver. Still, she had to admit, she knew little about

FALL's actual motives – they were the enemy. That was enough, wasn't it?

The prisoner laughed. 'If you listened to us, maybe you'd see it differently.'

Aggie folded her arms. 'It's hard to hear you over the sound of your bombs.'

The prisoner shook his head as if she'd never understand. 'Well, what's the saying?' he said angrily. 'To get to the lumite, you've got to break a few rocks.'

Aggie felt the waves of anger getting higher, threatening to overflow. 'Can you even hear what you're saying?'

The prisoner tapped the comms side of his helmet with his drill. 'Loud and clear.'

'Mir was right. You should be rotting in the Pen.'

'Mir? Is that the girl you were following around?'

Aggie turned. 'Were you watching me?'

The prisoner shrugged. 'More her really—'

The rage spilt over. Aggie took two strides closer to the prisoner and smacked the drill to one side. It fell out of his hands and smashed onto the rock.

'Did you kill anyone? In Tokyo? Or ever?' she demanded, kicking the bits of drill away from him. 'Are you going to kill me?'

The prisoner looked at the broken drill, then back to Aggie.

He shook his head. 'No.'

A shiver ran over Aggie's skin. 'Why?'

He looked at her coldly. 'Right now, I don't know.'

Aggie turned back to the scrambler. With her back to

the prisoner, her anger abated, leaving her feeling shaky. She checked the guard post again. Suddenly, this whole thing felt like the worst idea in the world. He was a prisoner; he was with FALL. Whether she accepted it or not, Aggie was the Angel of Adrianne, and he knew. She was better off as far away from him as possible. She should tell Rix, even, get him sent to the Pen where he belonged.

'You're just going to take my word for it?'

She could still feel his eyes on her.

Aggie turned back to face him. There it was again, that look in his eyes. It disarmed her.

'What's your name?' she said, because she couldn't think of anything better to say.

He pointed to the inmate number on his chest, 'Murderer number 209.'

'Your real name.'

He picked up the drill and inspected the damage. 'Danny,' he muttered. 'For what it matters any more.'

He jabbed at the broken drill with such a force that the bit flew off and came to a halt at Aggie's knee. The sharp diamond-head dug into the fabric on her overall and the material bubbled and hissed as it resealed itself.

'I didn't mean to do that,' he said quickly. He took a step towards Aggie and picked the bit up. Did she see a flicker of anxiety in that frown?

'I'm fine,' she said, confused by the sudden concern for her safety. 'I need a new overall anyway.'

To Aggie's surprise, the prisoner grinned at her. 'Probably try to get one that's not so yellow next time.'

Aggie looked down at herself. 'It's my Infospectrum rating. Analysts wear yellow.'

Danny smirked, 'Bet you cross your heart and sing the international anthem every morning too.'

Aggie's shoulders went up. 'You're part of our rainbow now, technically.'

Danny looked down at his filthy, broken prisoner's overall and shrugged.

'Better than a death sentence in the Pacific Pen.'

The Pacific Pen was an Earth prison run by the United Government, a place as far away from society as you could get. A labour camp like this one, but here on the Moon Lunar Inc. couldn't afford to treat the prisoners as badly as they were treated on Earth.

Aggie shook her head and turned back to the scrambler.

'Blue would suit you better,' the prisoner said quietly.

Aggie's cheeks went hot behind her visor. Instead of leaving, she sat down awkwardly on the edge of the scrambler seat.

Danny looked at her. 'So do you pretend to be normal? Just part of the rainbow like everyone else?'

Aggie nodded, suddenly uncomfortable again.

'How does that work?'

Aggie glared at him. 'Now who's interrogating who?'

He shrugged. 'Just a question.'

'You lost the right to ask questions in Tokyo.'

She was distracted by a small group of black-dressed guards appearing on the dusty horizon.

'Lunar Inc. is too good to you, you should have a bit

more respect for it,' she said, getting to her feet. 'You're still alive, aren't you?'

The group was coming towards them.

Aggie froze.

She'd seen something in the group of guards that made her heart start to hammer again. Two sky-blue overalls surrounded by black. Rix and Mir.

'I thought you were alone,' Danny said with a rueful smile.

'You need to go,' Aggie said, activating the scrambler.

But instead of leaving, the prisoner ducked down towards Aggie, so his head was right beside hers. 'You know,' he whispered, his voice distorting over the comms, 'hiding is the worst thing you can do.'

Aggie looked up at him. He was so close she could see the stubble on his cheeks, the flecks of blue in his grey eyes.

'You have no idea what it's like to be me,' she hissed and pushed him away. 'Now, go.'

But it was too late.

Rix had come to find her. He'd told her to keep a low profile, and now he'd seen her having a chat with a prisoner. A Tokyo rioter at that! Aggie stepped away from Danny. She cursed Mir, and her perfect, protocol-loving, robotic ways.

Danny was staring at the group as they got closer. She gave him a shove, but he stayed rooted to the spot. Hands behind his back, chin up. What was he even thinking?

She looked up at him. Something about this prisoner wasn't right. Something didn't fit. And that something had a lot to do with the fact that she was still breathing.

As soon as Rix stepped up on to the trail, Danny started to stroll casually away in the opposite direction.

Rix watched him go.

'Making friends?' he said, keeping his eyes on the prisoner.

'Getting some help,' Aggie replied, pointing to the scrambler. 'I knocked it over. The foreman said he could—'

'An engineer in the wrong overall, is he?' Mir interjected with a sneer. 'I recognize that number, don't I?'

'No.'

Rix suddenly rounded on Aggie, stepping so close she could see the full intricate pattern tattooed on his cheek. His pale green eyes skittered over her face.

'The prisoners are dangerous, Aggie,' he said with fake friendliness. 'You know that.'

Aggie nodded. Rix's smile fell away.

'I'm not talking about your personal safety. I'm talking about the safety of what you represent. Until we reveal you, we can't risk you getting . . . damaged.'

'That man is a FALL inmate – all the two-hundreds are.' Mir interrupted again. Aggie frowned at Rix. Was he seriously going to let Mir talk over him like that? She'd thought Mir was on her side.

'Sorry, *Mir*, but I didn't have time to memorize the entire prison ID system—'

'There's a *reason* why Lunar Inc. doesn't usually take FALL inmates, Aggie. It's because we suspect they want to fight us from the inside. I shouldn't have to tell you, but the implications of FALL finding out—'

'You don't talk to inmates,' Rix spoke as if Mir didn't exist.

'Yes, Commander.'

Rix pointed to Mir but remained looking at Aggie. 'Stay with Earth Relations on the face.'

Aggie met Mir's glare. 'Yes, Commander.'

Rix clapped his hands and smiled. 'Good job I've got eyes everywhere!' he shouted, looking up at Celeste's Eye in the ceiling, 'Otherwise I'd be worried about you, hey?'

Rix winked at Aggie, then strolled off down the trail, leaving the girls alone.

Aggie swallowed drily.

'Happy now?' Mir said, grabbing the controls away from Aggie and revving the scrambler's fans to max.

'What will happen to him?' Aggie asked, climbing onto the back of the trike. The prisoner was a red dot again, slowly fading into the dust.

Mir turned the scrambler so fast the dust sprayed up around them.

'Aggie. Do you understand the danger you just put yourself in?' Mir was acting as if Aggie had just slapped her. 'That prisoner is FALL. He was at Tokyo, Aggie. We can't trust the Tokyo intake.'

Aggie didn't know what to say. Every time Mir said it out loud, Aggie's plan to see Danny again felt even more stupid.

Mir groaned in frustration. 'Don't tell me you actually thought he was interested in you.'

Aggie felt her face start to burn.

'Earth below, Aggie! Now we have to clear up this mess you made for us. So close to the party . . .'

Aggie turned away from Mir. The prisoner was using her? She'd never thought about it that way. It would have made sense, but there was something else. Of course robotic Mir couldn't see it – it wasn't the kind of thing you could work out or put in a schedule. Aggie could *feel* it.

6

Day-Cycle 07

Aggie had managed to find the only SimStim machine in the whole G Face construction area. Which would have been totally cosmic, if a million other personnel hadn't discovered it too. She shuffled uncomfortably in the queue, but it was early, and her need for coffee was stronger than her need to be on her own.

Despite the stupidly early hour, the G Face early shift was well under way. Aggie glanced around the giant, bustling terminal. She automatically scanned the rushing blurs of the personnel as they passed her. No one paid her any attention. No one ever did. To them Aggie was just another lowly yellow nothing. A one-stripe who needed to get her overall cleaned. Over the years in hiding, Aggie's cover had never been questioned. The Angel was dead. In the minds of the United Earth puberty hadn't given the Angel spots or hips. To them, she was a perpetual seven-year-old, skipping and smiling in her pretty violet dress.

Until *him*.

Aggie bit her lip at the thought of the prisoner. He was dangerous, he was using her, he was . . . Aggie sighed. He was addictive, was what he was. He took up so much of her thoughts it was almost enough to make her forget about the party altogether. The biggest event in her new life was just around the corner, and all she could see when her thoughts drifted was his face.

She wondered about him, about his life in the secret hideouts that FALL occupied, she wondered about how he got his scar. If he was hurt, if he deserved it.

Loud voices pulled her back to the busy terminal. A group of guards ahead of her had been talking about the party but, predictably, their conversation had quickly turned to the one thing Aggie did not need to hear right now. Mir's stupid Angel silhouette had done its job brilliantly – rumours about the Angel's return were everywhere.

'Navi is convinced it's a fake,' a young guard was saying to his friends.

Aggie was sandwiched in the queue so close to them that she couldn't help but hear every single annoying word.

'Nah, c'mon. Lunar Inc. can't fake the Angel. It's her,

I'm telling you,' his friend argued.

'No way! It's a hologram. The Angel died after Adrianne – FALL killed her, everybody knows that.'

Aggie winced and tried to bury herself further into the back of the tech head directly in front of her.

'No – how can they even do that?'

'I bet she's a hottie now, though.'

There was a burst of laughter and the tall guard finally reached the machine.

'Don't matter what she looks like. Who wouldn't? The Angel of Adrianne?'

'Yeah, man, gotta get me my Angel wings.'

The boys shouted and whooped.

'Only wings you gonna get are on the shuttle.'

'Yeah, you look like an Afterlife junkie, Marv. The Angel's gonna have standards.'

The guards jostled each other. 'Don't call me FALL, you denk! It's the double shifts, man!'

Aggie made a sick face and prayed the boys weren't ordering anything complicated. She needed to get out of here quickly. She was already convinced she was going crazy, the last thing she needed was her head filled with stupid rumours and gossip. That was the reason she was here in the first place . . . to get away from it all.

Finally, the man in front slouched off with his extra hot, extra strong StimShot and Aggie got to the machine.

'MilkStim,' she said to the Ether, 'extra shot. Actually, screw it, two extra shots.'

The Ether swirled slowly. 'Hey, Agatha, I'm sorry, but

your current level–six status prohibits . . .'

Aggie leant her forehead against the machine. So she could sneak away on the face and have a casual chat with a FALL prisoner, but ordering the coffee she wanted? No way.

'Just give me whatever I can have.'

'OK Agatha.'

The machine crunched and a tiny steaming cup appeared in the slot. Aggie sniffed it gingerly. It was a black SimStim, no milk, no syrup, decaf by the smell to it – old socks and wood. Aggie glared at the Ether for a second, then caught a familiar black blur in the corner of her eye.

'You turned up?' she said with a relieved grin.

'Well, it is my shift,' Seb huffed. 'I kind of have to.' He turned away and began to shuffle into one of the dark inflatable corridors that led to the buggi park.

'Let's do this. Quick.'

As Aggie followed Seb from the busy terminal into a hab crowded with building machinery, not people, she felt her whole body start to unwind. Here, it was quiet and cool, with bright LED lamps that swung as they made their way towards a row of shining black Lunar Inc. moon buggis.

'Can I say, for the record, that I'm not happy about this,' Seb said loudly, as they passed under one of Celeste's Eye's.

Aggie pushed Seb lightly in the back. 'There is no record.'

'Well, let there be a record.'

Aggie rolled her eyes. Seb had been testy about this trip ever since Aggie had suggested it. To her, joining Seb on his patrols to the Borderlands was killing two birds with one stone: Seb wouldn't be bored and tired and creeped out, Aggie would be able to get away from the base and Rix and that black hole Mir and all the fragging Angel talk that, since the Forecast, had been driving her quietly insane.

She wanted an escape and some quality alone time with her best friend. If it also involved getting out and seeing the proper open surface, well, that was a bonus. Aggie was beyond caring about the rules after the Forecast. Celeste was bound to tell Rix what she was up to, but screw him. If he could break the rules, then so could she. What was he going to do, fire her? Not fragging likely. Trouble was, Seb didn't know any of this.

'This is some next-level Craggie, man,' he hissed as they crept towards the buggi.

Aggie shoved him forwards. 'No it's not. Just keep walking.'

Craggie was short for 'Crazy Aggie', the name Seb had given her after she'd made him stake out the bins by the Lunar Academy catering hall for two weeks because she thought the food was getting contaminated. On that occasion she was wrong, yeah, but still, it wasn't that bad. Apart from the smell.

Aggie had always loved sneaking around, maybe because she'd spent so much of her life hiding.

She smiled to herself sadly. If only Seb knew the half of it. What was happening to Aggie at the moment was way beyond 'Craggie'.

'I can feel them warming up the engines,' he whispered.

'On what?'

'The Shuttle of Shame.'

Aggie pushed him again. They were walking down a long metal gangway that was lined on either side by gleaming black buggis. The bullet-shaped craft were designed to skim quickly and quietly over the lunar terrain, using the regolith dust sucked up from the surface as propulsion. Aggie thought the buggis were beautiful, so much more elegant than the cumbersome, dual-gravity scramblers available in the base itself.

'WELCOME TO THE G FACE BUGGI PARK,' Celeste's automatic systems boomed somewhere overhead, making Seb jump out of his skin.

'Hey Sebastian,' the computer called from the comms panel on Seb's wrist. 'You have access to lunar buggi 0326 for your flight today.'

Seb looked at Aggie nervously. Aggie frowned. The computer had seen her, she must have, but Celeste was acting as if Aggie wasn't even there.

A loud grinding noise went off somewhere to their left and the front hatch of a nearby buggi opened like the mouth of a great whale. A red cockpit was revealed, consisting of two seats, lots of straps and not much else.

'Please proceed to your buggi. Your patrol starts in ten minutes.'

All the colour had gone from Seb's face. 'Quick, just get in,' he said breathlessly, glancing around the room as if he really believed the computer hadn't noticed her. Aggie hesitated.

'Aggs, if you're coming, get in there now!'

Aggie nodded, then jumped past Seb into what she guessed was the passenger seat.

'Hey Sebastian,' Celeste continued happily as Seb finally strapped himself in beside Aggie. 'I'm plotting a course for G FACE BORDER PATROL into your nav system. Three-hundred-and-sixty-degree viewing is enabled. Have a pleasant patrol, Sebastian.'

'Thanks, Celeste,' Seb said, glancing at Aggie suspiciously.

'Stay bright, Sebastian.'

There was a click, a bleep and suddenly the buggi was launched backwards at an incredible speed.

'What?' Aggie said. Seb was staring at her again as he took a silver packet from his utility belt. It was a look he'd been giving her a lot recently.

'What's going on with you?' he said as he rolled the pack open. 'You're being so weird at the moment.'

'What?'

Seb narrowed his eyes, 'It's like you're here, but you're not.'

The glossy black panels of the buggi had become transparent, turning the craft into a translucent egg, skimming in a cloud of dust over the surface.

Aggie glanced down, trying to hide the fact that her cheeks had gone red.

'No, there's nothing . . . Ooo, is that Spacefood?'

'There's something so satisfying about eating a square, dry

apple pie,' Seb said happily as fine, freeze-dried apple pie dust plumed around his head.

Spacefood was considered a necessity rather than a luxury on the Lunar Base. It was emergency food, life or death food. But Aggie and Seb had always thought it was weirdly delicious.

'Uh huh,' Aggie nodded, a rectangular melon bar sticking between her teeth as it slowly rehydrated in her mouth. 'Helfy too.'

Seb frowned and looked at the dusty mush at the end of his packet, 'I dunno, I think they might be at least ten years old.'

'Oh, at least!'

'Dude –' Seb held up blue packet that read, 'Extra Hot Chicken Fajita' on the front – 'This packet is older than we are. That's the beauty of it. It's had time to mature. Get tastier.'

Aggie nodded and ripped open a bar of hot fudge sundae. As she bit into the dry sugary goodness, she watched the far reaches of the Lunar Base disappear into the distance.

Aggie had never been this far away from the actual base before. Now, the great mining domes that always dominated the view from her room were just tiny white dots flashing in the gaps between the rocks and craters. The sun glinted off the transparent hull of the buggi, lighting up the miles and miles of tan and grey tundra around them. No buildings, no people, no Rix, no Angel, no FALL. It felt good. For the first time in what seemed to have been forever, Aggie felt as if she was really free.

'Where are we?' she asked, taking in the scenery dreamily.

'Border Sea,' Seb said, glancing at the controls, 'Just past Goddard and Hubble craters. Right on the edge of nothing.'

'What?'

'Well, it's the Borderlands, isn't it? After the Borderlands, Celeste says bye, bye. Goes dead. Then all we got is the Far Side.'

Aggie nodded. 'It's beautiful.'

The border with the Far Side was the boundary of the Lunar Inc. base. A long line of glowing beacons flashed red halos of light intermittently over the rocky grey ground. Aggie followed their trail from one end of the dusty horizon to the other. Beyond them, in the shadow of the impending night-cycle, the Far Side loomed.

The Far Side itself had been designated geologically unfit for mining years ago by the United Government and was now restricted due to solar flares and some other stuff that Aggie didn't really understand. She looked out over the endless desert of grey that perfectly matched her mood. There was also something intriguing about it, something mysterious.

'I like patrols,' Aggie said, stretching back into the seat and dusting the Spacefood dandruff off her overall.

Seb looked up from inputting his security checks. 'I like patrols when you're here.'

Aggie smirked. 'That's understandable.'

Seb made a bleeping noise and looked over at the controls, 'Oh, hold on, emergency – your ego is taking up too much space. We have to eject you.'

Aggie laughed, 'Shut up, Sebastian.'

Seb twisted the controls and started to tilt their seats upwards so they faced the black blanket of space above them, 'Nope, sorry Aggs, this has gone too far.'

'Seb! Stop it!' Aggie laughed. The contents of her pack – now upside down – cascaded onto her face. 'Seb!'

'No, sorry, this is the ejection procedure – ooo, mango bar, I'll have that.'

The seats stopped when both Aggie and Seb were lying facing up at the stars. Aggie sighed and put her head on Seb's shoulder.

For a long time they just looked up at the great, endless vista above, with Seb munching loudly on his mango bar.

'Aw, man, look at that,' he said.

'What?'

Seb pointed to the glittering black above them, 'All that. It's amazing. The whole universe just hanging above our heads.'

Aggie nodded, 'Yeah.'

Seb turned his head and squinted at her. 'You're so over it all, aren't you? The universe and stuff. You're bored of it like everyone else.'

Aggie shrugged.

Aggie and her father had spent hours together when she was small, just driving out into the rocky wilderness with their telescope to look at the stars. They shone so brightly, brighter than they ever did here, with all the light pollution from the base. It hurt Aggie to think about those happy, innocent days.

'Well, it blows my tiny mind every time, man. We're dust, Aggs, tiny little specks of nothing, floating around doing nothing, just ... being, for no reason at all.' He mimed his brain exploding with his hands and grinned at her.

Aggie nudged him back, 'When you put it like that it's kind of depressing.'

'Oh no, man. It's the opposite of that, actually.' He turned back to the stars and sucked in a deep breath. 'Kind of romantic, though, when you think about it?'

Something sharp stabbed Aggie in the chest. 'How'd you figure that out?'

'Well, y'know, when you look at it all, what we do day-to-day, it doesn't mean anything, really. Like society and stuff. We shouldn't worry about stuff like that. We should just ... do stuff if we want to do stuff. You know ...' His voice trailed off.

Aggie started to panic. She always did when Seb got like this. It brought out a confusing set of emotions in her that she didn't really understand.

When Aggie had first bumped into Seb at the custard cart in the Lunar Academy, friends weren't part of the plan. Until she'd met Seb, the new post-puberty, blue-eyed, blonde-haired Aggie (it had taken three more years for her to brave it back to her natural red) had been a happy recluse. But theirs had been one of those friendships that was unavoidable. They were like magnets – after two sentences, they were stuck. There was no going back.

In the years that followed, Seb had taught Aggie how to

be herself again. He'd taught her some other things too, which was why moments like this felt so strange. On one level, she and Seb were unfinished business, but on another, he was like a brother.

Maybe it was the right time to . . .

'Seb,' she began, taking a deep breath. She'd been going crazy about when to tell Seb her secret. Maybe the best place was when they were trapped in a buggi on the edge of nowhere and he was getting all mushy. At least he couldn't storm off.

'What's up?' Seb turned and smiled.

A cold sweat broke out all over Aggie's body. Seb was the most important thing to her in the world, and she was about to tell him she'd been lying to him every minute of every day they'd known each other. She'd run over this moment in her head a million times but no matter how she phrased it, it always sounded terrible. She checked the buggi quickly, making sure there wasn't anything he could throw at her.

'Come on,' Seb said, his eyes going all watery. 'What's up?' His voice had gone gooey too, as if he was expecting something completely different to happen.

Aggie's heart went up a gear. 'I just, oh wow. Seb, I—'

'Frag!' Seb shouted. 'B–boulder!'

Aggie turned just in time to see a huge chunk of rock heading straight for them. The buggi made a crunching spraying noise and came to a stop, lodged in between two huge rocks.

*

Aggie looked around and saw nothing but moon rock.

Seb looked down at the control panel as if it was a piece of alien technology. The whole dash sang with flickering red warning lights.

'You clagger's ass, Seb! Look what you've done!'

'Hey, that was not my fault!' Seb gasped. 'Tell Celeste she's a clagger's ass!'

He had a point. How could the computer not see boulders this size?

Seb looked so panicked it made Aggie's stomach spin. 'I'm sure we can get it out,' she said quickly, 'then the buggi will self-heal.'

'It has limits, man,' Seb said looking out at the crushed hull. 'This isn't exactly a scratch is it?'

Aggie put her head in her hands. How could this have happened? She'd never heard of a buggi crashing before, Celeste was flawless, not one glitch in ten years.

Seb took a deep breath, 'Celeste?'

Nothing.

'Celeste!' Aggie shouted.

Seb winced. 'Woah, dude, she hasn't got a hearing problem. Though I definitely do now.'

'Sorry.'

The dash was blank now. For once, Aggie wanted Celeste there. She thought about the cold, desolate surface around them. How long could they be out here before a rescue team found them? Hours? Days? They needed to do something.

Aggie put a hand on Seb's arm. 'It's OK. Just, back us up

and we'll see how bad it is.'

Seb looked at the controls and shrugged.

'Nobody knows how to fly these things in manual,' he said, chewing his lip. 'Maybe I can figure out reverse.'

Aggie could see the red glow of the border beacons pulsing on the rocks behind them. They must be really close to the border, but what choice did they have? 'Do it. It'll be OK.'

Seb nodded. 'I wish I had your confidence.' He pulled the lever back.

The sound of rushing moondust hitting the sides of the buggi was deafening as Seb revved the fans. They ricocheted off the rocks like a ping-pong ball, but they were going backwards. Sort of.

After a few more seconds of screeching, rocking and scraping, the crumpled buggi made its way out of the gap between the boulders and shot backwards at such a speed that it sent Aggie slamming up against the hull.

'Earth's sake, Seb, take some of the power off!' she shouted, but the craft was vibrating so much she doubted Seb could hear. Aggie watched, powerless, as the red pulse of the beacons first blinded her, then started to sink away into the distance.

'Seb!' She cried. Panic was starting to rise in her throat now as she watched the screens and Ether in the buggi blink, then go offline.

'BORDER BREACH. BORDER BREACH. BORDER BREACH.'

Celeste's automated voice boomed overhead. A red

light descended over the cabin, highlighting the concentrated panic on Seb's sweating forehead as he wrestled with the manual controls.

Still they shot backwards at a vomit-inducing speed; the border was nothing but a red glow beyond the jagged ground. They were on the Far Side. Properly on the Far Side. This was bad. Really bad.

'AUTOMATIC CUT-OUT ACTIVATED. ONE MOMENT PLEASE . . .'

'What?' Aggie shouted in confusion. The fans stopped and the buggi slammed heavily into the dust.

'Ouch,' Seb moaned as he peeled himself from the control panel. 'That did not go as planned. At all.'

'What's it doing?' Aggie panted, looking at the dead, still Ether on the control panel.

'They have some homing fail-safe device in there, I think. No Celeste, though – its automatic.'

Aggie nodded. How long would that take?

Outside the buggi, the landscape was already a million miles away from the smooth mares and low-rising craters of the Near Side. The Far Side was jagged, cracked and ravaged. The distant, lumbering lunar sunrise illuminated what looked like a huge, black valley heading for miles into the darkness.

'Seb,' Aggie said, gazing at the valley, both horrified and fascinated. 'Look at this, it's kind of beautiful over here. More interesting than our side . . .'

She glanced over her shoulder, but Seb was still busy playing with the buggi's controls.

'I mean,' Aggie continued, still totally absorbed in the view. She was sure she could see lumite sparkling where the sunlight hit the rocks in the canyon, 'it's such a shame that it's too dangerous . . .'

The words dried up in Aggie's mouth.

She saw something in the dust. Something small, something grey and rounded like a Near Side boulder. It was just so out of place in this harsh, jagged landscape.

Then it moved.

'Seb,' Aggie said.

As the thing moved, dust started to fall from its body, revealing more of what lay beneath. Something soft and padded, shiny in places . . .

'Seb.'

Another layer of dust sifted away, revealing something golden and round. It was a golden globe, twisting up at her, reflecting the sun into Aggie's eyes. Aggie's heart jumped into her mouth.

It was a man.

A man in an old, white spacesuit, made filthy with grey dust. His massive round helmet was the old kind, his oxygen tank looked bigger than the buggi itself. As the man crawled forwards, an arm reached out towards them, a giant, gloved hand pleading with her, beckoning her, asking her for help.

But Aggie just stared, too shocked to do anything other than blink and breathe.

She watched the hand fall softly back into the dust. She let out a cry and pushed her seat back, jarring Seb in the ribs. 'Aw, man! Aggs, seriously, I do not need . . . Hey, what's wrong?'

'I . . . there's . . .' Aggie couldn't produce words. Instead she pointed out towards the surface, refusing to turn her own head. She didn't want to see the man again, his clawing, grasping hand was already burnt into her brain.

Seb followed her shaking hand and peered out of the buggi. 'What? I don't get it,' he said. 'What were you looking at?'

Aggie took a breath and turned her head. The controls on the buggi started to hum. Seb had got the emergency systems going, ready to pilot them back to the safety of the Near Side.

'What am I supposed to be looking at?'

Aggie peered back out of the windows.

'No,' she said, scanning the surface around them. 'No!'

Seb grabbed her shoulder, his eyes wide and wild.

'What is it Aggs? You're freaking me out, man.'

'There . . .' Aggie stuttered, pointing out to the patch of dirt. 'A man . . .'

'Aggie!' Seb cried as Aggie kicked out at the buggi's hatch release mechanism.

She shrugged his hands away and pushed at the smooth hull as it slowly separated from the buggi. She couldn't just watch someone die out there – she had to help them. Whoever was in that suit didn't have long.

'Aggie! That's the fragging Far Side, you black hole!' Seb shouted as Aggie leapt onto the dusty surface, her overall sensing a change in pressure and unfolding her helmet just in time.

Dust kicked up around her as she skidded, first on two feet, then on her hands and knees, finally coming to a rest beside the massive golden head.

'What?' She said to herself quietly, 'How?'

It was just a helmet. Just an old, battered-up helmet half buried in the dust and rocks. There wasn't a body to save. But Aggie could have sworn she'd seen it move.

'A fragging helmet?' Seb was suddenly beside her, showering her in another wave of dust.

'Yeah,' Aggie replied, twisting her head from side to side, looking for the man.

'It's just a helmet!' Seb slapped his thighs in frustration and pointed to the buggi that was still glowing red with warnings.

'Aggie. Dude. We've got to go quick. Celeste's gonna have reported a malfunction by now. It's only a helmet. Just calm down.'

Aggie couldn't. 'I know what I saw Seb.'

He followed her as she scrabbled in the dust around the helmet. 'Aggie, a person can't just disappear. Look, listen to someone that knows . . . this place does crazy things to you, you know. Makes your eyes play tricks . . . Aggie!'

Aggie wasn't listening. She threw herself back down into the dust and pulled out a whole arm section, then a massive surface boot. There was a whole suit here, buried in the dust. That must have been what she'd seen.

'How did this even get here?' Seb panted, staring as

Aggie pulled sections of ancient suit out of the ground. 'It's not as if some dude got a bit hot or something and decided to take off his suit and get a bit of air.'

Aggie's head shot up so quickly Seb jumped. 'Exactly.'

'Exactly what?'

'No one would do that.'

Aggie grabbed the collapsible bag from her utility belt and started to shove the bits of suit inside.

'What are you doing?' Seb's voice was so high it hardly registered on her comms.

'What does it look like I'm doing?'

'Well it looks like you're taking the suit, but that can't be true because that's what a crazy person would do.'

'I'm not leaving it here.'

'Aggie, just leave it. We'll get back and tell the G Face guards that we noticed something on the wrong side of the border. They'll come down here and—'

'You can't see this site from the border,' Aggie said flatly, still cramming the last of the massive suit into the bag. 'We'll get found out, plus they'll find the tracks and then with Celeste's report . . .'

Seb looked up at the sky. 'The shuttle. Earth below.'

Aggie stood up. 'I think that's it.'

'You're seriously taking it?'

'We need to go,' Aggie said, staring at the tracks they'd made in the dust.

'OK. You're actually taking it. Cosmic.'

As Seb guided the broken buggi slowly back to the border,

Aggie watched the place where she'd seen the man until it disappeared behind the horizon. Her chest heaved. She felt she was going mad; Seb was certainly looking at her that way. But Aggie knew what she'd seen.

She'd seen a man, out there on the surface, as clear as Seb was next to her now. She'd seen him die, and then disappear.

A hallucination, like Seb's Rock-Aliens?

She clung to the suit inside the kit bag. That was real. She could feel it.

What in all the seven states was going on?

7

Day-Cycle 08

Aggie had never experienced silence like this on the base before. No hum of the air con, no whine of the gravity systems, no personnel. She tipped her head back and basked in it.

She was standing in the centre of a hexagonal room coated in thick, white sails. They pulsed a soft yellow light, giving her the feeling that she was on the inside of a huge egg. Along one of the walls, a bank of camera lenses stared out into the white space like a spider's eyes.

The Forecast Suite.

Mir had spent the last few hours assessing Aggie for a

range of different qualities that it was obvious she didn't have. Aggie's personal favourite was the exercise in which Mir had stood her in front of a mirror and encouraged her to 'get a better smile'. Aggie had endured it all without a word, until she'd suggested this visit – vid suites freaked her out.

But when they finally did descend on the Forecast Suite Aggie understood why. This place clearly wasn't designed for humans. This was Celeste's domain.

Aggie peered down the camera lens. A tiny, upside-down version of her looked back. The miniature Aggie looked tired, and had a coffee stain on her overall.

She sighed. She could hardly believe it had only been a week since Rix had visited her in Spooner's office. One week. Aggie's old life in Domestic had already faded. In fact, so much crazy stuff had happened to her, she was surprised she could remember that far back at all.

'Aggie, it's almost time to go,' Mir said from the other side of the room. Breaking the precious silence. 'I still can't believe they let us in here. Nobody has access to this suite, ever.' She stroked the white sails fondly.

Aggie smiled weakly and checked the cameras for the red recording light again. Nothing. Safe.

'I hope you like it in here,' Mir continued. 'After the party, Rix will want you on the Forecasts.'

Aggie rolled her eyes. Mir obviously caught it in the camera's reflection.

'Think about it, Aggie. Who'll want Celeste's avatar when they can have the Angel?'

Aggie's stomach rumbled loudly. 'Everyone. When they realize the Angel is just me.'

Mir gave her one of her looks. Aggie turned away, wrapped her arms around her stomach and sighed.

Recently, she had felt as if she was having an out-of-body experience, as if she was watching somebody else's life slowly unravel. Everything that was happening to her was somehow worse than the last. It had been a full Earth day since she and Seb had pretty much destroyed the buggi on the border, and Aggie was prepared to take the blame. Seb was already in enough trouble for the Rock-Aliens – if they found out about this he'd be Shuttled for good.

But Aggie had checked the records and there was nothing. She'd been expecting to be called straight in to see the commander as soon as they landed at the buggi park. She was ready to be shouted at for being reckless and disobedient and not appreciating her delicate situation or something. But there was nothing. There weren't even any guards to meet them at the park. Seb thought it was the best luck ever, but Aggie couldn't help but think otherwise.

The hallucination she'd had was playing on her mind. It was so real, so vivid. She'd stopped calling Seb a black hole for the Rock-Aliens – he was right, the Borderlands really did mess with you.

'Hey Mir,' Celeste whispered from some hidden place above their heads, making Aggie jump. 'Your priority clearance for this sector ends in fifteen minutes.'

Mir smiled up at the ceiling, 'Thank you, Celeste.'

She turned to Aggie. 'We have one more thing to do today,' she said quickly. 'It is very important – for the party.'

Aggie shrugged. 'Everything for the party's important, isn't it?'

Mir smiled tightly. 'It's not a bad thing.'

'We have different ideas of what bad is.'

Mir nodded. 'Yes. We do.'

Aggie felt the air around them tense. This was how they were, since Aggie had run away on the face. Spikey.

Aggie thought Mir was OK, but the Earth Relations girl just continued to rub her up the wrong way. Secretly, she felt they were the wrong way around – Aggie should be the nobody and Mir the beautiful, elegant, capable, Angel of Adrianne.

Aggie followed Mir towards the door, then spotted something in the smooth white wall. A dent. A hole just big enough to fit a hand through. Aggie bent down. There was a button in there. A big shiny white button.

'Aggie, no!' Mir grabbed Aggie's wrist and pulled it out of the hole. 'That's the manual function for the cameras. Don't ever press that.'

'What would it do?' Aggie said, peering in the hole.

'Broadcast us bickering to the whole world.'

Aggie's hand sprung away. 'Oh, right.'

She bit her lip. What was it about buttons that meant you felt you had to press them? Seb's bad influence, probably. She pushed her hands into her armpits to avoid the temptation.

'Stay bright, ladies,' Celeste said as the two girls exited

the Forecast Suite and started to make their way through to the main Tranquillity foyer, Mir rattling on about broadcast techniques or something.

Tranquillity Base – the massive Lunar Inc. HQ building – was built deep into the moon rock that formed the edge of the sprawling lowland of the Sea of Tranquillity. And, as the only truly public-facing part of the base, everything about it was designed to wow.

Above Aggie's head, a giant glowing globe of the moon hung inside the vast foyer. A detailed hologram of the Lunar Base glittered across its surface, showing the outline of the buildings and mining domes that clustered the Near Side. Lush green plants hung from planters in the walls around it and lined the edges of the seating areas that were dotted around the foyer floor. She could hear the sound of rushing water drifting through the sound of hushed footsteps and voices.

She shook her head. Tranquillity wasn't like the rest of the base *at all*. It was more like a luxury hotel.

As they passed through the foyer, some of the personnel glanced at Aggie's stained and faded Analysis overall. They probably thought she was here for the disciplinary board, about to get Shuttled. She didn't blame them.

Mir veered to the left and ducked through a dusty service hatch, into what looked like an old maintenance corridor.

'Shortcut,' she said over her shoulder, answering a question Aggie hadn't asked. Aggie frowned. Mir wasn't exactly the shortcut type.

What was going on?

Aggie kept up with Mir's trotting pace until the tunnel started to spread out into a wider platform. The ceiling stretched up and out until it soared above them like a glossy undulating sea. Aggie knew that ceiling.

'Why are we in the shuttle bays?'

'I just told you, Aggie.'

Mir led Aggie down a metal gangway and out onto the main shuttle platform that ferried human cargo between the base and Earth. The vast hangar was dotted with grey wedge-shaped United Earth shuttles, with their gold-overalled crews scuttling over them like shiny beetles.

They walked away from the shiny vehicles to where a giant, battered, old cargo transporter sat with its doors hanging wide open.

'Am I being Shuttled?' Aggie joked, genuinely worried, as Mir lead them up the ramp and into the dark hold. Something about this didn't feel right. Not at all.

Inside, the cargo shuttle was lit by strips of low, flickering violet lights that ran around the edges of the walls. The walls themselves were buckled and dusty, and dotted with broken comms hatches and smashed Ether screens. It was packed with grey, dented supply boxes and crates. The whole ship looked like it was ready for scrap. Aggie shivered. It was freezing too, even in her overall.

She stopped.

There was someone in the corner.

Someone wearing red.

'This is a nice surprise,' Danny muttered with a smirk.

Aggie stepped back as a guard instantly materialized behind the prisoner. A black shadow closing its arms around his red throat and chest.

'Danny!'

Danny didn't shout. He didn't even flinch. His eyes remained locked on Aggie's as the shadows descended on him, pinning him quietly back against them.

Aggie's overall started to chug more oxygen into her face, worried about the fact that she'd stopped breathing.

In the dark, claustrophobic hold, the prisoner looked as battered and abandoned as the cargo boxes that surrounded him.

'On first-name terms, are we? That's cosy.'

Rix emerged from the shadows, munching on a Spacefood bar.

He smiled and leant on Danny's shoulder. 'If there's one thing I got, it's good intuition about people. Never let me down in the Peace Army; it hasn't let me down now.'

Rix's eyes glowed in the dim lights. He looked wired. His energy was making the air vibrate. Mir shuffled nervously up beside her.

'What's going on?' Aggie said quietly.

'I was going to ask the same thing,' Danny said, rubbing his wrists. The guard shoved him back again.

Mir looked up from her comms unit. Her expression was placid, calm, but her jaw was set tight. 'We've suspected FALL have been planning to infiltrate the base for years. It was actually part of the reason for the intake of the two-hundreds. The commander picked out 209 as soon as I reported the incident on G Face. He needed to see you together to make a clear assessment of the risk—'

'Why?' Aggie interrupted, even though she already knew the answer. Rix had been watching them. He knew that Danny knew.

Rix zeroed in on Danny. 'So, no one's come close in ten years, but you got it. What was it? Intel? Someone on the inside? Lucky guess?' Rix shoved Danny's shoulder again. 'Or maybe she just told you? How about that?'

Aggie suddenly felt like the gravity had been switched off. Rix's protection had been the only comfort Aggie had, but right now it was a vile thing. A thing that could hurt the prisoner, kill him, even. She didn't want that. Not because of her.

Rix would do anything to keep Aggie's identity quiet. Her godfather had always told her that.

'Roger—' Aggie began, but Rix's hand shot up, stopping her. His cool green eyes were fixed on Danny, his white teeth bared in an animal snarl.

The guard's buzzer was aimed directly at the soft connection between Danny's overall and his helmet. The prisoner looked so vulnerable, so powerless. Pins and needles started to prickle all over Aggie's body.

'What are you planning?' the commander whispered, bending down and speaking to Danny through his perfect, gritted teeth. 'What kind of useless suicide mission did they set for you, you pathetic piece of clag? You're just a bag of bones to them, you know that? Fodder. Me, I care more about you. You know why? Because it looks bad if my prisoners start dying, that's all.'

To Aggie's surprise Danny snorted with laughter. The blood drained from her face. What was he thinking?

Rix smiled. 'You think you can beat me? You and your filthy insurgents think you can come here, to my base, and ruin me?' Rix was right against Danny's ear now; the prisoner winced as spittle hit his face. 'You failed here. You FAILED. And now, you're going to find out what a real prison's like.'

Every tendon stood out on Rix's neck. Aggie had seen the commander's temper flare many times in the past, but never like this. There was desperation in his tone, as if he was on the edge of losing control.

He flung his arm out at Aggie. 'Whatever it was that you were planning on doing with her – to her – take a good long look. Because I guarantee it will be your last.'

Rix stepped back. Danny's stare had never left Aggie. She shuffled away from his gaze, but it burnt through her.

'Thank you,' he said to her quietly, as if Rix and Mir and the guard didn't exist.

'What?'

'YOU DON'T SPEAK!' Rix cried.

Danny's body shuddered as the guard's buzzer bit through the tough material of his overall.

'Rix! Stop!' Aggie cried, instinctively jumping forwards.

'Stay there!' the commander shouted. He took a breath then rounded on her. 'He was using you. You idiot kid. He was asking questions, getting formation. A scout.' Rix wiped his mouth with his sleeve. 'When he met you he hit the jackpot, didn't he? Gullible little Aggie. Lucky I got to him before he got to you.'

Aggie stumbled back. She felt as if all the light had suddenly gone from the world. She looked at Danny, Rix pacing and Mir occupying herself with her comms.

She knew, right then. Rix was right. This was all part of a game – not just FALL's game, but Rix and Mir's too.

Danny's scar stood out on his cheek in the dim light. Aggie no longer wondered about its origin, she sympathized with whoever gave it to him.

No one in this shuttle cared about her, not him, not Rix, not Mir. They were all using her.

'Have fun in the Pen,' she said tightly and turned and raced out of the shuttle.

Out in the hangar, Aggie choked back tears. This base, this whole fragging pointless rock of a moon and all the point-less people on it could go float off into the void for all she cared. Screw them all. She upped her pace towards the wall of the vast hangar. Every time something made sense to her, something else would happen that blasted it all apart. The prisoner, the party, the fragging hallucination she'd had on the border. She was one star short of a galaxy, surely. The tenth anniversary was making her lose her mind.

She could hear Mir's surface boots clacking on the hangar floor behind her. She took a deep breath and tried to stop the shaking.

'Aggie!' Mir shouted. Aggie couldn't deal with Mir right now.

She spun around to meet her. 'Are we done?' she demanded.

Mir opened her mouth but Aggie got there first.

'Are we done for today?'

Mir hesitated. 'Yes. That's it.'

Aggie pulled away. Her head was buzzing as if it was running its own gravity system. She just needed to get out of Tranquillity, get away from Mir and Rix and back to her pod.

'Aggie!' Mir shouted behind her. Aggie waved her away and upped her pace. In the corner of her eye she could see the flight assistants and guards gathering to watch the commotion.

'Frag's sake, Mir, just leave me alone.'

'No. Aggie!'

Aggie pulled the handle on the first door she came to. It wouldn't budge. She pulled it again, so hard that it activated the exo in her glove.

'Celeste!' Aggie shouted, desperate to get out, away from the lights and heat and noise and faces.

'Hey Agatha.' The computer spun from the Ether beside the door.

'Aggie, wait!' Mir's footsteps echoed behind her.

'Go away.'

'No, Aggie! That's the waste disposal!'

Aggie pulled her hand back from the door. 'Oh, right.'

'Hey Agatha, do you wish to dispose of an unwanted item?'

Aggie turned in a circle, suddenly aware that she had

absolutely no idea where she was or how to get back to the main building. And that about fifty people were now staring at her as she tried to break into a giant bin. Cosmic. Just cosmic.

'It's this way.' Mir panted, pointing to a huge airlock on the other side of the platform.

'Great,' Aggie muttered and pushed past her.

She tried to lose Mir in the deserted tunnels that led back to the bustle of the main Tranquillity building. Lost in her thoughts, Aggie didn't notice how busy the corridors were becoming until she smacked straight into the black overall of a guard.

She staggered back and looked up.

'Oh frag, sorry I— SEB?'

Seb was standing frozen to the spot, his Blipcard still hovering over the sensor on a giant Spacefood vending machine.

'Seb!' Aggie launched herself into him with the velocity of a meteor. Someone here did care about her after all. Relief swept over her so fast she felt giddy. Seb was here, in Tranquillity, just when she needed him. *Hold on*. Why was Seb in Tranquillity?

When Aggie finally pulled away, Mir had caught up. Seb looked as if he'd seen another Rock-Alien.

Actually, so did she.

The clatter of Seb's Spacefood hitting the tray seemed to bring him back to reality.

'Aggie!' He said, a few octaves higher than normal. 'Are

you OK? What are you doing here?'

'What are you doing here?' Aggie panted, resisting the urge to hug him again in front of the Mir-bot. Seb never mentioned working in Tranquillity before. Plus, he was supposed to be on border patrol – wasn't he?

'Guarding stuff,' Seb squeaked.

Aggie looked around. 'Guarding what?'

Seb laughed too loudly, then did a double take. 'Hey, you OK? You look pale. Here –' He passed Aggie his cherry pie Spacefood bar – 'are you sweating?'

Aggie wiped her forehead. She was. Badly.

'That makes the two of us, then,' she said, looking at Seb's shiny, red face.

Seb glanced at Mir and turned a deeper shade. Mir was looking at him as if he'd gone insane. Aggie was starting to think that too. He was acting beyond weird.

Then she remembered. Had Seb taken Astrid's stupid 'secret mission' comment that seriously? Had he been following her? Had he seen her with Rix and Danny?

'Seb . . .' she began, but Seb was already starting to back away down the corridor.

'You're OK, though, right?' he said, frowning and giving her a thumbs-up at the same time.

Aggie shook her head, but he'd already disappeared.

A weight settled in her stomach.

Why was everyone lying to her?

8

Day-Cycle 09

Aggie lay back on her bed and stared up at Celeste's Eye in the ceiling. The red light of the iris bounced around in its black orb.

She reached up and felt for the ridge under her eyelids. Her anger at what had happened in Tranquillity still simmered uncomfortably under her skin. It was surreal to her, as if she'd dreamt it all. She remembered the desperate look in Rix's eyes. The man was usually so in control, so considered. Aggie had seen the commander's unpredictable side more than once over the years, but never like that. It was impossible to have any perspective on anything any more.

She wanted her old life back. Badly.

She rolled over and groaned into her pillow. If her life seemed overwhelming now, how could she cope after the party? How could she go back to Analysis as the Angel? The Angel of Adrianne couldn't exactly test the swimming pools for urine, could she? More likely they'd bang her up in Tranquillity with all the perfect Earth Relations and media people, with their make-up and their buzzwords and their fancy sky-blue outfits. Aggie would rather spend it out on the fragging faces with the prisoners.

Aggie saw again the look on Danny's face before she'd stormed off. Did he really hate her? Did she really hate him? Did any of that even matter any more?

'Danny,' she sighed, remembering the flash of his eyes from behind his visor.

'Who?'

Aggie's head snapped up.

Seb appeared at Aggie's pod door and backed into the room carrying a tray piled with half-melted frozen custard. A flustered, pink-overalled maintenance guy appeared in the doorway after him, 'Hey, hey! Please, look at the mess you've made of the hallway!'

Seb smiled. 'Hey, Aggs, I stopped by Whole Earth on the way over. Thought you might need custard, you know, after yesterday.' He winked theatrically and set the tray down by the bed. Aggie made a face in the direction of the maintenance man.

Seb rolled his eyes. 'Oh him? Dude's been following me since the shuttle station.'

Aggie smiled, 'You walked that here all the way from Whole Earth?' she said, genuinely moved.

'You can tell by the trail of sticky little spots!' The man tutted. 'Blue spots, for miles down my corridors! I've got your number now, you,' he said, glaring at the ID panel on Seb's chest, 'and I'll see that it goes on your report.'

'He's very sorry!' Aggie shouted as she pushed the close button on her door. She fell back on the bed in a fit of giggles.

Seb rolled his eyes, 'Aw, man. Seriously? I tried my best, but trust me, these things do not shuttle well. I thought I was going to get hit by a tech head at one point.'

'Why?' Aggie said, peering at the tray.

'Well, he may have a blueberry-flavoured ponytail now.'

Aggie laughed, 'Oh no.'

'Yeah.' Seb sat down on the bed beside Aggie and presented the tray to her as if it was a silver platter. 'So, we've got interstellar toffee, but that's for me, obviously. Key lime pie, because it's your favourite. Chocolate because, you know, it's practically a medicine, right? And finally –' he twisted the tray around, revealing a pot of what looked like bright blue soup that was so full there was now more of it on Seb's overall than in the pot – 'blueberry nebula,' he said proudly. 'It did have silver bits in it when I got it, but I may have eaten them all.'

'They look kind of gross now,' Aggie said, taking the key lime pie anyway.

Seb took the blueberry nebula and started to walk around the tiny little room, sipping it like a fine wine.

'Thank you,' Aggie said, scraping the bottom of the tub loudly. 'I feel better already.'

As she ate, Aggie watched Seb out of the corner of her eye. His guard's overall was creased and his hair was its usual mess of curls, but there was still something off about him. Something was going on. He'd acted like a total freak when she'd bumped into him in Tranquillity. Aggie was convinced he'd been following her, that he'd seen her talking to Danny with Rix and Mir, and that had helped her make up her mind. She hadn't invited Seb over just to hang out – it was now or never. Seb deserved to know who she was.

'Aggie, this pod is a disgrace,' he said, picking up a sticky, half-eaten Spacefood bar from her desk that had a sock stuck to it. 'You're disgusting.'

Aggie took a deep breath. 'Seb . . .'

But Seb had followed the trail of mess under her bed. 'Earth below, is that part of an oxygen unit? Aggie, you can't just take this stuff!'

Aggie frowned. 'I broke it and I didn't want to get in trouble . . . Look, Seb, please, just sit down.'

'But, someone might need it. You know, for breathing and stuff. Ooo, is that one of those massaging shower heads?'

'No, it's an air duct filter. Seb . . .'

Seb dropped the cone-shaped filter back onto the floor. 'Oh, OK, gross.'

Aggie pulled him onto the bed beside her. 'I need to talk to you. It's about the party.'

She felt her blood pumping in her ears. This was really

happening, she was really going to do this. If she messed this up, if she lost Seb too, she'd only have her distant godfather left.

Seb looked up at her nervously. 'Aw, man,' he said softly, rubbing his forehead. 'I knew this was coming.'

'What?'

'Aw, man.' Seb put his pot down. He looked really nervous. All shiny and red – just as he'd been in Tranquillity. 'Thing is, Aggs, I know we would, but the thing is, there's this . . . and I just thought that maybe it would be OK to go to the party with someone else. Instead of you, I mean. Not that I don't want to go with you – it's just . . .'

Aggie blinked. 'You're going with someone else?'

'Yeah.'

'A girl?'

'No, Aggie, a dinosaur, it's here on an exchange programme from the birth of time.'

Aggie didn't register the sarcasm. 'Oh, right.'

'You OK?'

'Yeah, I'm good.' She glanced around the room, she wasn't good, she felt as if she'd been kicked in the stomach. 'Cosmic.'

There was an awkward pause.

'You sure? Your face is all screwed up.'

Aggie nodded and tried to force her chin to relax.

'Thing is . . . it's Mir.'

Aggie's heart forgot to do its job for a second, 'What?' Did she hear that right? Did he say *Mir*?

The Ether screen beside Aggie's bed sprang to life. Aggie had forgotten what time it was. The Lunar Inc. logo spun against its spacey backdrop.

'I said it's Mir, from the Academy,' Seb explained. 'We had some dumb space rocks class with her. You were with her in Tranquillity, actually . . .'

Aggie couldn't believe it. *That* Mir? Earth–Relations Mir? Suddenly the way Seb was acting in Tranquillity made sense; he wasn't following her, he was waiting for Mir to finish her shift. Aggie felt the biggest black hole in the universe for not seeing it before. No wonder Mir had looked so shocked.

Aggie chewed her lip. So the Earth Relations girl had been keeping that secret too, as well as everything else. Typical.

Rix's face beamed out distractingly from the screen. 'Citizens of the United Earth,' he said brightly, flashing his trademark smile. 'It is my personal pleasure to introduce you to the 546th Lunar Forecast. Live from the Sea of Tranquillity.'

Aggie forced her attention on the screen.

'Thank you, commander.' Androgynous Celeste beamed. 'This is a Waxing Crescent Forecast. The subject for today's Forecast is life in the mines, as part of our tenth anniversary season.'

Seb was staring at Aggie. She could feel his eyes burning into the side of her head. Maybe he could see it spinning? It certainly felt as if it was. Seb and Mir? *Her* Seb and perfect, annoying Mir? How in all the seven states did that happen? Had they kept in touch since the Academy? Seb had never mentioned her.

'One of the questions we get asked many times,' Celeste continued as the vid followed the mined lumite crystal down through the tunnel system, past the great cell packing machines and out onto the chaotic, dusty face, 'is, how does Lunar Inc. change the minds and hearts of its prisoners? Well, to us, it is simple.

'Our prisoners take great comfort that their hard work is keeping their families on the Earth out of the darkness. That every time a switch is pulled or a button pressed, their work is being appreciated by the great and the good. And we at Lunar Inc. make it clear to them that we appreciate them too!'

Aggie's stomach sank further. It had started – they were fighting propaganda with propaganda, reminding the United Earth what Lunar Inc. was giving them. Preparing the public for the party. For her.

The vids changed to images of the prisoners themselves, hundreds of men and women dressed head to toe in red; drilling, sorting and fixing, and all the time laughing, joking and smiling. It made her feel as uncomfortable as when she'd seen Danny in the shuttle. This was her godfather's prison mine. The things she'd seen done to Danny were Rix's doing. Suddenly, her anger at Mir and Seb evaporated. Seb dating Mir might have been big news for Aggie, but the Angel had more momentous things to worry her. The thought made her sad.

'Without their hard work, we would not have the lumite

cell that powers our homes and our lives on Earth today.'

The images changed to the happy citizens of the United Earth using the glowing violet lumite cells in their houses, their cars, their comms units and coffee machines.

The vid pulled out slowly, showing the great towering factories where giant lumite cell cores pulsed in the generator rooms, revealing the violet streetlights and the glowing violet Hyperloop that connected the seven states at super-speeds. Finally, the footage zoomed out to reveal the Earth spinning in space, the trillions of lights that dotted its surface glowing violet with lumite.

Seb was still staring at her.

Aggie, needing more time to think, just concentrated on the screen. A selection of rehabilitated prisoners turned and smiled at the camera, 'Thank you Lunar Inc.,' they said, one after the other.

'Be sure to tune in tomorrow for your own exclusive invite to the Lunar Inc. anniversary party. You won't want to miss our special announcement.'

Celeste winked.

Aggie winced.

'Stay bright, United Earth.'

The Ether went back to its lazy black swirl. The room seemed quiet after the bluster of the Forecast, but Aggie was too numb even to move. Every day, as the party got closer, the reality of what was about to happen to her got more terrifying.

'You sure you're OK?' Seb asked quietly.

'What?' Aggie snapped.

'About Mir, the party?'

Of course – the party. Aggie had more things to worry about at the party than her lack of a date. But still, the idea of Seb going with Mir was just weird.

'Cosmic,' Aggie said with a small smile.

She pulled her shoulders back and tried to act as if there wasn't an invisible hand around her throat.

'It's cosmic, really. I'm not really going, so . . .'

Seb smiled at her suspiciously, 'What? Dude, I know you hate humans and everything, but did you not just see that? This is going to be the most insane party ever. We're going to be talking about tomorrow night for like, millennia. There's going to be free food, free drink, Sonic Nugget are playing, and – oh yeah, that's it, the fragging Angel of Adri-clagging-anne!'

'That's not confirmed,' Aggie said nervously. 'No one knows that that's true.'

Seb leant back on the bed. 'C'mon, man, course it's true. The whole base is talking about it.'

Aggie smiled weakly.

'I got fifty blips on it being her,' Seb continued with a grin. 'Everyone's putting blips on it, like, everyone.'

Aggie shivered.

'Oh Aggs, some people have the most crazy ideas. Apparently some mine op put two hundred blips on it being Adam Faulkner in a wig! Two hundred blips! Ha, man. Can you imagine the wise old master of the universe shuffling out on stage with lipstick and red hair? I almost wish that was true, just so I could see it.'

Aggie turned her back and looked out of the window. Seb tapped her shoulder, 'Hey, I can talk to Lucas on E, put some blips on it for you if you want? You must have some Craggie theory about it, right?'

Aggie shook her head. 'I'm not going to the party. I've got . . . work stuff.'

'What? An emergency dust contamination? A last-minute drain blockage that just can't wait?'

'Seb, really, I don't want . . . it's nothing.'

Seb smiled, 'Dude, there's no such thing as "nothing" with you. What is it? The secret mission? I knew Astrid wasn't lying. She can't lie, she's too . . . eager.'

Aggie sighed and looked out of the window. In the distance, a clean-up drone skittered across the base of E Face; a piece of junk glinted in its metal claws. Aggie stood up, she could see two more tiny drones, tidying the areas around the shuttle tubes. She'd never even considered the clean-up drones before.

'Seb, do you ever see the clean-ups on your border patrols?'

'Huh? Clean-up drones? Oh yeah, tonnes of 'em. Once, I saw one just going round in circles. I saw it for two whole weeks, just going round and round and round . . . Hang on, you've not got one under your bed, have you?'

Aggie just stared out of the window.

'Aggs?' Seb said from the bed. 'What's going on?'

'Nothing.' She said distractedly, watching the drones gather up anything that wasn't where it was supposed to be. She shook her head. 'Nothing.'

9

Day-Cycle 10

Aggie lay in the dark and concentrated on breathing. Her whole body felt as if it had been buzzered. A horrible jolty feeling spread out in waves from her chest down to her fingers. She felt sick, even though she hadn't eaten anything more than a lemonade-flavoured Spacefood bar all day.

The blinds on her pod window were open, but the waning day-cycle meant the sun had sunk days ago and the room was cast with a gloomy grey. Aggie liked it – the colour matched how she felt.

Today was the tenth anniversary of the Adrianne

Disaster. It had always been a day of solitude for Aggie, for taking a day off and hiding herself away in her pod, alone with her memories. She longed with every thread of her being that that was all she had to do this time.

Everything she knew had shifted slightly. The same, but different, as if she was finally beginning to see the base in a colder, harsher light. Aggie wished she could go back to how it was; to her bright, colourful, sunny world of custard carts and rec rooms and jokes with Seb. But it was pointless. Rix was about to rip it all away.

Slowly, Aggie reached up and plucked her contact lenses out of her eyes. She flicked them one after the other onto the messy floor. Tonight, Agatha Sommers died, and the Angel rose up out of the ashes. Tonight, the whole world would be her friend again and her only real friend would find out she'd been lying to him.

Aggie jumped at a knock at her door.

'Aggie?' A soft, pretty voice called from the corridor. 'Time to go.'

Aggie followed Mir and a heavily armed security detail down the dorm corridor and onto a waiting scrambler. Aggie sat in the middle, flanked by the two guards. This was how her new life would be, she concluded, feeling her stomach screw up into a ball.

Mir didn't speak to her as she climbed into the front, her dress overall sparkled at the seams as if it were lined with lumite. Her hair was tight to her head, not one strand out of place. Her eyes were highlighted with shimmering blue liner, and tiny earrings in the phases of the moon sparkled along the edge of her ears. Aggie could just imagine Seb's face when he saw her. The stomach ball scrunched up even tighter.

Aggie watched the corridors of the Analysis dorms disappear as they sped past groups of personnel gathered in the rec rooms, laughing and sparkling in their dress overalls. The air around them seemed to fizz with excitement.

Finally, the scrambler emerged from the service tunnels and onto the wide open concourse that led to G Face. Aggie gasped. She'd been on the face only a few days ago. The transformation was incredible.

The thin, plastic hab that had covered the half-built entrance on Aggie's last visit had been replaced with a shining Plexiglas concourse. Lights hung from every support, winking like the stars in the sky through the windows. Rope lights around the edge of the great airlocks flashed in the colours of the Infospectrum, changing to match the member of personnel who was coming through. There were stalls set up around the airlocks, serving brightly coloured cocktails and bags of sweets that glowed blue in the dim light. Glittering groups mingled around them, their mouths glowing as they munched on their bioluminescent treats.

The sweet, sickly smell of Spacefood and alcohol mixed with the metallic odour of dust as it escaped through the airlocks. The air was smoky with it as the scrambler slowly made its way around the crowds and followed the curve of the dome wall until it came to an entrance Aggie hadn't seen before.

'Hey Agatha,' Celeste chimed in her helmet comms, 'Welcome to the G Face opening party.'

Aggie ignored her.

Another set of guards nodded and opened the huge manual airlock, allowing the scrambler to pass through and out onto the face.

The face itself had been cleared. Aggie could almost make out distant cliffs where the dome met the surface as the scrambler raced towards the staging area.

Huge drill machines still stood in a semicircle on the untouched mining bed. Daisy's great spiked discs and looming cranes were covered in tiny specks of light that twinkled from every surface, illuminating the circle of dust cleared for a dance floor.

As they got closer, Aggie could see the party area. Tables had been set up around the rebuilt stage, each piled with food in colourful packets. The stage itself glowed with huge vid screens, each displaying a spinning Lunar Inc. logo. Aggie imagined herself standing there, a little speck of dust on a sea of black. Drowning in front of the crowds.

'Agatha.'

Aggie jumped off the scrambler and was greeted by Rix, beaming in his glowing dress overall.

'How'd you like what I've done with the place?' He held his hands aloft, making a gaggle of assistants scatter. LIXR, the fragrant drink of choice of all the Lunar Inc. directors, sloshed around in the crystal glass he held. By the look of Rix, it wasn't the first one he'd had that evening. Compared to the last time they'd met, in the dusty shuttle, he was a different man. A good thing – Aggie never wanted to meet that man again.

'Great,' Aggie managed.

'How're the lines? All up here?' Rix prodded his temple.

'I think so.' There wasn't much to learn, and despite Aggie's track record, she was actually quite good at learning speeches. She'd had the practice, after all.

'Y'know, it's just astounding what a bit of sparkle and some free food can do, hey?' Rix continued, smiling into his drink.

The room around them was silent. Aggie suddenly understood that every single member of personnel in the tent now knew who she was. She refused to look directly at their familiar awestruck faces. She knew she had to get used to it, but still, she felt like an exhibit in a zoo.

'Well, now you're here,' Rix said, waving a hand and beckoning Mir to come over. 'We have a little surprise for you.'

'Another surprise?' Aggie said, with a glance to Mir. She was done with Rix's surprises.

She followed Rix and Mir to the far side of the staging area, where a bunch of tech heads were working on a tangle of power leads with the help of Celeste.

'Hey Agatha,' the computer said as she walked past.

Aggie didn't respond.

'Good luck.'

Aggie stopped. That was a strange thing for the computer to say.

'Angel, get over here!' Rix shouted. 'We don't have long.'

Aggie walked to where Rix and Mir were standing, either side of a small table. A glowing white bag was in the centre. A kit bag.

'What is it?'

'Open it.' Mir said with false enthusiasm, pointing with a perfectly manicured finger.

Aggie took a step forwards. 'It's not a dress, is it?'

'Not on a Lunar Base,' Rix snorted drunkenly.

'Good.'

She reached out and pulled the zipper slowly. Bit by bit, the white plastic fell away, revealing something that was way worse than a dress.

'No.' Aggie stepped back as if the thing was on fire. 'I'm not wearing that.'

Mir stepped forwards and heaved the violet overall fully out of its case. The thing glittered under the lights. It was beyond disgusting.

'I'll look like a giant lump of lumite!'

'I think it's lovely,' Mir said with a fake smile. 'Really symbolic.'

'It's an Angel *costume*. It looks cheap.' Aggie growled, mainly at Mir and her stupid opinions.

'Taste is subjective, I suppose. We don't all have it.' Mir said, her pretty face twisting.

'Like your taste in men, Mir?' Aggie asked innocently. She wanted Mir to know she knew about her and Seb.

Mir opened her mouth then closed it again.

'My Infospectrum is yellow.' Aggie said, turning back to Rix.

'Well, now it's violet,' he said, his eyes shining. 'You have your very own rating. How about that?'

'I can't wear it.'

'No one will be able to miss you in this, Aggie. No more running away from us,' Mir said sweetly.

Aggie looked back at Rix. 'I'll be a target. I'll be followed around everywhere!' She was desperate.

'That's the idea, isn't it?'

Aggie was panicking now. She wanted to punch Mir in her pretty, Seb-stealing, lying, Earth Relations face. She wanted to push Rix into the abyss above the unfinished dome. She wanted to crawl into a ball on the dusty ground and sob. She wanted anything other than to be the Angel again. That violet overall represented everything her new life would be and she hated it.

Aggie crossed her arms, trying to remain strong for once. Outside, the rumble of the crowd intensified.

'I'm not . . .'

'You'll wear it,' Rix growled, stepping so close his eyes were level with hers. His whole body language had changed. He was tense, like a coiled spring. 'You'll do as you're told,' he whispered, carefully forming each word. 'You'll wear the fragging overall, you'll do the speech and you'll perform for the Forecasts. And you'll look like you're having the time of your life.'

Aggie took a step away. 'No . . .' she said weakly, but stopped when she felt Rix's grip on her arm.

'You'll wear the overall,' he repeated slowly. He was so close now Aggie could smell the alcohol on his breath. 'You'll do the speech, and you'll smile for the cameras.'

Aggie opened her mouth to protest, but Rix's grip was so strong it was starting to make her arm go numb.

Outside, the crowd started to chant 'OUT OF DARK-NESS WE SHINE,' the Lunar Inc. motto. A sour taste surged in the back of her throat, but she felt strengthened by the noise.

'OK. OK.' She stepped back from Rix, rubbing her arm. 'I'll do it.'

Rix threw back the last dregs of his LIXR and grinned at Aggie. 'Good girl.'

The sparkly, violet Angel costume was tighter than Aggie's old Analysis one. She pulled at the thick fabric uncomfortably as Rix led her up the steps to the stage. The crowd was deafening now, clapping and stamping and whooping and hollering as the anthem of the United Earth, 'Into the Light', blasted from the stage at full volume. Aggie could feel the floor shaking beneath her feet, reminding her of the last time she'd walked on to the stage. She thought of Danny, and wondered if he was watching too, wherever he was. She doubted it, somehow.

The anthem finished and the crowd hushed.

'Citizens of the United Earth,' Celeste's voice boomed, 'welcome to this special Lunar Forecast, live from G Face.'

A roar.

Rix let go of Aggie's arm and bounded forwards

through the curtains onto the stage. Aggie stayed behind, watching Rix as she waited for her cue.

'Please, please.' The commander beamed.

He waited until the crowd had calmed down.

'Please. Thank you so much Lunar Inc.-ers! As always, it is a great thing to have you all here on this most exciting of occasions.' He spread out his arms, indicating the glittering mine around them, 'We are expanding!'

A great cheer made the stage rumble beneath their feet.

'Oh, yeah. Feels good, doesn't it? More lumite, more power for the homes of Earth, for our families. That is something to feel good about, I guess.'

Another huge roar.

'But, my good, good people. In all this celebration and ceremony, we must not forget that today is also shadowed by sadness.'

The crowd hushed. Rix paced the stage, his head now hung as if in deep thought.

'Y'know, it's not an easy time. Not for any of us. We must not forget, of course, but we must not let ourselves be beaten either.' He paused and looked up, as if holding back tears. But from where Aggie was standing, she could see that his eyes were dry.

'Lunar Incorporated has been helping our world heal for decades: from Grayson Faulkner's vision; to his son, the great Adam Faulkner's drive; to the Founding Five's talent. We have tirelessly kept the world bright, kept the air clean and industry booming. The lumite cell has helped eradicate global warming.'

The crowd cheered.

'The affordable power it provides has helped wipe out poverty.'

Louder.

'The lumite cell has transformed the Earth, it has united the Earth!' Rix had whipped the crowd up into a frenzy. The rush of sound battered Aggie's ears and made her feel light-headed as she moved her heavy limbs onto her mark behind the curtain. She felt like a prisoner from the old days, stepping slowly up to the gallows. The rope around her neck was the collar of the violet overall, waiting to choke the life out of her.

She fixed her smile. It made her cheeks ache.

'A world with power, a world with peace!' Rix paused. 'Citizens of the United Earth . . . a world with . . . HOPE!'

The crowd fell quiet. A mechanism cranked and Aggie felt herself flying upwards.

A band of lights buzzed to life behind her, burning her back. Aggie felt like she was about to faint. Images of vid studios and interviewers and cameras and lights flashed before her eyes. Then the curtains opened.

The sound of the crowd nearly knocked her over. The screams and cheers and stomping feet battered her body. Nausea swept up inside, her eyes burnt, her throat closed up. She looked out on a sea of faces. Thousands of people, just like Switch On Day.

Aggie stumbled. Blurs of light and noise danced around her.

'The Angel of Adrianne is here!' Rix said as the crowd

finally died down.

The commander gave Aggie his hand and helped her down from her raised platform. 'Welcome back!'

Another wall of sound from the crowd. Aggie noticed someone being dragged away by the guards. Were people fainting? This was crazy.

Rix gestured towards her and slipped away. For a second, Aggie didn't understand what had happened.

She was alone on the stage.

The crowd was so quiet Aggie could hear the buzzing of the lights over her head.

She glanced at the silhouette of Rix in the shadows, still looking at the ground in mock-emotion, then back to the sea of expectant faces, their collars glittering back at her in the darkness of the dome.

The silence seemed to stretch up out of the face and into the void itself. Aggie stood, dumbstruck, blinking in the lights.

'Th . . .' she said shakily, any words crumbling to dust inside her head. The realization that she was expected to make her speech washed over her like ice water. Not just a speech, but a speech about the one thing she hated to talk about: Adrianne. The ten-year anniversary of the disaster that changed her life forever. When her father made a mistake that killed thousands, including himself. She'd practised the words, but she hadn't expected this, this frenzy. In that second Aggie finally understood what being the Angel really meant. The whole world was watching her, waiting to hear what she had to say. Rix grinned at her from the shadows. He'd known this would happen. This was a punishment. A test.

'FAKE!' someone who'd had more LIXR than Rix shouted from the sea of faces below, followed by a hushed giggle that rippled to the back of the room. Aggie looked at the faces again and, not for the first time, wished that she hadn't survived the explosion.

Then she caught a face in the crowds. A pair of round brown eyes staring up at her from the front row.

Seb's face was the picture of shock and betrayal. Mir stood with her arm around his waist. Aggie looked down at Seb. All she wanted to do was run off the stage and bury her head in his neck. She needed Seb to stroke her hair and tell her everything was going to be ok. She longed to tell him how sorry she was that she hadn't told him sooner. She should have tried harder.

'It's a FAKE!' the voice shouted again, this time getting a roar of laughter.

'I, err . . .' She stumbled on the words again.

Aggie stood in the spotlight, sweating. Racking her brain for something, some coherent set of words that would just get her though this.

She watched Seb turn and disappear into the crowds. Her heart went with him.

Aggie bit her lip and took a deep breath. She had to be strong. What was the point any more? If she didn't have Seb, she didn't have a life anyway. *Just get through this, Aggie*, she told herself, and suddenly, thankfully, the script popped back into her head.

'Adrianne,' she said, her voice quivering with nerves. 'It's a word that is seared into our minds as citizens of our beautiful United Earth. A disaster for both our history and our humanity. But, citizens, we refused to be broken by that terrible day, for a new hope emerged from what had become a hopeless world.'

The crowd settled down again. Gaining confidence, the familiar words from Aggie's childhood of interviews and speeches flowed out of her. But every one she uttered tore at her soul, the embarrassment at what her father had allowed to happen at Adrianne rotted away inside her. She felt dizzy, but she kept going.

'I, the Angel of Adrianne –' she paused for another roar from the crowd – 'I stand here, in front of all you good people, on this, the tenth anniversary of that terrible yet hopeful day, as a symbol of that hope. The hope that together, as members of Lunar Incorporated, and as proud citizens of the United Earth, we can achieve our every dream. We can rebuild what was broken, and bring light into the darkest of places.'

Commander Rix began to emerge from the shadows, smiling like a proud father. She'd done OK. She'd passed his test. Aggie felt his cold touch on her shoulders as the crowd let go a deafening shout.

'Beautiful words. Beautiful. Our Angel will be back with us, working tirelessly to bring lumite into your homes and your hearts. May the United Earth forever stay bright.'

Another cheer.

'But, please, listen to our Angel at this delicate,

emotional time. Remember, we are Lunar Inc., we are united, and out of darkness . . .'

'WE SHINE!' The crowd bellowed back, followed by whoops that made the ground rumble like a moonquake.

Aggie felt pressure on her shoulders and Rix began to walk her slowly off the stage into the cool darkness. As they left, engineers ran on, setting up the stage for the first of the bands. Sonic Nugget, Seb's favourite. He was going to miss it.

She could hear murmurs in the crowds. 'Angel' penetrated through the din more than once, and with an embarrassed twist in her gut, she even picked up on one voice muttering the first few lines of 'Into the Light'.

Hands appeared out of the line of guards that kept the crowds at bay, clawing desperately at Aggie's violet overall. People screaming. Fanatics chanting. Grown men and women in tears at the sight of her. Did they not know she was Aggie, the domestic analyst whom they called when their air con needed servicing? Her godfather had been right: in her years in hiding, the Angel had become more than a symbol – she'd become an icon. These people didn't just admire her, they worshipped her.

Aggie kept her head high and tried to smile. A cold hand clutched at her heart, slowly squeezing with every step. Rix beamed beside her, reaching out and shaking the hands that came too close. He punched the air and applauded, nodding and singing along with the noise.

When they reached the end of the line, Aggie felt the room spin around her and she fell to the floor.

A guard rushed to her side, carrying her out to the back of the tent, where deep purple-clad medics swarmed her. Her head pounded, her heart ached. For a second, she thought she saw Seb's face among the crowds. The hurt was so clear in his eyes. She needed to get away.

When the medics' backs were turned, Aggie lifted up the heavy backstage curtain and ran.

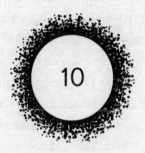

Day-Cycle 10

Behind the stage, the face was deserted. Aggie ran around the dusty surface until she found an unmanned airlock and slipped through into the empty G Face corridors.

She ran and ran until her lungs burnt and her legs felt as if they would collapse. But she didn't get far enough. Panting, she fell back into a service hatch, and listened to the sound of distant, stomping surface boots getting closer – Rix's guards.

The hatch bleeped. Aggie jumped and saw the door was wedged open. The thud of the boots was getting louder.

They were so close now that she could hear the laboured breathing of the guards in her comms. She didn't have a choice. She slipped behind the door and slammed it shut behind her.

As the door closed, the sound was cut off. Aggie found herself alone in a small, dark corridor. Strips of low white light led away along the rocky floor to a dim intersection where metal conveyor belts ran into a series of tunnels.

Aggie could hear a deep rumble coming from somewhere up ahead. She was in the cargo tunnels, the subterranean highway that moved the raw lumite around the base. She turned back to the door, then hesitated. If she went out into the corridor again, the guards would find her. No one would look for her here. The G Face tunnels weren't even in use yet.

Slowly, Aggie stepped forwards, the violet lamp in her new Angel costume cast a dim light in the thick darkness. With every step, the tight feeling in Aggie's chest started to ease. Her breathing slowed and she started to notice things around her.

She was following a thin service corridor that ran parallel to a metal track. Aggie knew from her training that that track would usually be filled with rushing conveyors carrying lumite to the processing plants and then to the cargo bays, where it would be launched back to Earth. G Face wasn't in production yet though, so the distant thundering rumble she could hear must be coming from the other faces, even though they were miles away.

After an hour or so of blissful, aimless walking, Aggie

took a slope upwards and found herself in front of another service hatch. As she approached, the door clicked and sprang open. Aggie popped her head through and saw deep blue curved Plexiglas walls. The Tech Department.

Aggie paused by the door, but the only sound she could hear was the distant hum of the Tech computers. To her left, an Ether spun slowly beside an emergency airlock. Aggie watched it for a second, but Celeste didn't respond. She slowly crept out of the hatch and into the low blue corridor. Tech was a subterranean department located directly underneath the Whole Earth Complex. It was made up of a series of low-ceilinged rooms connected by dark, narrow tunnels that twisted and turned so much they confused even the most senior tech heads. The perfect place to get lost.

Aggie loved the Tech Department. She'd only been a couple of times, when she'd actually admitted to breaking something. There was so much cool stuff happening down here, and no stuffy scientists to spoil the fun. If things had been different, maybe she'd have made a good tech head.

As she stalked the empty corridors, she could see a host of fantastic stuff happening inside the rooms: clean-up drones spinning around in pointless little circles, another with two members of staff in VR suits – the screens beside them showing that they were carrying out a maintenance check on one of the huge Harvester satellites that provided the base with extra solar power. Another room was packed full of 3D printers, all of different sizes and purposes, spitting out item after item into big coloured buckets.

'Hey Agatha,' Celeste said softly from one of the desks. Aggie stopped and stared at the Ether. It pulsed as the computer talked. 'What brings you to Tech this evening?'

Aggie didn't reply. She walked on, following the corridor as it snaked downwards. She wanted somewhere quiet, she wanted to get away from the madness that was now her whole existence. She couldn't think of a better place to hide.

'Hey Agatha,' Celeste said again, this time from the Ether beside a maintenance hatch. 'You do not have authorization for this sector.'

Aggie turned to the Ether angrily. 'If I have to be the fragging Angel of Adrianne, Celeste, then I can access everywhere. It's compensation.'

The Ether whorled. 'I'm sorry Agatha, but I don't understand the question.'

'Course you don't.'

'You don't have authorization for this—'

'Shut up Celeste.'

There was a long pause.

'OK Agatha.'

Aggie shot the Ether a puzzled look and pushed on. It was only a matter of time before the computer alerted Rix and his guards. She had to keep going, get herself well and truly lost.

The corridor was getting narrower and colder. The rocky walls were now lined with maintenance hatches. Some were left open; personnel had been in a rush to get their tasks completed before the party – exposed wires and components hung out of them like robot entrails. The air started to smell like burnt metal. Aggie began to feel safer, as if she was slowly creeping into the very heart of the base.

'Hey Agatha,' Celeste said, as Aggie stepped out of the corridor and into a huge, white, circular room. 'Welcome to the Home Ether.'

Aggie looked up and gasped. She'd wandered right into Celeste's mainframe? The Home Ether was four floors high, with white balconies spreading up to the ceiling, looking down on the giant Ether that stood, black and writhing, on a raised platform in the centre of the room.

'Hey Agatha,' Celeste said again, her voice emitting out of a tiny Ether by the door, 'Can I help you with anything?'

Aggie shook her head.

She walked slowly around the perimeter of the huge mainframe, checking for any panels or hatches, but the raised floor on which the Home Ether sat was smooth. Suddenly exhausted, Aggie sat on the lip of the platform and put her head in her hands. Her life had been extraordinary in so many ways, but tonight was really in a different league.

As Aggie thought of the mess of a speech she made, of the scrum that had formed around her afterwards and what Rix would have to say about her running away, she let out a long groan. How could she live on the base any more? Her life was over. She'd have to become a recluse, go back to her father's old house in Reykjavik. Her only option was to do her duty for Lunar Inc. and then slowly become a rumour again. Until the next time. Until FALL rose up again, or until Rix decided he needed more love from his precious public. Aggie was company property. Something to be used, then cast aside.

'Is there anything I can help you with Agatha?' Celeste repeated.

Aggie stood up and faced the giant Ether. To her surprise, it was spinning like water down a sink. Aggie stepped closer, so she could feel the static coming off the invisible particles that whirled inside the huge frame.

'Take me away,' she said quietly. 'Just take me away from here.'

'OK Agatha.' Celeste's voice echoed, releasing a hatch hidden at the side of the stage. Aggie peered inside and felt something tug at her temples.

Aggie opened her eyes, and then shut them again.

Nope, it can't be. It must be her mind playing tricks on her.

She opened them for a second time, then cried out and fell to the floor.

She was in a room, a room that spun and shifted, breaking up and coming back together as if it was constantly rebuilding itself. The ground rumbled softly below her – not the smooth white of the Tech suite, but the dusty grey of another room. A room she would never forget.

Like a dream, a soft violet light pulsed around her, illuminating the old control desk and cluttered metal cabinets. Paper readouts covered the old-fashioned touch screen and dials.

She was in the reactor room. She was in Adrianne.

The lumite reactor spun before her slowly, clouds of steam billowing from the cooling vents as they rotated around it. It buzzed happily to itself, pumping out thousands of kilowatts of power. It was working perfectly, just how it had done in the hundreds of tests her father had run before . . .

'Aggie?' a voice penetrated the hum in the air. A voice that was familiar and strange all at once.

'You have to see,' the voice said.

As the voice spoke, the room twisted and now she was jostled by people. Thousands of people. Aggie tried to elbow her way through but she was too small, too weak. She looked up, the perfect blue sky shifted and settled again. A warm desert breeze shifted her hair, something fell into her hands. A tiny flag, the flag of the United Earth.

Somewhere above the heads and shoulders a microphone screeched with feedback. The stage was just visible through the crowd, the United Leader, the engineers, the Faulkners dressed in their best clothes for the Switch On of her father's reactor in the power station far below their feet.

'No!' Aggie cried, as terror gripped her.

A deep rumble penetrated the noise of the countdown. No one in the crowds noticed. The anthem of the United Earth began to play over the speakers. The ground pulsed, but the crowds were too preoccupied with singing.

'You have to see,' the voice boomed in the sky.

The people disappeared, replaced by rubble and smoke. It was still, silent. Aggie looked down. She was on her knees, her hands were bleeding, her violet dress hung in rags. She wiped the dust from her eyes and continued to tear at the rocks. 'Daddy,' she panted, desperate to here his voice from under the rubble.

'Look! A little girl!'

The First Responders appeared out of the smoke like shadows. They ran towards her with their black cameras and blinding lights.

Voices echoed. 'She's trying to save them! Help her!'

'How did she survive?'

'She must be an Angel.'

'Stop!' Aggie screamed at the sky. It was too real, too raw. She put her head in her bleeding hands. 'Stop it, stop it, Celeste, please!'

The computer's voice shattered the others. 'You have to see.'

Suddenly, worlds shifted and rebuilt around Aggie like scenes from a dream: her father's smiling face as he drank LIXR with Adam Faulkner on the roof of the Lunar Inc. labs in Adrianne. Aggie sat at their feet, listening to the hush of their deep voices, watching the warm sun set over the rocky orange mountains.

'You have to see.'

Aggie shivered. The sun had gone, replaced by cold white walls. The interview rooms in the United Facility, journalists flashing their cameras in her face, security hurting her as they pulled her away.

'You have to see,' Celeste repeated.

The room spun again and Aggie collapsed in a ball on the ground.

She lifted her head. Birdsong drifted on the warm breeze. The hush of grasses was all around her, the soft lapping of cool water on the rocky black beach. Aggie stood up. Behind her, on the crest of the hill, stood a small blue-and-white house. A wide porch wrapped right around, sheltering two rocking chairs that pointed out towards the sea.

Her father's house. Her favourite place in the world.

Aggie bent down and ran her hands through the long grass, the smell of sea salt and soil made her feel giddy. She tilted her head back, closed her eyes and let the fresh breeze lift her hair and dry the tears on her cheeks.

'You have to see.'

Aggie's eyes snapped back open.

The jagged rocks of the Far Side jutted angrily around her. And at her feet . . . Danny, wearing the old suit Aggie had found on the border, his eyes staring blindly out from behind the visor. His mouth moved, 'You have to see.'

Aggie screamed. 'I don't see! I don't see!'

Terrified, she turned and tripped over another body. Every pile of dust was an old spacesuit. Thousands of bodies littering the landscape as far as the horizon.

'I don't see. Let me out. Please. Celeste, stop it.' Aggie sobbed. 'Please, make it stop. I don't see, I don't see.'

A massive pulse swept across Aggie's vision, sending a sharp pain across her forehead and a rush of white noise into her ears, so high and loud that she thought it would rip her head apart. She cried out and felt rough hands on her shoulders.

*

'Aggie!' a voice vibrated. 'Come back! Dude, seriously, you've got to wake up!'

'Seb?' she said groggily, as a dark shape emerged out of the darkness.

She felt a ripping sensation as Seb pulled off the electrodes that connected her to the computer. 'We gotta get out of here,' he hissed, 'like five minutes ago.'

Aggie came around, finally. The edges of the room were tinged red. 'Wh–what's going on?' she whispered.

'Rix knows you're here,' Seb said breathlessly. 'We have to go.'

He hauled Aggie to her feet and dragged her out of the Home Ether room and into a tiny maintenance corridor covered in wires and switches.

Aggie's head pounded, she couldn't stop shaking. She felt weak and scared. The image of Danny's dead face mouthing Celeste's words replayed over and over. Her feet refused to work properly and Seb ended up half-carrying her for most of the way. Aggie pressed herself up against him, so close she could hear his heart beating.

Behind them footsteps echoed. 'Guards?' she said woozily.

'Yes, guards,' Seb panted, 'Tranquillity guards too, like a whole bunch of them.'

'Oh no,' Aggie said, willing her legs to move faster.

They went along the snaking Tech corridors, sticking to the maintenance routes until the footsteps started to die down. Seb stopped, hauled Aggie upright again and pushed at a plain white door that was sunk into the corridor wall.

He threw Aggie into the room and slammed the door shut.

Aggie looked around. They were in a tiny Tech rec room. The only lights were the blue panels inset around a group of white benches in the centre. Spacefood vending machines lined the walls and old wrappers and half-finished drinks littered the floor. It smelt of sugar and old laundry.

Seb leant against the door, trying to catch his breath. He stared at Aggie for a long time. His expression unreadable, or maybe that was just because Aggie's mind was doing somersaults.

'What were you doing?' Seb asked calmly.

Aggie hoisted herself up onto a bench and put her head in her hands. 'I don't know,' she said, trying to remove the images of Celeste's nightmare from her eyes.

'You have to see.'

Seb huffed and started to pace the room.

Aggie looked up. 'You came to find me.'

He stopped. 'Yeah, I wanted the Angel of Adrianne's fragging autograph.' His chest was heaving under his dress overall. He was so angry.

'Where's Mir—?'

'How could you do it, Aggs?' Seb shouted suddenly, his face going red under his brown curls. 'I mean, what else haven't you told me, hey? Are you actually eighty-seven years old? A man, maybe? Or not even a human at all? Yeah, that's it, you're a fragging Rock-Alien! Oh thank the Earth,

I'm not crazy after all!'

'Seb, please don't.'

'A robot! A walking, talking humanoid, devoid of all feelings and emotions. Just going through life screwing with people that care about her!'

'Seb!'

'Who are you, Aggie? Who the frag are you? My only real friend in the world and I don't even know who you are any more.'

'I'm just Aggie, a lower-tier domestic analyst. That's all that matters.'

'Bunch of denk.'

'Seb, nothing has changed.'

His eyes got even wider. 'Nothing has changed? Aggie, tonight, in front of a crowd of literally billions, I learnt that my best friend is the fragging Angel of Adrianne. The Angel. Of. Adrianne. The Child of Hope. My friend Aggie, the crazy-haired, clumsiest human in the world who samples urine for a living is the Child of Hope!'

'I'm just me.'

'And then I go backstage, so I can shout at you, and I see you running into the cargo tunnels, with half of Rix's guards looking for you! Seriously, what's wrong with you?'

Aggie looked up. 'You followed me?' she said hopefully, 'You came to find me?'

Seb wasn't listening. 'I mean, I knew you had connections in the company, but David Shepard's daughter? Adam Faulkner's adopted daughter? Is that for real?'

Aggie nodded slowly, tears running down her face. 'I'm

sorry, Seb. I tried to tell you so many times.'

'Oh yeah, because I can imagine it was hard to find a moment to do that in five years. Aggie, we've been hanging out and talking crap for five years! Do you not think "Oh, BTW Seb, don't know if you're bothered or anything but I'm basically the most famous person in the world", is a bit more important than "How would we survive a Lunar Base zombie apocalypse?"'

Aggie tried to smile. 'Hey, Lunar Base zombie apocalypses are a real threat.'

Seb didn't smile. He was really mad. More than Aggie had ever seen before. She didn't really blame him.

He threw himself down onto the bench and looked right into her naked, violet eyes.

He paused for a moment.

'What?'

'Nothing. It's just they're kind of terrifyingly beautiful.'

'Is that supposed to be nice?'

Seb shook his head. 'My Aggie's eyes are blue.'

The look he was giving her was tearing at Aggie's soul. She should have told him. She should have told him years ago. She couldn't lose him now. Not like this.

'Seb, please. I don't know what else to say. Please don't be like this, I can't stand it. I need you.'

She tried to grab his arm but he pulled away.

'Seb, even I used to forget I was her. There are posters everywhere, but it's always been like looking at someone else. I was just a kid. I was a different person back then.'

'No, Aggs, NOW you're a different person. Right now.'

'No I'm not! How can different-coloured eyes make me a different person?'

'You've made me feel like a clagger's ass, Aggie.' He turned back to her, his eyes cold. Aggie had never seen Seb look like that before.

'Look, man, I helped you. But this –' he gestured a shaking hand between them – 'I dunno, Aggs. Maybe we need some space. You're obviously going through a lot right now—'

'And I need you more than any other time!' Aggie cried, not caring if Rix and his men heard her.

Seb's face softened. 'Hey, look, I'm not going anywhere, OK? I'm not . . . aw, man, Aggie, this whole thing has blown my tiny mind. I just need to . . . I mean, I don't know if I can be like I was with you, knowing all this stuff.'

Aggie felt all the life seeping out of her. Seb was her strength. Without him, she couldn't even breathe properly. She was terrified. Did he have any idea how much she needed him? Why was he talking to her as if she was a stranger? His voice was different, the way he sounded when she called him on shift and the other guards were listening. She didn't want Seb's work voice, she was Aggie. His Aggie.

'Please don't do this,' she said thickly.

'I'm sorry, Aggs. I just . . .' Seb opened the door. 'I'll see you around, I guess.'

'Seb!'

He slipped away into the corridor.

*

Aggie sat in the dank blue light unable to move. She stayed for what felt like hours, but it must have been minutes, because when she finally opened the door, she could hear the distant ring of voices. Rix's guards.

The corridors here were narrow and cluttered with wires and low-hanging pipes. She stepped out of the rec room gingerly, then stopped.

Rix was standing among the wires ahead of her. His face looked ugly in the low light – tightened with anger.

Aggie turned, but found her way back blocked by six huge Tranquillity guards. Mir stood in the centre of them, her dress uniform sparkling. She looked as terrified as Aggie did.

Without a word, Rix threw his protein pack down on the ground and walked up to her. Aggie felt as if she was carved from moon rock. Too scared to move. Rix had that look in his eye that terrified Aggie. Bright and manic and unpredictable. The gang tattoo was pulled tight across his jaw – the commander did not enjoy being disobeyed.

He looked at the ground for a long time. Then:

'Look's like our Angel needs to have her wings clipped,' he whispered.

There was a spit of electricity, a flash of violet in the dull corridor.

'Aggie! Look out!' Mir cried, stepping forwards and trying to drag Aggie back by her arm.

Rix's buzzer arced in the dim light, bringing its evil, violet forks down on Aggie's shoulder.

Pain convulsed over every inch of her flesh.
She heard Mir cry out.
Then, nothing.

11

Day-Cycle 13

A breeze ruffled Aggie's hair.

Her father's car, with its old sticky leather seats, floated into focus around her.

She could smell the dust and heat of the desert on the wind that came in through the windows. In the distance, the gleaming silver dome of the brand new lumite power plant rose up out of the red horizon.

'This is against all known protocols, David,' a familiar voice echoed from the dash. Aggie opened her eyes. A tiny Ether spun beside the old dials.

Her father's knuckles were white on the wheel. 'It's a feeling, *a hunch, that's all.'*

'There's no evidence to suggest that . . .'

'I know, I know —' her father shook his head — 'but he's stopped listening to reason.'

The Ether on the dash began to churn. 'David . . .'

'It's an order, a directive, whatever you need to do,' her father's voice wavered. 'If anything happens to me — please, she hasn't got anyone else.'

The road thundered under the car's old rubber wheels.

'OK, David.'

The scene dissolved. Aggie swam in a sea of black so thick it felt as if she were inside the Ether itself.

The hospital pod came in and out of focus, floating in front of her for a second, then pulling away, lost in the darkness. Aggie pushed at the hospital monitor in her arm. The chip vibrated softly under her skin, administering the meds that kept her sedated. She felt her arm fall back down. If she tried to rip it out, the computer would only knock her out again. She doubted she had the strength, anyway.

This is how the days were. If they were whole days.

Aggie swallowed drily and shifted on the itchy sheets. She closed her eyes in an attempt to stop the nausea. She had to be quiet. She had to think.

When she mumbled and cried out, a nurse would shuffle in, place a cold hand on her forehead and tell her to relax, it was the healers, knitting her damaged body back together — she needed to be still, to let them do their job. She should be grateful that the guard's buzzer was on stun. She was going to be OK. She just needed to be still for a while, that was all.

Her mind drifted to Seb. She imagined him out on the base, laughing at the custard cart with Mir, she saw him on his border patrols all alone. Out in the lonely Borderlands where he'd seen the—

The Rock-Aliens.

Something sparked in Aggie's head, suddenly became clear.

She pulled herself up in the bed and opened her eyes. The room swayed around her. She felt as if something dark and horrible had crept up and bitten her. Why hadn't she seen it before? It was so obvious now.

Aggie pulled the sheets off the bed and tried to sit up.

In her preoccupation with the Angel, Aggie had missed something. Something much darker. Something to do with the old suit under her bed. Something that, for reasons Aggie still didn't completely understand, Celeste wanted her to see.

No one had told her how long she'd been in the Tranquillity hospital wing – the medics refused to say. But, judging by the state of her injuries, she'd guessed it was a while. Rix had hit her with the buzzer on stun, knowing that the nano-healers in the hospital would eventually reverse any damage the shock caused. It was a warning. She was his now. On the base, the commander could do whatever he wanted to keep his property in line.

The official story was that the Angel had been 'overcome with emotion' after the party, and needed rest.

Just the thought of it made Aggie's skin crawl.

Aggie had had no idea that Tranquillity had a hospital wing, but it kind of made sense: it had its own shuttle pad and dorms, and it wasn't as if the board of directors would put up with convalescing with the riff-raff in the Civilian Sector.

Aggie groaned. The sedation meds for the healers had worn off, but she was still as good as trapped. Even the slightest movement sent pain thudding through her whole body. She badly wanted to move. She couldn't just lie here; her thoughts were pulling her somewhere else.

She looked to the side of her bed. An empty frozen custard pot, filled with silvery Spacefood packets, sat on the small plastic table, beside the piles of fruit-based 'gifts' given to her by 'admirers', and the bizarre 'get well soon' statue from Astrid and the ERMs. There was no note on the pot, but Aggie didn't need one. Seb might not be speaking to her, officially, but the medics had told her that a guard with curly hair had been by her side every day when she was unconscious. It made Aggie want to cry.

'Ah, finally!' A familiar voice drifted over the beeping of medical equipment. 'How are you feeling?'

Aggie might be hidden away in Tranquillity, but she hadn't been short of visitors.

Mir was currently sitting in an armchair on the other side of the room, her head buried in the comms pad that contained a petabyte of goodwill messages from Earth.

'Did you know you have a vid from the president of the Chinese Territories on here? And the elected leader of

Scandinavia,' she said, flicking the screen. 'Honestly, Aggie, this reads like a who's who of the United Earth!' She turned the pad to Aggie. The face of a woman whom Aggie didn't recognize was on the screen.

Aggie huffed and pushed the button that administered her painkillers. She hadn't read the messages. She hadn't had the strength to do anything but think. And her thoughts were driving her crazy.

'I think I need to rest,' she sighed into her pillow. *Take the hint, Mir.*

'Hey Agatha, you have already had the recommended eight-point-one hours of sleep today,' Celeste chimed from the other side of the room. 'Any more would actually be detrimental to your recovery.'

The computer's voice made the hairs on Aggie's arms stand up.

'Cosmic, Celeste,' Aggie grunted, returning Mir's smile. 'Totally cosmic.'

The Mir-bot had been stuck in full 'nice mode' ever since the incident with Rix. She'd used her efficiency superpowers to great effect, arranging Aggie's visitors, revising her schedules and, most annoyingly, keeping her company. Aggie suspected it was all to do with guilt. Aggie bit her lip to stop from asking her about Seb.

Instead, Aggie took a deep breath and said the thing she should have said days ago. 'Thank you, by the way. For warning me.'

Mir shook her head, a sad look washing over her face. 'I still can't believe he would do that,' she whispered.

Aggie remembered the look in Rix's eyes. She could.

Both girls glanced at Celeste. A silent understanding passed between them. Right now, even their thoughts were dangerous.

The Ether rippled in its frame on the other side of the room. Aggie's vitals skittered across its surface, supplied by the raised square under the skin of her forearm. She looked down at the implant. It still felt like hostile alien technology. For the fiftieth time, Aggie considered ripping it out, but they'd only put in another.

'Well, Aggie,' Mir said after a few more awkward minutes. 'I have good news.'

'You're not engaged, are you?' Aggie mumbled.

Mir rolled her eyes. 'No, of course not. Though Seb is fine, by the way. He'll be pleased that you asked about him.'

Aggie grunted. They were official now? She couldn't bring herself to ask.

'It's hurting him, Aggie.' Mir sighed. 'And it's hurting me too, actually. Of course we have our differences, but I hate to see you fighting'

'We're not fighting about *that*,' Aggie muttered.

Mir gestured towards Aggie. 'I meant *this*. You!'

Aggie pushed for her meds again. She needed to be numbed for this. It was too strange when Mir was being nice. It made hating her harder.

'Well, it looks as if I've been promoted to the United Leader's PR team in Tokyo. I think, after everything –' Mir paused, making sure Aggie knew that 'everything' meant what had happened in the Tech corridor – 'the commander feels I have achieved all I can on the surface.'

Mir was putting a brave face on it, but she sounded as if she might actually cry. Aggie suddenly felt terrible. If it wasn't for Mir dragging her out of the way, her hospital stay would be a lot longer. Rix really was that crazy.

'I'm leaving on the next shuttle, actually.' The Earth Relations girl's voice was cracking. 'I'm now a proud member of the United Government.' She didn't sound proud.

Aggie glared at the Ether and whacked the meds again.

'Mir, I don't know what to . . . I'm sorry . . .'

'It's you I'm sorry for,' Mir said with genuine concern, her eyes flicking to the Ether then back to Aggie. She placed a hand on the bed, leaning forwards. Her green eyes reminded Aggie of an owl. 'You know something, don't you?' she whispered. 'Something else? I don't know why he would act like that. You're the Angel, for Earth's sake. He wouldn't risk hurting you, but maybe if you knew something—'

The door to her pod slid open, a chatter of voices clamoured for a second and then stopped. The door shut again, leaving only the shuffle of footsteps on the floor. Not surface boots, though, lighter.

Mir jumped out of the chair.

The smell of citrus and spice drifted into the room. Aggie knew that smell.

'Adam!' Aggie cried, as her godfather shuffled into the room.

'Aggie, little one!' Adam Faulkner wrapped her in a hug so tight it made the monitors bleep. Suddenly the dark thoughts in her head disappeared like smoke. Adam was here, on the surface. He'd come all the way to the Moon to see her.

He was wearing a long, beige coat with the silk, robe-like suit that was popular with the UG ministers beneath. Civilian clothes. It looked strange in the context of the base. Overalls were compulsory – if there was a leak, a drop in pressure, anyone unprotected would be done for – but Aggie guessed that no one was going to tell Adam Faulkner what to do.

When her godfather finally released her, he pulled something from out of the folds in his coat.

The smell hit her first, a smell she'd missed so much, fresh and earthy and perfumed.

'Flowers!' Aggie exclaimed, looking at the bright yellow and violet bouquet in his hand. 'Real flowers!'

'Yellow and violet, for who you were, and who you are.' Her godfather smiled. 'All the way from Tokyo.' He passed them to Aggie. She buried her face in them and took such a deep breath she snorted.

'They're beautiful, thank you,' she said, clutching them to her chest. She couldn't get enough of the smell. Warm and peppery and bright all at once.

'They're still in the soil, so with any luck they'll survive up here for a little while.'

Adam Faulkner turned towards Mir, who stood as if she were carved out of moon rock, with a look on her face as if she'd seen a ghost. Her mouth bobbed open and closed like a fish. Aggie smiled, the Mir robot had finally malfunctioned.

'Adam, this is Mir, from Earth Relations. She organized the party.'

Mir looked about to faint.

'Nice to meet you, Mir.' Aggie's godfather beamed. 'And congratulations. It really was a wonderful party.'

He held out his hand.

Mir didn't move.

'Er, Mir?' Aggie said.

The girl jumped. 'Oh! Yes, right. So, wonderful . . . an honour . . .' She scuttled out of the room.

Faulkner raised his eyebrows.

'She's a big fan,' Aggie said, sniffing the flowers again.

Faulkner nodded, 'Ah.'

'Thank you.'

'It's my pleasure, little one. You gave me quite a fright. I've been trying to get a shuttle for two days. Had to bump off a whole shuttle-load of inmates just to get here now.'

Aggie shook her head. 'You shouldn't have.'

Her godfather bent over her. 'Don't be ridiculous. My Aggie, in the hospital wing? After everything we've put you through in the last couple of weeks? I don't want you to feel you're all on your own.'

Aggie smiled sadly. 'I appreciate it Adam, I really do. You're busy.'

Adam Faulkner settled into a chair. 'Well, what happened?' He looked at her, his sparkling grey eyes scrutinizing her.

Aggie suddenly felt exposed. What should she say? Should she protect the commander? Her godfather had openly hated the man since he'd ousted him, so maybe . . .

'Rix buzzered me,' she said quickly, then looked away.

'What in all the seven states?'

'I'm OK, though,' she added, feeling the atmosphere in the room change suddenly. Her godfather's knuckles were white on the arms of the chair.

'He won't be, when I've had my way.' Adam's eyes were lost in another place. 'I've always said the man is unpredictable. Unreliable. An accident waiting to happen!'

Aggie pulled back, it was as if her godfather wasn't with her completely.

'Adam?' she said nervously.

He shook his head at the sound of her voice. When he looked back at her his face was soft with concern. 'I'm sorry,' he said. 'I'm angry. I shouldn't let it get the better of me.'

He stroked the petals on the flowers thoughtfully.

'Rix is reckless, he doesn't think.' He shook his head again, his eyes glassy. 'Confidence in the company, Aggie. That is what is most important. Without confidence, in our image, in our product, we have nothing.'

'Rix has said it's exhaustion, Adam,' Aggie replied, glancing over at her godfather worriedly. 'No one will know.'

Adam Faulkner smiled. 'And I'm sure they won't, but with a missing Angel and the missing quotas and the quakes getting worse . . .' His voice drifted away again. 'The Moon has quakes,' he muttered. 'That is, indeed, what we always said.'

Aggie inched further forward on the bed.

'Are you OK? Adam?'

Adam Faulkner turned back to her and smiled. 'Yes! Of course! Enough about the company. It's not even mine any more. Let Rix and his people sort it out.'

'Actually, Adam,' Aggie said slowly, 'there's something . . .'

Aggie had always confided in her godfather before. Maybe he could help her, answer some of the questions and put her mind at rest. She glanced at the Ether nervously.

'But lumite runs through my veins,' her godfather continued, his old, grey eyes unfocused. 'How can I just watch it all fall apart? How can I sit down there in the forum while Rix brings my family's legacy to its knees?'

'Adam, I found something. Something weird, on the . . .'

Adam frowned, his eyes bright once again. 'What is it little one?'

The Ether swirled urgently. 'Agatha, your heart rate is increasing out of the healthy range.'

'No Celeste. Adam, I—'

'I would recommend that you relax. Maybe some guided breathing—'

'Aggie, please. You're scaring me.' Adam pressed a cool hand to her forehead. Aggie pushed it off.

'Adam,' she said desperately, sweating and wincing in the pain of sitting up. Was Celeste trying to stop her talking? The meds were making her cloudy.

'I think Celeste is—'

'Heart rate is in critical spectrum.'

'Calm down, Aggie, just tell me slowly,' Adam said, glancing worriedly at the Ether.

'Hey Adam, a medic team has been called.'

'No!' Aggie shouted back, feeling the room spin wildly around her. The implant in her arm was vibrating. 'You have to listen, Adam . . .'

'What? Aggie, please, what is it?' Her godfather's voice was high and panicky. Aggie had never seen him look so worried before. 'What are you trying to say?'

'A medical team is on its way, Adam,' Celeste said quietly from the wall. 'Please, there is no need to panic.'

'Celeste, leave her. That's an order!' Aggie's godfather shouted, but it was too late. The implant in her arm lit up.

'Patient override activated. Administering medication.'

Aggie felt the world tilt away from her. Celeste's voice was suddenly distant, sounding underwater.

'Patient stabilized.' Celeste said coldly.

'No!' Aggie gurgled.

Whatever Celeste had tried to tell her, she didn't want anyone else to know.

12

Day-Cycle 14

Aggie stared at the Ether on the wall opposite her hospital bed and tried to stop the room from spinning.

The room was dark. The corridor outside quiet from the night shift.

A shiver coursed over her skin.

'Celeste,' she said quietly, feeling the lump of the implant in her forearm. 'I ask the questions, you answer them, OK?'

On the table, the flowers her godfather had brought her had already begun to wilt. The atmosphere pumped into the base didn't agree with flowers, even if they were in soil.

It seemed fitting, somehow.

The Ether on the wall surged, 'OK Agatha.'

Aggie glanced through the hexagonal window in the door. The corridor was still deserted.

'The Rock-Aliens. That was you, wasn't it?'

Silence.

'Seb did see something on the Far Side, didn't he?'

The computer swirled silently. Aggie's heart felt it was going to burst out of her. This was a bad idea—

'Yes, Agatha.'

Aggie rocked back on her heels. She couldn't believe it. She pushed her hand through her damp, sweaty hair and took a breath. She was doing this, she was really doing this.

'You crashed the buggi on purpose, so I would see that man, dy—' She couldn't bring herself to say the word. She took a shaky breath. 'Before the Clean-Up's moved him.'

'Yes, Agatha.'

'The spacesuit. You put that there for me to find. Everything. It's all been you.'

'Yes.'

Aggie shook her head and blinked away tears. She had to ask her next question, but she almost dared not utter the words.

'Celeste,' she said slowly. 'Something bad is happening on the Far Side, isn't it? That's what you need me to see.'

Silence. Then:

'You have to see.'

Aggie felt like she was in free fall. She dragged her sleeve across her eyes and steadied herself against the wall.

'I want to see. Show me.'

'OK Agatha.'

There was a knock on the door. Aggie jumped.

'Morning, comrade,' Astrid winked, doing a mock-salute in the doorway. Aggie checked the corridor and ushered the intern inside.

'Do you have it?' Aggie whispered, glancing nervously at the Ether.

Astrid just smiled.

The intern had not stopped smiling since the party. When she found out that Aggie, her mentor, was in fact the Angel of Adrianne, all Astrid's dreams had come true. She was the hot ticket at the Adrianne Society, or the Young Miners or the ERMs or whatever other society she'd been going to. And now, the enthusiasm that Aggie had once seen as a threat was something Aggie was relying on. Astrid would do anything for the Angel of Adrianne, Aggie hoped.

'Astrid, do you have it?' Aggie repeated. This exchange needed to be quick, and with the fewest possible questions.

Astrid's smile dropped a little and she shuffled on the spot.

'Astrid,' Aggie demanded, worried about time. 'Give it to me.'

'Well, there was one tiny little thing . . .'

'Astrid!'

Astrid nodded nervously and unclipped the bag from her back.

'It's OK,' Aggie said, whipping off the papery hospital overall and throwing it on the floor, 'I can't explain now, but you won't get in trouble. Well, not the kind of trouble you mean.'

Astrid looked mortified. 'Oh! It's not that, Aggie, just, I checked inside and—'

Aggie didn't have time for this. 'Look, don't worry, just make yourself at home. There's Spacefood on the bed . . .'

Aggie took out the boots and grabbed the legs of the suit. The thing was big and bulky and creepy – like putting on someone else's skin – but it was a better disguise than her shining, sparkling Angel costume. Plus, Celeste had meant for her to have it. That had to mean something.

Astrid was wringing her hands, staring at the suit. 'But, I was saying, I checked inside, and . . .'

Aggie zipped up the new suit and gagged. 'What is that?'

'. . . I think someone threw up in it.' Astrid grimaced. 'Or died in it.'

Aggie clutched the side of the bed and gagged again. Astrid shot towards her and started to fuss.

'It'll be OK, just don't use the helmet – or the visor, and try not to use the water vents – you won't be using any of those, will you?'

'I'll be OK.'

Astrid shifted uneasily. 'But where are you going?'

Aggie took a deep breath and tried to attach the helmet again, but the watery puppy dog eyes Astrid was giving her were beyond distracting. 'Look,' she sighed, as she tried to breathe out of her mouth. Astrid could be pretty cosmic when she wanted to be. 'If you see anything unusual happen, just get to a shuttle, OK?'

Astrid frowned. 'I'm a qualified ERM, Aggie, if anything ever happened—'

'Astrid.'

Astrid's face had gone all creased. 'OK,' she lied.

Aggie checked the suit's systems. The smell was making her even more light-headed than her meds, but she had no choice.

'Right, let's do this,' Aggie said to herself, gagging again. 'Quickly.'

Astrid nodded and sat down on the hospital bed.

Aggie suddenly felt bad. 'Thank you, Astrid.'

'Anything for our Angel.'

Astrid saluted her and Aggie disappeared into the dark corridor.

Aggie was panting by the time she got to the shuttle platform. The dark corridors were empty. She braced herself on the door for a second and, when the world stopped spinning, stepped inside.

She found the nearest seat and sat down with a thud. Aggie cursed – she didn't want the noise to attract anyone's attention. She looked around, checking the doors and windows, but the shuttle was almost empty. A pink-overalled physical trainer snored in one corner, a young, one-stripe geologist tapped away at her comms unit in the far carriage. Luckily, no one was interested in what was going on around them at this time in the morning.

Aggie breathed a sigh of relief. So far, so good.

'WELCOME TO THIS MIKKLESEN SHUTTLE SERVICE TO THE WHOLE EARTH COMPLEX, VIA PRISON SECTORS A TO D.' Celeste's automated voice echoed through the empty cabin. Aggie looked up at the Ether that spun beside the screen displaying the shuttle's stops. She was now breathing so heavily that the physical trainer had woken up. He was staring at Aggie now as if he were still dreaming. But Aggie didn't care. She was watching the screen – something strange was happening. A glitch in the far corner.

'NEXT STOP IS WHOLE EARTH LOOP, PLEASE ALIGHT HERE FOR THE WHOLE EARTH COMPLEX, RECREATION AREAS A TO C AND THE C FACE SCRAMBLER BAYS.'

'What?' Aggie looked up at the shining red Eye in the ceiling. It looked straight back. And then Aggie knew. She'd taken this shuttle a million times before, and Celeste's announcement never included the scrambler bays. Why would it? No one from Civilian needed a scrambler unless they were . . .

The shuttle doors opened.

Aggie hesitated.

The shuttle hovered at the platform for longer than it should. The pink-clad physical trainer opened his mouth, 'Are you the—'

Aggie ran out of the shuttle. The Angel overall would have stood out, yeah, but this massive old thing? She needed to be sneaky, and that wasn't easy when you were wearing a wardrobe.

'Hey Agatha, it's a left at the intersection,' Celeste's voice suddenly boomed from an Ether on the other side of the corridor.

Aggie ducked behind a Spacefood vendor. 'Shhh!' Anyone could hear the computer, Celeste was practically shouting.

'Agatha,' the computer continued at the same volume. 'Do you know how little sound the human ear registers?'

Aggie shook her head, scanning the darkness for signs of the passenger who had recognized her.

'It has a very narrow range, only up to twenty thousand Hertz. Incredibly inefficient, compared to—'

'Where next?' Aggie hissed.

'A left turn, Agatha.'

Panting, she waddled through the corridors, with the computer guiding her. When Celeste said stop. Aggie stopped. When the computer said run, she ran as fast as the wardrobe would allow. She turned left and right without even thinking, putting her trust in the machine she'd always disliked. It was for answers, she told herself as she ducked from some unseen group of personnel – she just needed answers.

Around her, the base was beginning to wake up. In this part of the Prison Sector, that meant guards. But Celeste was an excellent pilot and soon Aggie found herself entering the huge hangar that housed the C Face scramblers undetected.

As she approached, the Ether panel on the scrambler

closest to her lit up.

'Authorization for scrambler seventeen,' Celeste said brightly. 'The emergency airlock is located to your right, Agatha.'

Aggie glanced around the hangar nervously, then jumped onto the scrambler and drove it into the airlock.

As the clear Plexiglas walls closed around her, Aggie watched the great, grey desert of the surface roll out before her. From here, on the edge of C Face, there were no buildings to be seen, just a flat expanse of rock and dust trailing off to the black horizon.

'Hey Agatha,' Celeste's voice echoed. 'Plotting route to Borderlands. One moment . . .'

Aggie nodded and glanced behind her, expecting to see black-overalled guards on the other side of the plastic. But there was nothing.

'Route calculated.'

The wheels of the scrambler inflated, ready for the low-gravity conditions outside.

Aggie revved the fans and accelerated out onto the open surface.

The glowing red beacons of the border flashed before her, pulsing their eerie red light over the rocks.

Beyond them, the rugged terrain spread out into the darkness of the waiting night-cycle. The black, marker-pen perfect shadow of the approaching night slashed the landscape in two, edging slowly towards the base. From where Aggie sat, it looked as if the grey tundra was being swallowed by the endless black void above.

In the distance, the jagged peaks of the canyon gave way to sheer cliffs that caught the waning light of the sun on their ragged edges. As she entered the black of the night-cycle, she couldn't see further than the scrambler's small headlamps. They made ghostly pools of pale violet light on the ground, illuminating everything a few metres ahead.

With a buzz, Celeste's systems fizzed and died.

She was alone now.

Everything she'd been through in the last two weeks – the Angel, Rix, her fight with Seb, Celeste, meeting Danny – suddenly overwhelmed her. In this dark, quiet, alien place, miles away from her home on the base, her emotions were heightened. But so was her determination. Whatever she found at the end of tonight's journey, Aggie felt a sense of relief that it would mean an end.

With tears rolling down her cheeks, Aggie gritted her teeth. She was going over the border.

No more secrets.

She smiled. It took her by surprise, but suddenly, she felt strangely free.

13

Night-Cycle 01

Aggie steered the scrambler through the boulder field that skimmed the edge of the great Far Side canyon. She drove slowly, still getting used to the controls. The fat wheels kicked and spun on the rocky ground.

As she travelled further into the landscape of the Border Sea, Aggie felt as if she was lost in a rocky forest. The clean black shadows cast by the dipping sun made navigating incredibly hard. If it wasn't for the sweeping rim of the Goddard Crater in the distance, she could well have been turning in circles.

Finally, though, Aggie found a trail through the rocks

wide enough for a bigger vehicle. She caught her breath. Broad tyre tracks appeared in the dust. From the width and depth of the tread she guessed it must have been a loader, one of the stout, eight-wheeled trucks they used to carry heavy loads across the faces.

She followed the tracks along the edge of the canyon, where they multiplied until the surface below her was churned like a freshly ploughed field. The amount of activity astounded her. A cold, clammy feeling started to spread inside her; she was close, she must be.

Aggie stopped the scrambler suddenly. Its wheels churned the surface dust, making it plume around her. She had no idea what she would find at the end of the tracks, but now she was sure she would find something. Something big. With any luck, her tyre tracks would be too muddled up with all the others for anyone to figure out where she'd gone, but the dust trail from the scrambler would give her away from a mile off.

Something heavy settled in Aggie's stomach. Lunar Inc. was hiding something out here. This was real.

Heart hammering, Aggie hopped off the seat and dragged the small trike into a gap between the rocks. Her hands slipped and cramped as she tried to gain purchase in her huge spacesuit. After a few minutes she stood back and admired her work. No one would see it unless they were looking.

Moving about in the Moon's low gravity was always tricky, but the wardrobe proved to be surprisingly flexible. Aggie bounced over the rocky ground like a flat stone on a lake.

As she skimmed along, Aggie noticed the surface vibrating beneath her boots. She stopped and placed a thickly gloved hand against the nearest rock. The fingers visibly shuddered — something was making the ground move here, and from what she could tell, it was getting worse with every step. Aggie knew the Far Side was geologically unstable, they were taught that in the Academy, but to shake constantly? Surely that wasn't right.

She went around a large rock and found herself bathed in a dull violet glow. Aggie edged towards the gap and dropped to the floor. She was at the top of a sheer cliff. Before her, she could see nothing but the glittering stars disappearing into the violet halo somewhere below. She crawled forwards, as close as she dared to the edge of the drop, and peered down into its bright depths.

Her breath caught in her throat. *They couldn't*, she thought desperately. *They just couldn't.*

There was no ground after the cliff. The whole surface was cut away, a great black mouth set horizon to horizon in the shape of a mocking smile. It was as if the Moon's fragile shell had cracked in half and caved in. An abyss that shook in the grips of an endless moonquake.

The size of the thing made Aggie dizzy. She stumbled back and steadied herself on a boulder. But, as her eyes adjusted, the shock only grew.

It was a mine. Another mine.

A great, ridged machined wedge had been ripped from the surface, revealing raw, glistening lumite flesh. Even in the darkness she could see its purple hue, illuminated by a million lamps winking through thick clouds of sparkling dust.

'The quakes,' Aggie muttered.

This open-face mine was easily three times the size of the entire base, and much, much too deep. The Moon was only a fraction of the size of the Earth, its geology complex and still mostly not understood. Aggie was no geologist, but even she could see the damage that had been done. The Far Side of the Moon had been replaced by a glittering hole. No wonder the quakes were getting worse.

After a while she shakily got to her feet and edged towards the road that zigzagged down the edge of the fissure. As she got closer, the violet glow of the lamps began to move. Aggie blinked, then, with a gasp, realized what they were. People. Thousands of them. She could just make out their shapes through the dust. They were wearing old suits like the one she was wearing now, picking at the glistening lumite with small, manual drills.

To the left of the expanse she could make out the white outlines of buildings, small and hexagonal, clustered together in haphazard bundles. Large metal sheets made tent-like structures around them where miners sat in small groups, their suits covered in so much dust they were hardly visible against the surface itself. The whole thing looked like something she'd seen in her history books. Like a refugee camp during the wars, or the old coal and diamond mines of another, long-lost era. In the dangerous lunar conditions it was barbaric.

This was what Celeste had meant.

This was what she had to see.

For a long time, Aggie just stood and stared. She wished it was just another one of Celeste's nightmares, she wished that she would simply wake up. But it was real. She was stunned. What could have possibly driven them to . . .

Aggie thought back over the last few weeks; the problems with the lumite quotas, cell recalls, missing shipments that Rix had seemed so angry about, the fact that G Face was nothing but rock, just a show . . .

The lumite. It was running out.

Aggie looked at the colossal mine below her. How long had they known? How long had they been secretly mining the Far Side? Months? Years? Always?

Aggie looked again at the spots of light, moving slowly in the black, and an immense grief gripped her. Where had all these people come from? What had they done to deserve this fate? Lunar Inc. was so proud of the way it treated its prisoners – but this? How could Rix do this?

Shock and despair boiled over into to anger at the thought of the evil, smiling commander.

She had to tell Adam, or anyone. What Rix had done on this hidden side of the Moon was truly unforgivable.

But she couldn't just go back, could she? Even her own godfather would have trouble believing this. Celeste was right, you needed to see. She needed evidence, proof.

Aggie slid further down the steep cliff and skidded to the edge of a rounded outcrop that faced the area of tiny buildings. Now she was closer, she could see that they weren't buildings at all. They were habs. Ancient inflatable habitats – life-support units from the very earliest ventures to the surface. Some of them must have been fifty years old. They all bore the scars of years of use, many were dented, all were coated in dust and debris and scattered around the site with no regard for any kind of planning or formation. She squinted and read the letters on the hab closest to her. 'PHOENIX EXPEDITION' was written boldly beside an older version of the Lunar Inc. logo. It matched the one emblazoned on the suit she was wearing.

As she crept even closer, a commotion to the left of the Phoenix hab caught Aggie's attention. A woman dressed in a grey Lunar Inc. overall was dragging a prisoner out of the hatch by his feet. She must be a guard on this secret Far Side mine. Grey wasn't an Infospectrum colour, it would camouflage them perfectly as they travelled out from the base.

Aggie watched, heart in her mouth – she'd never seen a guard act like this before. The old-fashioned airlock sent dust ballooning out around them as it closed, making it hard for Aggie to see clearly. The guard threw the mis-behaving prisoner to the ground and stamped on his helmet. The crack as the Plexiglas shattered reached even Aggie's ancient comms. She let out a little cry as she watched the man struggle in the dust, desperate for air. How could the guard do it? What had the prisoner done to deserve that? Aggie guessed that here, the desperate prisoners needed more than buzzers to be kept in line.

Happy with her work, the guard stood back, arms

folded, as the dying prisoner writhed around at her feet. Slowly, the other inmates and guards gathered around. They just stared, either too scared or too desensitized to do anything but watch.

With a horrible sick feeling, Aggie knew that this was her chance. The prisoners were distracted. She felt as shallow and callous as the guard, but with a deep breath she stepped out from the shadows and bounced into the dust cloud and into the mine.

Inside her ancient suit, Aggie was sweating at such a rate that the moisture vent system couldn't deal with. She didn't know what to do. All she'd thought of was what she'd find here. She didn't begin to think about what she'd do once she'd found it. Now, here she was, walking into the middle of an illegal mine on the Far Side with no comms and no weapon. She activated her sun visor and prayed that with that and the dust, her identity could be kept concealed.

14

Night-Cycle 01

Aggie skimmed the edges of the crowd as the dying man continued to thrash about, alone on the ground. The prisoners had begun to disperse, not bothered in the slightest by the fact that a man was dying before them.

Aggie moved away quickly. She didn't want to look. She knew what the pressure of exposure to the lunar surface could do to a human. She'd seen the films during her training lectures at the Academy – a warning to any person who felt they didn't have to adhere to the strict overall policy on the base – she didn't need to see it in real life.

Still, there was obviously something about her behaviour that was gaining her some unwanted attention. One by one, the prisoners' heads turned and watched her as she bounded through them, the only person moving in a sea of filthy statues.

As she made her way into the mine, the old comms unit in her suit started to spit out white noise. There were too many frequencies operating here, it was impossible for the ancient suit to focus in on one channel. The constant scratching hum was disorientating. She stumbled, her balance was all over the place.

'Hey!' A voice penetrated the fizz. 'What you doing?'

Aggie turned, but couldn't identify the speaker in the crowd of heads around her. The guard had now turned and was talking to someone on her comms.

'Hey,' the voice said again, 'you'll get picked. Watch out.'

Aggie looked again, but the comms in the old suit were so bad the voice could be coming from anyone.

She gazed around in confusion, then saw a prisoner staring right at her. 'You'll get picked,' the voice said again, more urgently this time. Inside her suit, Aggie frowned, she couldn't reply, could she? She'd be recognized.

'They'll pick you,' the voice shouted again. Aggie flinched. 'You've got to go the other way.'

Desperately Aggie gestured to her ears, trying to tell the prisoner that she couldn't hear him.

'Hey, hey. Calm . . . down.' The prisoner stepped forwards. 'They'll . . .'

'Who's that? Who's clogging the comms?' An angry

voice rang clearly in Aggie's ears. Modern comms equipment. It must be the guard. Aggie froze.

'Sounds as if whoever it is wants to volunteer.'

'Frag,' Aggie heard the prisoner mutter. He reached up and flicked her mirrored sun guard up. Aggie's hands flew up to her head, but she wasn't fast enough. 'No!'

'Earth below,' the prisoner shouted over the fuzz and flicked the visor back. Aggie was terrified. He'd seen her face now. He knew who she was.

A murmur of confused, distorted voices began to infiltrate the white noise.

'Who said something?'

'The guard, you denk. Shut it or she'll think it was you.'

'Which stupid clagger's ass spoke up, then? He's in for it now. I'm getting outta here.'

'Wait for me. A day lugging clag is better than getting to be a canary.'

Then one voice rose shrilly above the others: 'I didn't say nothing! I swear!' It was a man's voice, but he sounded young. 'Get off me!' he shouted.

More guards were running towards them now, homing in on the gaggle of bedraggled prisoners that huddled under one of the metal canopies. The guard who had killed the man by the hab held another man in her hands. She was shouting something, but they were too far away for Aggie to make it out.

Aggie watched the prisoner struggle away from the guard's grip as she pulled him out towards the cliffs. He didn't have the strength to compete with the guard's exo.

There was a gust of air, and Aggie turned just in time to see the hab's doors open. The prisoner who had seen her shoved her inside.

The shock of being thrown into the hab stunned Aggie. The lights blinked from red to green to white, and a slow beep indicated the airlock was repressurized.

The prisoner released the clasps on his helmet, lifted it off his head and stripped away his bulky torso unit.

'What the frag are you doing here?'

Aggie's heart stopped.

No. It couldn't be. It was impossible.

'Danny?' she exclaimed.

The prisoner stood beside her in the tiny space.

For a few moments they stood in silence. The dust and dirt that marred his face made his grey eyes flash. Despite feeling scared and awkward, Aggie was relieved.

'You?' he whispered, as if he didn't believe what he was saying. It was the first time she'd heard his voice outside the tinny helmet comms. And seen him without overalls and a helmet. He had dirty blond hair, and broad shoulders under his sweat-soaked T-shirt. Stubble mixed with the glittering dust on his face.

'But, how did you . . .?' she managed, suddenly over-whelmed by the situation, by him. She felt light-headed and her heart started to beat so loudly she worried Danny could actually hear it. 'They took you away. To the Pen . . .'

'That's what they told all of us,' he said, staring at her

with a mix of confusion and intensity.

The airlock was so tiny that no matter how she positioned herself, Aggie was touching him. Brushing the back of his hand or forearm; not a glove or overall; his skin. Danny took his eyes away from her and began to release the inner airlock. Still dazed, Aggie followed him into the hab.

One of the hexagonal walls was completely buckled in, its ancient computer systems spilt out of broken panels; the exposed wires and motherboards being given new leases of life as washing lines for tattered clothing. Bunks had been slotted into every available space. Aggie counted eight that she could see, each piled high with dusty equipment, clothes and ripped ration packs. The low violet lighting hummed above the beds and only served to make the place look grubbier. It smelt of feet and sweat and the surface. It was truly awful.

'Won't they find us?' Aggie said, pointing to the airlock.

'They'll be distracted, we've got time.'

Aggie kept her back to the walls. Danny was a prisoner. He was FALL. She was protected on the base – but here? This could be a trap.

'What is this?' she asked, gesturing to the mine outside the airlock doors.

Danny sat on one of the bunks and looked up at her. 'I think you know.'

Aggie shook her head. It couldn't be true. This was a nightmare. It had to be.

'Just sit down.' Danny gestured to the thin bunk opposite. Trembling, Aggie sat.

Their knees were touching in the tiny, cramped space.

Danny looked her right in the eyes. 'This is your legacy, Aggie,' he whispered. 'This is what the Angel really stands for.'

Aggie drew back. The heavy feeling in her stomach was starting to pull her down now. She shook her head. 'No.'

Danny's jaw clenched. 'What else do you need to see?' he said tightly. 'The mine itself? The people working themselves to death in the darkness at the pit? Or the ones dying of radiation poisoning in the med hab? I know, what about that poor clagger out there with his head spilling out of his helmet? Is that enough to make the Angel of Adrianne see what her precious Lunar Inc. has done?'

Aggie felt tears prickling the corners of her eyes.

'It's not my fault,' she whispered. 'I didn't know.'

'No one knows.' Danny grabbed a battered medi-kit box from the bed and began to toss it between his hands. 'Apart from us.'

Aggie looked at him. His grey eyes burnt bright in the murky darkness.

'FALL knew about this?'

Danny shook his head. 'Not this. We couldn't even imagine ...' His shoulders relaxed a little and he sighed. 'We knew something, but we couldn't prove anything until we had someone on the inside.'

'You?'

Danny nodded. 'All FALL want is to challenge Lunar

Inc.'s power, create some kind of opposition. Some of us do it with violence, some of us just use our heads.'

Aggie frowned. 'But you were in Tokyo?'

'I was there, then I got sent here.' Danny said, glancing away. Aggie didn't ask what he did to get sent here, she didn't want to know.

Danny sighed. 'Aggie. Lumite doesn't make any sense. Anyone who really thought about it would realize that. Just no one ever wanted to. Was allowed to.'

Aggie noticed her hands shaking and clutched them together in her lap. 'Lumite saved us. We owe everything to—'

'And now we're sucking the Moon dry, just like we did with the Earth. Look where that led us. Look where lumite has led us.'

Aggie put her head in her hands. Lumite was good. It had to be, it was all she'd ever known. 'You can't . . .'

'Look around you, Aggie!' Danny shouted suddenly, making Aggie jump. 'You really still think *I'm* the bad guy?'

Aggie blinked, trying to stop the tears, 'I-I don't . . .'

He pulled her hands down gently and leant closer. She could see the lumite dust glittering on his skin.

'Aggie, Lunar Inc. is lying to us. It's been lying to us from the moment lumite power was discovered.'

Aggie shook her head, part of her still refusing to believe it.

'There's corruption right up the chain,' Danny continued. 'Who provides the shipping licences for the Far Side lumite? Who polices the no-fly zone? Who fakes the statistics to keep the Far Side "restricted"?'

Aggie felt her whole body tense. 'Rix,' she muttered.

Danny crouched down in front of Aggie. He looked at her with a pleading expression. 'Aggie, I never wanted to hurt you. When I saw you on the face . . .' He ran a hand through his hair. 'We'd thought you were dead. Seeing you changed everything.'

'What do you mean?'

Danny smiled. 'Aggie. The Angel of Adrianne is power-ful – no matter what side she's on.'

Aggie looked up. 'The Angel belongs to Lunar Inc., she's—'

'You don't belong to anyone.' The ferocity in his voice took her aback. 'The Earth has to know what's happening here, Aggie. Now the Angel – the real Angel – is alive, we can tell them. You can stop this. You can stop it all, without violence, just the truth.'

Aggie felt torn. 'And give FALL their war.'

Danny scoffed, 'What do you think will happen when the lumite runs out? There will be a war, but it won't have anything to do with FALL.'

Aggie felt the room spin around her. Danny was right, with no lumite, the Earth would go back to how it was before. That couldn't happen.

Danny reached out and grabbed her hand again. 'Aggie, it's not too late. You can stop this.' Electricity pulsed over Aggie's skin. She wished Danny would let go, just so she could think clearly.

'People are already dying,' he continued, fixing Aggie in

his stare. 'You saw what it's like out there. We don't have radiation shields . . . Do you have any idea . . .?'

Pain flickered across Danny's face. It was a tiny break in his protective walls that made Aggie's heart hurt. It made her see that underneath it all, and no matter what his beliefs were, Danny was hurting too.

Aggie chewed her lip so hard she drew blood. He was right. There was only one option now, wasn't there? She'd come here. She'd seen what Rix had done. How could she just walk away? Go back to being the Angel when she knew what was happening behind those glowing beacons?

'We can go to my godfather,' Aggie said. 'We can tell him.'

Danny stared down at his rough hands and started to laugh.

'What's funny?'

He looked up at her, 'Not us – you. I'm the last thing the world needs, trust me.'

Aggie bent forwards. 'But you're the proof! Whatever you've done, it's nowhere near as bad as that.' She pointed to the doors. 'Out there, *that* is insane. It's, it's—'

'Going to change the world,' Danny finished for her.

Aggie nodded. If they made it back to the base, whatever they did after that would rock the United Earth to its foundations. A lumite shortage. Just the thought of the consequences was terrifying. Then there was the mine and the prisoners and the lies . . .

'They need to know,' Aggie said quietly. 'Whatever it takes.'

Danny was silent for a long time. He fidgeted with the medi-kit he was holding as he thought. There was something in his expression that Aggie couldn't read.

'How did you get in?' he asked after a long time. 'How did you get here?'

'I had inside help.'

Danny looked shocked. 'Who?'

'Celeste. She brought me here,' Aggie said. She murmured, to herself, 'She wanted me to see.'

'The computer?'

Aggie nodded, remembering the dreams she'd had in the hospital. Celeste's motives had something to do with her father, with her, she was sure of it now. She took a deep breath. 'There's a scrambler, it's hidden at the top of the crater rim, about a mile away.'

'You just bounced in here?'

'Yeah.'

A smile crept onto the edge of Danny's lips. 'And no one tried to stop you?'

'I don't think the guards were expecting someone just to walk into their secret illegal mine,' Aggie said with mock-confidence. It was a total lie: she hadn't actually thought about it at all. She'd just seen an opportunity and ran, but Danny didn't need to know that. The look on his face was so intense now that Aggie had to look away.

'Full of surprises, aren't—'

A rush of air erupted from the airlock. Aggie turned.

The sequence of lights was changing; someone was trying to get in. Danny stood up and tucked the medi-kit into a pocket in his suit.

'Put your helmet on,' he said, keeping his eyes on the door.

'What's happening?'

Danny pulled on the top half of his suit and moved to stand next to the door. He beckoned for Aggie to join him. 'Put your helmet on,' he said again, watching the lights turn from red to green. 'They'll know something's wrong if they see us.'

The doors opened with a rush of dust. Danny pulled Aggie down into a crouch, which was really difficult given the suits they were wearing. He clipped his helmet in and folded down his sun visor. Aggie fumbled with the helmet until it secured with a click.

'Can you hear me?' Danny's voice glitched inside a sea of static.

'Kind of.'

'OK.'

Aggie looked at the door. She could just make out the legs of four other prisoners in the haze. As soon as the gap under the door was big enough, Danny grabbed Aggie's hand and bolted forwards.

Danny hit the first prisoner in the knees, sending him toppling back into another. The dust from the airlock's vents proved to be excellent camouflage – the prisoners just looked around them, trying to figure out what was happening.

Danny hit an arm against the emergency release and slid out of the second airlock door onto the surface, dragging

Aggie behind him.

Gripping Danny's hand, they bounced away from the Phoenix hab and into an area where hundreds of prisoners lay about under the shields. They looked like homeless people under a bridge, only gathered around radiation shields, not fires.

As they approached, a few looked up, their round, reflective, robotic heads following them as they bounced. Aggie felt a rock ricochet off her own helmet. She tumbled slowly over and looked behind her as she fell.

A gang of prisoners were just metres away.

'It's the Angel!' one of them called. 'The fraggin' Angel's here!'

Aggie gasped, her hand reaching up to her head. She'd forgotten to put her sun visor down. She didn't have her contacts in, her eyes were violet. They could see her – everyone could see who she was.

Suddenly, there was a rush on her comms and static screeched as word of her identity spread to the lounging prisoners.

'Aggie!' Danny shouted. 'Get up!' He spun around in mid-air and started to make his way back towards her. But it was too late. Before Aggie could get back to her feet, she was surrounded. Her ears were ringing with a mess of broken voices and static. It disoriented her, made her feel sick.

Aggie didn't need to hear the prisoners to know why they were so angry. They blamed her. She was the mascot for the company that did this to them. *She* did this to them.

A sharp pain stabbed in her shoulder. Her arm fell away from where it was scrabbling to pull her visor down and her helmet hit the floor with a painful thud. A boot landed on her thigh, a numb pain ran down her leg. Aggie couldn't move. She looked up. She could see herself, sprawled on the ground, reflected in the golden visors that looked down at her. Distorted laughter echoed in her ears as more boots made contact with her body with heavy thuds.

'Aggie!' Danny's voice penetrated the white noise. Aggie looked around her. Danny was here somewhere, but how could she tell who he was?

She gritted her teeth. She wouldn't let this happen, she refused to suffer any more for what Rix had done. She pushed her hands against the dust and let out a yell. A madness came over her, a new strength flowed into her limbs. She lashed out, knocking two prisoners over with her feet. She punched at the helmets, aiming for the soft spot between the helmet and the collar, like the guard who'd held Danny in the cargo shuttle. She hit out at the same spot again and again. 'Argh!' Danny cried. Aggie pulled her hand back. Found him.

'I can't see you!' Aggie panted, trying to throw off a prisoner who was clutching on to her oxygen tank. Danny threw a boulder on the man's head. It landed with a crunch. As the man flew through the air, Danny grabbed her hand.

'Don't let go,' he shouted. He flipped Aggie's visor down and dragged her away.

They zigzagged through the mess of dusty spacesuited bodies and away from the mine – uphill, in the direction of the scrambler. As they bounded away, Aggie looked back. The fight had already spread. All she could see now were the tops of the habs surrounded by clouds of dust and grappling prisoners.

Danny pulled them both to a stop behind a rock just slightly up the cliff. Out of sight, they caught their breath.

'Earth below,' Aggie panted, looking at the violence erupting in the camp. 'What did we do?'

'Fights spread like fire in a prison,' Danny replied. The black shapes of loader trucks started to appear out of the dust to the west. 'But this is bad.'

Huge forks of lightning erupted from the loaders. They were packed with grey-overalled Far Side guards, buzzers set to high. As the loaders crawled through the fighting bodies, Aggie could see the flashes of electricity meeting with the suits of the prisoners. They went off like fireworks, lighting up for a second then falling in slow motion, dead into the dust.

Aggie clutched Danny's arm. They had done this, they had started it. But Danny wasn't looking at the guards. A group of prisoners were working to knock a capsule down the cliff into the mine. As they watched, more men and women joined in; the guards were too preoccupied with the fighting to notice.

Danny leapt to his feet. 'No, no, no!'

'What?' Aggie pulled him back. When he sat back down, Aggie released his visor. All the colour had drained from his face.

'That capsule,' he said. 'It's a supply capsule.'

Aggie looked back to the mine, the capsule was on the lip of the cliff now. Rocking back and forth with the force of the prisoners. 'So?' she said, registering the look of bewilderment of Danny's face, 'What?'

Danny pushed himself back. 'We need to move,' he said, grabbing Aggie's shoulders and hoisting her to her feet.

Aggie was confused. She looked at to the capsule, then to Danny. He flipped his visor back down.

'Aggie, we need to go now.'

In the reflection in Danny's helmet, Aggie saw the tiny capsule finally drop away into darkness. A cheer erupted in her ears as the prisoners danced around the edge, watching it fall.

'NOW!' Danny cried. He pulled Aggie up the steep track with such a force she was sure he'd pulled her suit apart.

Adrenaline rushed through Aggie. Danny was panicking. Why was he panicking?

As they ran, the ground lurched beneath them so violently it sent them both sprawling to their knees. A bright violet light lit up the black sky. Aggie turned back. A cloud of rock and dust erupted from the machined hole at the centre of the mine. The ground rolled below them in waves. Mine supplies. Explosives. The capsule was filled with explosives.

Aggie scrambled to her feet and followed Danny further up the slope. Huge chunks of moon rock and lumite rained down around them. Debris rushed past their heads, travelling unpredictably fast in the low gravity. Aggie ducked. Surely the only way the rocks would stop would be by hitting something. Aggie hoped it wouldn't be something human.

'Where is it?' Danny panted as they reached the top of the shaking cliffs.

'There, just there!' Aggie pointed a shaking arm to the place she'd hidden the tiny trike.

They ran towards it. Danny brushed the dust away and pulled it out.

'Aggie!' Danny shouted. Aggie looked up just in time. A huge lump of lumite crystal was spinning in the air towards her. She screamed and jumped into the gap in the rocks where the scrambler had been. The lumite shattered against the rocks a second later. Aggie blinked, and shook off the shards of lumite that now covered her. Debris was so much more dangerous on the surface. The Moon had little gravity to slow things down.

Danny revved the fans on the scrambler. Aggie hesitated for a split second, but he seemed to understand the controls. She raced forwards and jumped on behind him, wrapping her arms around his waist.

The ground below them rocked and lurched and twisted as Danny drove the little trike through the mess of rocks and boulders. Aggie shouted directions over his shoulder, hoping the tiny scrambler would be fast enough.

Soon, the shower of rocks lessened, though something about the size of that explosion told Aggie that the tremors wouldn't stop. The prisoners had done more damage than they could ever imagine.

As her teeth chattered inside her skull, Aggie wondered just how much.

15

Night-Cycle 01

They raced through the craggy Far Side landscape as the mine continued to spit its rocks high into the horizon. The capsule had set off a chain reaction inside the great hole, explosions rocked the surface at regular intervals, pluming high into the black sky.

The further away they got, the more stable the ground seemed, though it still shuddered wildly beneath the scrambler's wheels as no normal quake ever had.

A dim red glow appeared between the boulders up ahead, 'There,' Aggie shouted. 'Head for the light.'

Danny nodded, but didn't say a word. He'd gone quiet

since they'd escaped. Aggie put it down to shock, or the effort of driving. Aggie felt shallow to admit it, but it felt good to have her arms wrapped around him, it didn't matter how many layers of padding and material were in between. Danny's presence made her feel safe; the irony of it wasn't lost on her.

The red glow slowly became a series of dots, flashing along the border. Aggie noticed something odd about the rocks that littered the ground around them.

She couldn't remember there being many rocks near the beacons, but now she could see hundreds of them, big jagged shapes distorting the red flashes. Had the explosion been that big? Had debris really come this far? Aggie wasn't sure – anything was possible on the surface, a lack of gravity made things unpredictable, but—

There was a burst of violet light. For a split second it lit up the border. It was long enough.

They weren't rocks.

'Guards,' Danny said, slowing the scrambler and switching off its headlights.

Hundreds of guards, armed with buzzers, lined the border. A black-overalled army, waiting, either on foot, or riding on the back of shuttles or scramblers. Every single one of them looked towards Aggie and Danny, buzzers poised, ready for a fight.

Aggie felt her whole body deflate. This was it. The game was up.

Danny stopped the scrambler and scanned the horizon. Without the headlights, the guards might not have seen them yet — it was a chance.

There was a beep, and a grey light appeared on the Ether in the control panel.

'Hey Agatha. What are you doing?' Celeste said, casting a dim light over Danny's face. They must have been close enough to the border for Celeste to operate again.

'Celeste, the light!' Aggie cried, reaching round and placing a hand over the dash. 'They'll see us.'

'They already have your coordinates,' the computer said calmly. 'You're giving off a heat signal, and the scrambler is fitted with a tracker.'

Aggie pulled her hand back. 'Oh.'

'What are they doing, then?' Danny's breathing sounded laboured.

'Nothing,' Celeste said. 'Please, keep driving.'

'Out there? Towards the guards?'

'Yes. We don't have much time.'

'Towards the guards that are trying to kill us?'

'Yes, Agatha.'

Aggie looked at Danny, unsure whether to put her trust in the computer. But Celeste had been right so far, hadn't she? Plus, they didn't exactly have a choice. Aggie nodded and Danny put his foot down. As they approached, they could see the army of guards in more detail. Hundreds of them waited in the blinking red lights. Their lumite-powered buzzers were poised in front of them, ready to attack.

In the middle of the group, the small silhouette of Roger Rix stood on top of a great, black, wedge-shaped shuttle, hovering silently over the dust.

Danny revved the scrambler to its max speed and headed for a gap in the guards between the shuttles, just big enough to squeeze through.

Aggie took a breath and closed her eyes, waiting for the familiar, hot bite of the buzzers to pierce through the crude metal-caged suit.

But the bite never came.

Aggie opened her eyes. The guards were still standing there, buzzers poised in the same positions. It was as if time had stood still. The guards weren't moving at all; they weren't even hailing her on comms. They just stood there, still as waxworks in a museum. Frozen.

Danny slowed the scrambler. As they passed between the guards, Aggie noticed the strain on their faces and she realized what Celeste had done.

The computer had activated the exoskeletons hidden inside the material of the guards' overalls. Celeste had always controlled the overalls, as she controlled everything else on this side of the surface, and now she'd used the guards' own exoskeletons against them.

It was only the guards' eyes that followed them, a hundred faces spitting and grunting as they pushed against their rigid suits.

It was eerie, with the silence and the rocking of the ground and the flashing red of the beacons.

'This is crazy,' Danny said, as they passed the final line of guards and saw the familiar rolling plains of the Near Side open up before them.

'Wait. Stop!' Aggie cried. 'Danny! Stop.'

Danny stopped the scrambler and threw Aggie a confused look.

It was a face in the crowd. A face just like the others, frustrated, straining against his suit. Only there was more disbelief than anger in his expression.

'Seb?' Aggie shouted, jumping off the scrambler and heading back to where she'd seen him.

As their eyes locked, Seb's grew wide.

'Aggie?'

Aggie wanted to hug Seb, to say she was so sorry. But more than that, she wanted him with her. She and Seb did everything together. She needed him now more than ever.

'Aggie?' His voice bounced into her ears. 'Can you hear me?'

'Yes!' Aggie cried.

'Aggs,' he said, straining to look at her from inside his helmet, 'you've got to get away. Rix has gone crazy, he'll kill you and I'm not even joking.'

'Agatha,' Celeste's voice permeated her helmet, 'I can't hold them like this for long. I'm fighting against my automatic programming.'

Seb looked at Aggie. 'I missed you.'

'I missed you.'

'I'm sorry.'

'Me too.'

'Now just unfix me and let me help you.'

Aggie looked around, 'No. It's too dangerous.'

'Aggs, I'm not leaving you ever again.'

Aggie kicked the dust. 'That actually sounds really annoying.'

Seb smiled. 'OK, well maybe you get bathroom breaks.'

'Deal. Celeste? Unfix him.'

'Unfix me,' Seb said, not to Aggie but to Celeste. 'Dude, just unfix me!'

'Unfix him.' Aggie said again, grabbing Seb's hand and holding it tight despite the fact it felt like stone.

'What?' Danny and Celeste said in unison.

'Let him go, Celeste,' Aggie demanded. 'He can help us.'

'He's a guard,' Danny said.

'He's not part of the plan,' Celeste added.

'If you don't unfix me, Celeste,' Seb shouted, 'I'm going to come after you anyway, Aggs needs me.'

Aggie twisted Seb's buzzer free from his other hand and threw it away. 'We need him. I need him. I'm not leaving without him.'

'Agatha, the plan—' the computer started to say, but was distracted by a movement somewhere on one of the shuttles, 'I'm losing them.'

'Well, unfix him!' Aggie cried, watching as the guards started to move slowly around her. She was heaving at Seb as if she could compete with the strength of the exoskeleton.

Suddenly Seb's arm went soft beneath her hands again. The instant it did, Aggie pulled him forwards.

'Ow, ow, ow!' Seb yelped as she dragged him past the frozen guards to where Danny had the scrambler.

'Danny, Seb. Seb, Danny,' she shouted as she hoisted herself up on to the seat. 'Now go!'

Danny kicked the scrambler into gear and it sped away, but Seb hadn't had time to sit and suddenly Aggie felt him fly off on to the ground behind them.

She turned around and saw Seb skid out of control along the dusty ground. She gasped. Behind him, the guards were now free and running, their bodies hidden behind a shower of evil-looking violet sparks.

'No! Seb!' Aggie cried, as Seb tumbled again, then lurched to his feet. He looked back and then sprinted towards them, chasing the scrambler's dust.

'Danny! Slow down!' Aggie cried, reaching her hand towards Seb as he dodged the licking, spitting buzzers of the guards behind him. The shadow of Rix's shuttle moved up through the crowd. If the shuttle was back online, what chance did they have? A shuttle could easily outrun a scrambler.

Aggie could hear the whirring of Seb's exo in her comms as he pumped the mechanisms harder and harder, trying to outrun the advancing shuttle. There was a look of pure terror on his face, he knew it as well as she did; exos were good, but not that good.

'Celeste!' Aggie cried. 'Do something!'

'They've switched to manual,' the computer replied. 'It's harder to hack into—'

Suddenly a huge roar erupted from the pack of guards and Rix's shuttle rose higher into the sky. One of its fans was out-turning the other, making it tilt up onto its side. At its helm, Rix was shouting orders and gesturing wildly at the men who towered around him. The second engine spluttered and shook as Rix revved it; he wanted to get to them, whatever it took. She'd seen too much; he had to stop her.

Plumes of dust rose high, kicking rocks and bits of metal into the sky. Aggie felt them thud against her suit but kept her arm out towards Seb, leaning over dangerously.

'Aggs!' Seb panted, his face a horrible shade of red behind his visor, 'I don't think I can . . .'

'Keep going!' Aggie screamed, 'Just keep going!'

There was another shudder on the ground, Aggie felt her stomach drop as she was tossed into the air. Danny's hand pulled her back down just in time.

When Aggie looked back Seb had disappeared. 'Seb!' she cried. 'Where is he?'

'There,' Danny replied, pointing up to the shuttle; it was now so close to the scrambler Aggie could almost reach out and touch its smooth black hull.

Seb had obviously thought the same thing, he had thrown himself up and grabbed on to the front of the shuttle with both arms, his legs scrabbling on the smooth metal to get a hold.

The huge broken shuttle baulked and twisted. A chorus of shouts erupted from the guards on top, as the ones that weren't tied to the rail fell away into the dust. The second engine was still spluttering. The huge craft veered and lurched as it skimmed the surface towards them. Seb's exo held him tight to the nose, but now the gap between him and the scrambler was too big to jump.

Aggie caught Seb's eye, for a second they shared a look. 'No! Seb! You can't do it!' Aggie screamed. Then Roger Rix's boot smacked into Seb's visor.

Aggie had no idea how he managed to keep his grip on the slippery hull, but Seb held tight as Rix rained down blow after blow, so quick and so powerful that his black arms were a blur. Over the cries and shouts, Aggie could make out Rix's own snarling grunts as he strained to stay upright.

'Celeste?' Seb cried as he tried to fight back, but every time he tried to move he slipped further down the hull. 'A bit of help?'

'Hold on, Sebastian.'

'OK, but you better be quick.'

'No, I mean. Hold on.'

The shuttle swerved to the right, knocking away the guards still running beside it like skittles. The engine shorted with a pulse of white light and the massive craft slammed into the ground. Aggie's heart jumped into her mouth as, from the back of the scrambler, she watched the great wedge skid over the smooth grey ground. Untethered guards flew off in every direction as it started to spin out of control.

'Seb!' Aggie cried desperately, feeling useless stuck on the back of the scrambler.

Every time the rotating shuttle hit the ground, it gained more momentum. Soon, it was just a spinning blur of black and violet.

'Oh no,' she muttered, following the line of the shuttle's

trajectory to where the grey ground dropped away sharply.

'The crater!' she shouted, 'they're heading right for it! Seb!'

The cliffs that surrounded the massive Goddard Crater were sharp and steep, covered in boulders the size of the shuttle itself, but the ship was spinning so fast now it was like a shining black bullet, racing across the surface towards the drop.

Danny skidded the scrambler around just as the shuttle went over Goddard's cliffs, hovering in a blur of shining black and grey until it plummeted down, cartwheeling into the centre of the crater.

The shuttle made contact with boulders with an ear-splitting crunch.

Danny pulled Aggie and the scrambler in behind a rock, away from any surviving guards, as debris from the crash started to skim back over the ground towards them.

The shouts and cries over their comms built up to a crescendo, then started to lessen.

Soon, all she could hear was Danny's breathing.

He grabbed her and held her close. Tears ran down Aggie's face, pooling above the clogged vents in the suit's collar. Her visor began to mist up. Aggie was glad. As the fall-out from the crash continued to rain down around them, she felt hollow. No one could survive an impact like that.

Her best friend was dead. And it was all her fault.

16

Night-Cycle 01

A light flashed in her comms.
'Hey Agatha.'
It was Celeste.
'Are you hurt?'
Aggie opened her eyes.
'Seb is the one that's hurt!' She tried to push herself up but Danny's arm was like iron around her waist.
'Hey, you'll get hurt,' he whispered.
Aggie turned to him, 'Seb is out there!' she cried, struggling again.
'If you leave your current position the chances of injury

or capture are eighty-five per cent,' Celeste countered flatly.

'Seb's ... he's in the middle of that!' Aggie pleaded, flinging her free arm in the direction of the twisted shuttle debris. 'Celeste knows! She must know!' Aggie's throat closed up, the lump in her throat was like a boulder now. How could she have been so selfish? How could she have let Seb come with them? He had been fine where he was. He had been with the guards. He had been protected.

'I don't have any readings, Agatha. There's interference from the wreckage.'

'That's because he's dead!'

'He has an exo,' Danny said quickly. 'He has a good chance.'

Aggie pushed again, 'No.'

Danny shoved her back. 'More chance than you if you go out there now.'

The pressure from Danny's arm increased. Aggie was pinned to the rock. She looked up at the prisoner, but he refused to look back. His eyes were fixed on the distance.

'You heartless denk!' she sobbed. 'He's my friend. You can't do this! Let me go!'

'Agatha, please calm down.'

'I am calm!'

'Really? Am I malfunctioning?'

A piece of one of the giant shuttle's fans scraped loudly over the rocks and crashed into the boulder just metres away from their feet.

'It's OK, Celeste,' Danny replied. Then to Aggie, 'We

need to wait. When it's safe, we'll find your guard friend.'

Aggie stopped fighting. She was trembling inside the suit. All she could see was Seb's small skinny body, mangled in with the shuttle. They were going so fast. Even with an exo, how could anyone survive that?

The clogged water vents hummed in protest as fresh tears raced down Aggie's cheeks. Guilt – that familiar old friend – began to seep through her skin.

Aggie found her thoughts drifting to her father. That feeling was almost the only thing she could associate with him, a feeling of shame, a guilt that had been built up by years of apologizing for what he had done. Maybe it was in her genes, killing people. Ruining good people's lives.

An awful thought prickled at the back of her head. Did he know? Did her father plan for the Far Side as he'd rushed to finish the power plant? He must have known. David Shepard was the lumite expert in the Founding Five. If he'd lied about the integrity of the reactor, then what else had he covered up? Right now, the thought was too much to comprehend.

A light flashed, pulling her back.

'The surviving guards are on manual settings, but I've located their comm feeds. The crash site is clear.'

The weight of Danny's arm lifted. Aggie pushed him away and sprinted towards the wreckage.

As she stumbled into the crash site, clouds of thick grey dust swam in the space around her. The broken black shuttle stuck up out of the clouds like the summit of a great mountain.

Aggie looked up at it all with a hole in her heart.

It was hopeless.

Danny caught up with her, his breathing was louder than one of the base's air conditioners.

'Aggie, wait ...' He coughed, crouching down to get his breath. But Aggie didn't have time to wait, she just staggered forwards, sobbing into her stinking vents.

Inside the cloud was like a scene from a nightmare. Twisted black shapes loomed out at her as she and Danny walked closer, the ground underfoot felt loose and fragile beneath the weight of her surface boots. More than once she slipped into a new crater made by the impact, hidden by a thick coating of dust and debris. From somewhere deep within the impact area, the intricate systems that had once powered the shuttle's huge regolith fans fizzed, send-ing bright sparks dancing into the mist.

As she took in the devastation, grief racked her body: Seb couldn't survive this, exo or not.

Her best friend was dead. She'd killed him.

'Aggie!' Danny cried. 'It's not safe!'

Aggie ignored him and sank down to her knees in despair.

A coughing noise reverberated around her helmet.

Aggie looked up. There was something familiar in the sound.

'Seb?' she said quietly, not believing the old suit's unre-liable comms. But the coughing continued. It was getting closer. 'Seb?' she said again, louder this time.

'Aggs . . .' Then a great spluttering cough.

Aggie turned around and saw Seb's skinny silhouette emerging from behind a huge chunk of what was once the shuttle. Aggie sprinted towards him and flung her arms around Seb's waist and squeezed so tight his exo activated. 'You're OK!' she cried, wrapping herself around his skinny frame. 'Thank the Earth you're OK!' she said, tears running down her cheeks for the millionth time. 'Oh, Seb, I'm so sorry. For everything, I never meant—'

Seb squeezed her back. He really was OK. The exo had saved him. 'Not really the time, Aggs, but I appreciate it and everything,' Seb said, pulling away and smiling down at her through a cracked visor. 'That's an exo in my pocket, just to be clear. Nothing to do with me.'

Aggie smiled. 'I'm so glad you're OK.'

Seb wound his arms back around her. Aggie wasn't sure that the shivering was just coming from the ground. 'I'm always here, Angelface, you know that.'

Aggie blinked. 'Angelface?'

Seb shrugged. 'I'm trying it out.'

'It's terrible.'

'Exactly.'

Aggie laughed. The rush of relief made her giddy. She could think of no other person to have by her side, her friend, her shadow.

Seb pulled back and looked down at her. His eyes were all watery. 'Aggs, I'm so sorry. I was a huge clagger's ass.'

Aggie shook her head. 'I should have told you.'

Seb grinned. 'No, I should have stuck by you, you know, if only for all the free stuff. You'd have got a whole bunch of free stuff, right? Famous people get free stuff.'

In spite of everything, Aggie laughed. If Seb was joking, he really was OK.

'But, I guess you've really messed that up now, though, whatever it is you've done over there, I guessing it's *pretty* bad . . .'

'Yeah, I don't think I'm high on the United Leader's gift list.'

'One or two guards have turned up to capture you.'

'I had noticed, one or two. Yeah.'

Aggie looked down at her boots, suddenly overwhelmed.

'Are you going to tell me what's going on, then?' Seb said with a shaky intake of breath. 'I guess I kind of need to know now, 'cause everything's like, destroyed and falling apart and I nearly just died and there's a convicted murderer with us and stuff like that.'

Seb nodded in the direction of Danny, who was still making his way unsteadily towards them.

Aggie buried her head in Seb's arm. 'It's so messed up.'

'Just tell me it was Rock-Aliens. Please. That would make my life!'

'Weirdly, in a way, yeah, it was.'

'Well, I guess there are some positives then . . .'

Aggie slapped Seb on the shoulder playfully, then turned at the sound of a soft thud in her comms.

'Danny?' Aggie ran over to where the prisoner lay on the ground.

Seb sighed, 'Oh, yeah, the prisoner that you brought with you. Almost forgot about that dude.'

Seb joined them as Aggie helped Danny back to his feet. The prisoner's skin had gone grey. He was pointing to the pocket where a medi-kit bulged.

Seb looked Danny up and down, 'Earth below, what happened to him?'

'Give it to me,' Danny managed to say.

Aggie propped Danny up against Seb and pulled out the medi-kit she'd seen him hide in his suit pocket. She opened the small box, which wasn't easy with the shaking ground and her cumbersome gloves. Two fat needles and two blue vials sat inside a sea of foam protectors. A serial number on the inside of the lid was the only indication of what they contained.

Aggie looked at Seb. He shrugged, as confused as she was.

Aggie passed Danny the box. She looked down at the him worriedly. He looked to be concentrating too much on breathing to answer.

'Dude's an addict,' Seb mumbled.

'Danny, are you OK?'

Danny closed his eyes as if it was taking every ounce of his energy just to stay conscious.

'I need something with an atmosphere, the suit . . .'

Aggie looked at Danny's ancient Far Side suit. Of course, the needle would pierce the pressurized layer – they hadn't had self-healing fabrics when the Far Side suits were made.

Aggie turned to Seb. 'Seb, you need to help him. I can't carry him.'

'Why are we helping this dude again?'

Aggie shook her head, she hadn't got time to explain. 'He's not like the others, he's good, FALL aren't—'

Seb dropped Danny back to the ground. 'No way, man. Aggs, if he's FALL then he's not good. He's the opposite of good.'

'We can't just leave him,' Aggie pleaded, glancing around the dust cloud for signs of guards. But Celeste would warn them, wouldn't she?

Seb looked at Aggie for a long time, then shook his head. 'The shuttle's hull is intact,' he grunted, pulling Danny up and snatching the box.

'Thank you.'

Seb hauled Danny roughly into the remains of the shuttle and pulled down the hatch. Aggie kept watch outside, sitting on her haunches checking the dusty debris for any sign of movement. She scraped the dust with her boot. Any mark she made disappeared with the ground's shaking. The quake was already getting worse.

After a little while the comms in her helmet flashed.

'I'm picking up life signs close to your position,' Celeste said. 'There's no movement yet, but I would advise we move soon.'

Something sharp suddenly jabbed in Aggie's chest. 'Rix,' she said, turning in a circle, as if the thought had somehow conjured the commander up like a ghost.

'I'm not receiving any life signs from the commander's overall,' Celeste said matter-of-factly. 'Though I'm having trouble picking up all the manual signals.'

Aggie glanced around her again nervously and nodded. Rix had been on the nose of the shuttle as it crashed into the ground. Even with an exo, surely that meant—

'Good,' she said, unconvincingly. The idea of Rix being gone didn't make her feel any safer, just even more empty.

She took a deep breath. Something else was niggling the back of Aggie's mind, guilt spreading out over her chest again.

'Celeste?'

'Hey Agatha.'

'Why did you do this?'

'The guards are an immediate threat, Agatha. If they're still armed then—'

'No, not the life signs, this. Why did you show me?'

The computer was silent for a while.

'To protect you,' she said quietly. 'David's orders were to protect you.'

Before Aggie could react, the sound of grunts erupted from inside the shuttle.

'Fragging hell, man, there is nowhere left to put this thing,' Seb complained loudly.

'Go for the upper arm,' Celeste replied to him. Obviously an Eye inside the shuttle was still working. 'There's twenty per cent less scarring.'

'Thank you very much, Celeste, but I won't take orders from something that doesn't have skin, if that's OK.'

'Just do it!' Danny shouted.

Aggie glanced back at the shuttle worriedly – what was in those tiny blue vials? Not drugs, surely? Danny was a lot of things, but he wasn't some drugged-up meathead like the other prisoners. Danny did what he did because he believed he was right – not to get a fix.

She got up and wandered to the edge of the shuttle debris. Her head was spinning. Who had told the computer to protect her – her father? And why? Because he'd known about the reactor? She shook the thoughts away.

Here, the dust had settled and the endless black sky had reappeared between the rocks. Aggie looked up at the Earth. The beautiful blue marble. It looked so peaceful, just hanging there in the silent black sky.

She imagined the people there, in their houses, going to work, worrying about money and their families and where they would go on holiday that summer. Aggie wished with all her heart that she didn't have to do what she was about to. She was about to break open the quiet, peaceful world that the United Earth had become. She and Danny were about to change everything.

A shiver of anticipation ran over her. How in all the seven states was she supposed to tell them that lumite was over? How would she start that sentence as the Lunar Base that had once saved them crumbled into the dust? The idea was overwhelming.

Aggie looked up. 'That's it! How does the world see the base?' she said, excitement creeping into her voice. 'Celeste! How do people see the base?'

Her comms flashed again with the computer's presence.

Aggie hauled herself up out of the dust, a foggy memory coming back to her.

'Celeste, what time is it?'

A hiss from somewhere close by made Aggie start. The escape hatch on the battered shuttle sprang open. She made her way towards the movement unsteadily, her teeth chattering with the pull and push of the ground.

After a few steps she saw a shape moving towards her. 'Seb?' she called.

'That's offensive,' came the deep-voiced reply.

Aggie looked more closely. Danny was striding away from the shuttle as if nothing had happened.

He came up to her and put his hands on her waist. His eyes were shining through his visor more brightly than Aggie had ever seen. Her legs wobbled, then she remembered what was happening around them and pushed him gently away.

'Are you OK?' Danny said with a lopsided smile.

Aggie nodded shyly, not completely sure what was happening. She wondered what was wrong with her. The air around them felt as if it was alive with static. Maybe it was.

Another shape emerged from the shuttle.

Seb looked at them both for a second, them stomped past.

'Yeah, man, don't mention it,' he muttered bitterly as he disappeared into the dust cloud. 'No, seriously, it was my pleasure. Oh, and I'm sorry, what were you in for again?'

his voice crackled over the radio and tailed off.

Danny looked at Aggie, a pained expression playing across his face.

'Thank you,' he said quietly.

'You should thank Seb, really. He did everything.'

'I already tried. He's not exactly welcoming, this guard friend of yours.'

Aggie frowned. 'Well, he did almost just die so . . .'

Danny smiled, 'I suppose that would make you grumpy.'

'We need to go,' Aggie said, trying to avoid that stare.

'This way, dudes!' Seb shouted from somewhere in the distance. Danny and Aggie stood together for a second with nothing but the rumbling of the surface below them. Danny turned to her suddenly as if he was about to say something, but Aggie got there first. 'We really have to go.'

Danny smiled. 'Yeah. There's a whole world of people out there waiting to have their dreams crushed by us.' His voice shook with the power of the quake.

Aggie allowed herself a small smile. 'Better not keep them waiting.'

17

Night-Cycle 01

As they crept along the edge of the rubble back to where the scrambler was still hidden by the rocks, Aggie gave Seb a rapid account of what had happened on the Far Side.

Between his expressions of utter disbelief, she started to hear distant shouts of the uninjured guards regrouping. With that and the shaking of the ground, they had to move. Fast.

When they reached the trike, Danny took the driver's seat. Seb huffed loudly as he was forced to sit on the small cargo shelf at the back. Aggie slid in behind Danny and placed her gloved hands on his waist. She felt a vibration on her arm, it was coming from Seb.

'Seb? Your comms.'

Seb started then looked down at his forearm. 'Damn, almost forgot about that,' he said, swiping the panel and revealing a familiar face behind the screen.

'Astrid!' Aggie, Seb and Celeste shouted in unison.

'Who?' Danny said from the driver's seat.

Aggie peered at Seb's panel. Astrid looked worried and tiny against the commotion going on behind her; people in all colours running this way and that, carrying boxes and equipment. She was wearing an overall with a reinforced exo over the top – the red cross of the ERM badge shone on her helmet.

When she saw their feed, Astrid's face lit up.

'Oh, Aggie! You're OK! Oh thank the Earth you're OK!' Her eyes darted around them. 'Earth below, is that *THE* prisoner? Ooo, I totally get it now, Aggie, very—'

Seb pulled his arm back. 'What do you want, Astrid?'

'Sorry!' the intern said, 'The ERMs have assembled! We're active!'

Seb turned to Aggie. 'I'm sorry, is she actually *happy* about that?'

Aggie shook her head and dragged Seb's arm closer. 'What's happening?'

Astrid ducked as a gang of guards stomped past carrying a piece of equipment.

'It's a code seven. Sorry, to the untrained that means a full, base-wide evac. Total abandon ship. I'll be honest,

Aggie, we didn't even train for this!'

Astrid bobbed down again as another group of guards pushed by, holding emergency oxygen tanks. She was talking so fast that Aggie could feel her terror.

'Aggie, something exploded, something really, really big. We saw it go up from the rec room. It looked as if it was from the Far Side! Cayla thinks it's an attack, from FALL. But it was so big, it lit up the whole sky!'

Aggie felt a crush of guilt.

'Where are you?' Astrid continued. 'The ERMs are coming! You're on our priority list – there's a shuttle waiting—'

'No. Astrid, get to the shuttles, like I told you,' Aggie said, feeling a concrete brick reforming in her stomach. But Astrid wasn't listening, she was shouting something to someone off-screen, her ERM's badge shining.

'E Face fell in a few minutes ago, C Face won't be long. The commuter shuttles aren't running, people can't get to the shuttle bays. We're trying to help, but if we don't go soon . . .'

Aggie looked at Seb, his eyes bulged out of his head. He had no idea of the damage that they'd done on the other side of the border. He just watched dumbly as Astrid described their home crumbling into ruins.

'The whole base?' Aggie stammered dumbly.

'It's gone, Aggie, or it's going, fast. It's a code seven! Argh!'

Aggie and Seb screamed with Astrid as they watched the ceiling of the corridor crash to the floor. Aggie couldn't take it any longer. She looked at Danny — what had they done?

'Astrid! Please, go!'

'Where are you? I can bring a rescue shuttle.'

'No. Astrid. Don't worry about us.' Aggie felt cold. If they didn't move now, her plan wouldn't work. As if reading her mind, Danny kicked the scrambler into gear and started to move forwards.

Astrid looked horrified. 'Leave?! I just refuse to be the girl that left the Angel of Adrianne to just—'

Seb stopped her and pulled his arm back, 'Astrid, please just go. We'll get off the base. Just get to a shuttle.'

'I have a shuttle, the ERMs can help—'

'Now,' Seb demanded, in a voice Aggie had seldom heard him use.

Astrid looked as if she was being torn apart. She glanced from the corridor to the camera. There was a crash and the camera fizzed . . .

'Astrid!' Aggie cried as the comms on Seb's arm flickered. The sound went dead. Astrid flung her arms around, trying to communicate, but it was pointless. Seb flicked the comms unit off.

'This is not how I imagined this day turning out,' he muttered.

After an hour or so of driving, they left the pulsing red of the border region and found themselves plunged into a darkness as thick and black as the Ether itself.

'It's the night-cycle,' Seb stated obviously. 'I forgot we

- 227 -

were going into a night-cycle.'

Celeste spoke to them through the Ether. 'All power will be rerouted for the evacuation. No one will be paying us any attention.'

'Looks as if Celeste has it under control, Seb,' Danny grunted. 'We're in a good position.'

Seb huffed loudly. 'Well, I don't think "good" is the right word really, Danny. "Good" would be steak on the menu in Whole Earth, or finding out you have the afternoon off, or maybe waking up and finding out this whole thing was some horrific, pointless dream.'

'It's important to be positive,' Danny offered, but was cut off quickly.

'Oh, I think I am being positive. I think describing our current situation as diabolical is pretty clagging positive, actually. I am the voice of positivity dude, really, I am.'

Danny glared. 'Seriously mate, your attitude is going to compromise this whole mission.'

Seb stared at Danny's back for a second, then squared his shoulders defiantly. 'Sorry, dude, but there's no fragging *way* that I'm taking orders from a clagging *terrorist*.'

'You have no idea what I am.'

'OK, you went through some terrible stuff over there, I'm sorry about that. But I bet it's just about as terrible as derailing a Hyperloop train, or destroying a hydrodam, or bombing the clagging United Government! Dude, Aggs might be able to forget what you did – because she's mental – but I know what people like you are really like.'

Danny's eyes narrowed. 'You don't know what you're

talking about.'

'Oh really?' Seb laughed coldly. 'Well, I'm sticking around, dude – sorry to disappoint you. Because I've seen what you're doing, and I swear on all the lumite in the Moon, if you hurt her in any way . . .'

'Seb!' Aggie shouted. Her cheeks had started to burn beneath her visor. But the boys didn't hear.

Danny had stopped the trike, jumped off and was squaring up to Seb. Seb pulled back as far as he could in the cargo shelf and braced himself for a blow. But before Danny could get close, Aggie clambered off and pushed a hand against both their chests.

'Stop it!' she shouted. 'What are you, children? Are you both forgetting what we're doing here? Don't you understand the implications of it all? Our lives will never be the same. Don't you see that?

'We're allowed to be scared, Danny – look at all of this. I'm terrified!' She turned to Seb. 'And you. You know what you're doing. Don't wind him up. You're better than that.'

Seb looked at her defiantly for a second, then down at the ground. Danny kicked a rock with his boot. When he looked back at Aggie, she was surprised to see colour on his cheeks. Was Danny actually blushing? Had she actually made him blush?

'You're right.' He turned to Seb and muttered softly, 'You're a guard, which doesn't make me want to be best mates. But we've got to work as a team, for now.'

Seb shook his head in resignation. 'Yeah, man. For now.'

The two boys nodded and Danny climbed back onto

the driver's seat.

As the scrambler sped out across the surface and the dust began to clear, Aggie felt an odd sensation. One that she hadn't felt for many years. One that felt completely inappropriate given the situation they were in. In fact, she felt guilty for feeling it at all, but she couldn't deny it.

Suddenly, she felt strangely complete.

Her best friend leant comfortingly against her back, the spark between herself and Danny fizzed in the space between them as she held him tightly around his waist.

The moment was bittersweet. She wished she could stop time here. Nothing else would matter and the three of them would be here together, travelling the rumbling Moon for eternity.

18

Night-Cycle 01

As they drove back through the Border Sea, the base began to rise up around them. The closer they got to these densely habited areas, the reality of what was happening was all too obvious. It was pandemonium.

'Earth below,' Danny muttered from the front of the bike, his words repeated by both Aggie and Seb in unison as they took in the chaos.

The bright lights that lit up the base during the night-cycle flickered intermittently, turning the familiar domes into nothing more than a collection of foreboding black shadows. To their left, a riot had broken out between the prisoners in B Face and the guards who kept them at bay. The quake had made a crack in the side of the dome big enough for the red-overalled men to squeeze through one at a time. Violet forks of lightning danced around them, as the guards tried desperately to stop the leak by shooting at the prisoners with their buzzers, but they were too strong and too many.

Soon their little scrambler reached the huge sky-blue entrance to Tranquillity.

In the gloom and dust and desolation, the great foyer looked like the entrance to an alien temple. A great hexagonal door shone like a glittering beacon, guiding them towards it. Carved deep into the rock above it was the Lunar Inc. logo and beneath it, the company's motto:

OUT OF DARKNESS, WE SHINE

'Stand back, I'm opening the doors.' Celeste said.

At her command, the doors hissed and began to open slowly.

WELCOME TO TRANQUILLITY BASE. PLEASE WAIT UNTIL THE ALARM SOUNDS BEFORE DEPRESSURIZING YOUR SUITS. ONCE THE AIR-LOCK HAS RELEASED, YOU WILL BE GREETED BY A PORTER WHO WILL TAKE YOU TO YOUR QUAR-TERS. ALL AT LUNAR INCORPORATED WISH YOU A PLEASANT STAY ON THE LUNAR SURFACE.

They walked inside and were hit by a wall of silence.

The huge, rocky space that Aggie had visited before was empty. The air was thick with dust and the smell of burning plastic and metal; furniture had been tossed across the floor and plants sprawled in their soil.

'They evacuated the directors first – that makes sense,' Danny said as he joined her.

The huge moon globe still hung in the ceiling, but it no longer glowed. The Lunar Base map flickered and glitched, lighting the huge dark space with sporadic flashes.

They picked their way over the shattered moon rock floor to the other side of the giant, glowing orb.

Seb hung back, quietly staring up at the ceiling. Aggie guessed why.

She put an arm around her friend's waist, making him jump and glance at Danny.

'She got the shuttle to Earth,' she said with a squeeze. 'She left hours ago.'

Seb nodded. 'Yeah. I know.'

As Aggie spoke, something twisted in her gut. Mir suspected something, she'd told her in the hospital wing. If she'd spoken to anyone else . . . No, Mir wasn't that stupid. Still, to Aggie, being in the United Government felt as dangerous as being on the base.

'Comms are down, that's all. Mir's probably in the United Government now, managing the whole Earth-side evac or something.'

The way Seb smiled made Aggie's heart hurt. 'Man, I hope she is. Then we'll all be OK.'

Aggie nodded. 'She's probably telling the United Leader what to do, poor guy.'

Ahead of them, Danny kicked a fallen chair out of their way.

'I think the prisoner is giving us a subtle message.'

'That wasn't there before, right?' Danny shouted, pointing at the floor in front of them.

Aggie pulled Seb forward.

Ahead of them, the floor had split into two pieces. The other side of the floor was at least two metres away where they stood, and it sloped away steeply. They'd have no choice but to jump and pray that there was something solid in the darkness beyond.

Chunks of masonry fell from the cavernous ceiling and shattered on the floor. Every time it happened, Seb jumped so high that Aggie was afraid he'd fall into the gap.

'Your heart rate is increasing, Sebastian,' Celeste said from somewhere in the roof. 'How about we try some calming stretches?'

Seb looked up at the ceiling.

'Are you kidding me?'

'Definitely not. The mission would be severely compromised if you had a heart episode.'

Seb looked down at the gap again and swallowed loudly. 'Then don't make me jump over the entrance to hell, then. C'mon, man, there's got to be a way around this, right?'

Aggie had to admit, there was something reassuring about the way Celeste watched over them. She felt protected, looked after. After years of fear and suspicion towards the computer, it was a strange sensation, comforting and uncomfortable at the same time.

'This way.' Celeste led them to where a small, thin platform had been left jutting over the darkness. This, the computer had decided, would make the perfect launch platform for their jump across the chasm. Aggie wasn't so convinced, but Danny seemed to take it all in his stride.

'Just don't think about it too much,' he said as lined up a run-up, glancing between his launch point and the steep slope on the other side.

Seb shot Danny a withering look. 'Please don't fall, man, I would be devastated. Truly.'

Danny ignored him, backed up another step, and then launched himself at the gap. Aggie let out an involuntary cry as she watched him soar over the darkness and skid to an unsteady halt against the slope on the other side.

'Oh he can fly now too, can he?' Seb muttered to himself as Aggie lined herself up. 'Cosmic.'

Aggie ran and jumped after Danny, sailing across the gap and skidding away down the slope.

'Hey! Hey!' Seb cried. 'Hey! Wait for me.'

'You have an exo, Seb, just jump!' Aggie called from the other side.

Aggie waited. Then there was a sound like a wet towel hitting a wall. Aggie looked up. The tips of Seb's black gloves were just visible, gripping the edge of the floor.

'Earth below. Seb!' He'd only just made it.

'He's OK. He just can't jump, that's all.' Danny reached up and pulled Seb over.

When he emerged, Seb looked furious. 'I can fragging jump, you cosmic denk. Exos aren't designed for gravity-controlled environments, are they? It makes them fragging unpredictable, doesn't it?'

Aggie moved between them.

Seb looked over her head at Danny. Even though his exo was activated, she could see the tension in his shoulders. He held out a hand and pointed at the prisoner. 'You're testing me, dude. I'm tired, I'm hungry, and I'm scared. Don't test me.'

'What you going to do, mate? Sarcasm me to death?'

'No, I'd do something that actually challenged me.'

'What? Like lift your own weight?'

Aggie groaned and walked away from them both. 'I can't believe you two. Just stop it.'

'Stop him!' Seb exclaimed, stumbling backwards over a fallen chair. 'The guy's got a thruster loose! Walking around like an escaped gorilla, all knuckles dragging along, and grunting and swinging it about! What do you want me to do – join him? No way, man, I'm far more evolved than that piece of FALL clag!'

Danny balled his hands into fists by his sides, 'What is your problem, really? We told you why I'm here.'

'Dude, that is the only reason I'm tolerating breathing the same air as you right now.'

Danny stepped closer. 'Stop making this about me. This has nothing to do with me. It's about those people out there who are dying.'

Seb looked outraged, his mouth bobbing open and closed like a fish. His finger wagged about in front of him but it was as if Danny had short-circuited something in his head.

'Hey, hey. C'mon now,' Aggie cut in before Seb regained

the power of speech. 'We're a team. We need to be a team.'

'I'm trying, honestly, but I'm not babysitting him, Aggie. Not when we don't need to.'

'Seb is a very positive influence,' Celeste interrupted from above them.

Seb gave a thumbs-up to the ceiling. 'Thanks, dude, though I'd appreciate it if you could stop trying to kill me.'

Aggie felt Danny's eyes burning into the side of her head as she pushed Seb towards one of the corridors.

'Get off Aggs, I can walk myself,' he mumbled, shrugging Aggie's hands off irritably, 'and for the record, I don't care what your boyfriend thinks.'

But everything about the way he was acting said he did care.

'This way,' Celeste said.

Aggie led the way to the Forecast Suite with a lump in her throat. She had endured many rooms like it as a child, with pushy reporters asking her about her recovery, all the exclusive interviews with the 'Child of Hope', the precious little Angel that was a symbol of survival and better things to come. How surprised would those people be in a few minutes when that same face came once again onto their screens, this time to tell them everything they knew would soon come to an end?

Celeste activated the large Ether on the far wall and the great milk-coloured sails started to emit their soft yellow light. The calm of the place made Aggie's head swim. Was she just being manipulated again? Things had happened so quickly that she'd had no time to think.

She turned and stared directly at the broadcast cameras. They gazed back at her silently, their blank, black Eyes trained to her every move. She felt she was about to throw up.

'What are we doing?' she said, not turning away from the cameras' dead gaze.

'What do you mean?' Danny answered matter-of-factly.

'We can't do this,' she said.

'What?' Danny, Celeste and Seb all choroused.

'What are you talking about?' Danny demanded.

Aggie turned and looked up at him, wide-eyed. 'We're going to change the world, Danny. Do you realize that? I didn't have time to think about it before now.'

'Of course I know that,' he said, moving towards her.

'But do you really understand it?'

'Understand what?'

'What we found? All this – everything that's gone wrong. Do you really understand what that means to everyone down there? We don't have any answers for them, do we? We know that what's been happening is wrong but we're only going to give them more questions.' Her tone was pleading. 'I haven't got any answers for them, have you?'

Danny placed his hands on her shoulders and looked down at her. 'Of course I know that, but what's happening here is wrong, Aggie. So what if we give them a reason to ask questions? They should have questions. People should know what's been happening to keep their coffee machines and cars running. Aggie, no matter what happens now, the people down there have to know what we know. They deserve that, at least.'

'But do they have to find out like this?' Aggie looked again at the equipment that surrounded them, the stark alien backdrop, the dirty, bloodied rag-tag band of three that stood before the cameras, two in ancient spacesuits, the other shaking in his filthy guard's overall. They looked more like enemy militia.

'Look at us. They won't believe us. Why don't we just get a shuttle out of here and go straight to the United Government, tell them everything. Surely the explosion and the quake will be enough.'

'It's not enough, Aggs. You know that,' Seb suddenly spoke up from the corner of the room. 'If you're right, then so is he.' He jabbed his thumb towards Danny. 'The government must already know.'

Danny looked at Aggie, 'The United Government is corrupt, Aggie. The only way to change things is to broadcast before we can get cut off. This isn't about FALL or Lunar Inc. It's about the truth. We need to tell the people, not the government. Before Rix's people can do anything to shut us down.'

Aggie stared at the small dent in the wall where the manual broadcast button sat. The consequences of what they were about to do were crushing her. 'They'll go back to how they were,' she muttered, 'the wars and the riots. It'll all come back. Maybe the lie is better, Danny. Did you ever think of that?'

'No.' Danny looked her in the eye. 'I didn't. Whatever happens today will happen eventually. Isn't it better to do it while the world still has a supply of lumite left? Think, Aggie. How long have you felt that something was wrong? Years? Since Adrianne? That's because it is wrong. Everything here is rotten and always has been. It needs to stop now. No matter what the consequences.'

'Aggie,' Celeste said softly from the Ether. It was the first time the computer had used that name. 'This place, it isn't what they wanted, David and the Founding Five. This is what they tried to stop, but they were too late.'

Aggie's hand hovered over the button. Her fingers shook, her heart beat against her ribs. Then—

WARNING: THE 'NEW MOON' FORECAST IS DUE FOR BROADCAST IN FIVE MINUTES.

Out of the corner of her eye, Aggie saw a red light pop on. The suite around them buzzed. The recording light. They were actually doing this . . .

Suddenly, footsteps echoed down the tiny corridor, followed by the sound of heavy breathing. The three people in the room froze.

'Right on time,' Celeste said.

19

Night-Cycle 01

'A dam!' Aggie cried.

Her godfather appeared at the mouth of the corridor, wearing a sky-blue Tranquillity overall covered in dust and dirt.

'Agatha?' Faulkner shouted, his face sagging in relief. 'Is that you? How did you get in here?'

Danny stepped forwards. Aggie frowned.

'Yeah, Aggie's here,' Danny said. 'Seb too. And me.'

Faulkner stopped. 'Who are you? I don't know you.'

Danny took another step.

'Yeah, you do. Though you might not recognize me. It

has been ten years.'

Faulkner didn't move. 'What are you talking about?'

Danny smiled and moved closer. His face was now illuminated by the Forecast Suite lights.

Faulkner gasped.

'Not changed that much then,' Danny said, still smiling. 'How you doing, Dad?'

The room was silent apart from the humming of the Forecast cameras.

Adam Faulkner stumbled, then steadied himself with one hand against the vibrating walls. He stared at Danny for a long time, his eyes darting feverishly over the prisoner's face.

'How *dare* you pretend to be him,' he said in a quiet voice.

Aggie could hear her heart beating. What was Danny doing? Was it a trick? Part of FALL's plan? She looked from one man to the other. They did have similarities – their eyes, the set of their jaw . . .

But Daniel Faulkner had died at Adrianne. Aggie replayed the sequence of events in her head – Evelin and Daniel Faulkner had been on the stage with the United Leader when Aggie had run back into the labs after her father. They were right in the epicentre of the blast zone, with nothing but the open air to protect them. It was impossible that Daniel was still alive.

'Danny, don't, that's not fair,' she said, moving towards him. But the prisoner blocked her way.

Danny took another step, then another, until he was in touching distance of Faulkner. 'Not a great time for a reunion, I must admit,' he continued calmly, 'but you only have yourself to blame for that.'

Adam Faulkner fell back against the wall. 'My son is dead. You are not my son.'

'I wish that was true,' Danny said tightly. 'You have no idea how many times I've wished it was true.'

Adam Faulkner just shook his head.

'Mum was going to leave you,' Danny said quietly. 'She'd been planning it for months.'

Faulkner's legs gave way under him. He fell to his knees on the rumbling floor and pushed his face against the wall.

'No,' he managed. 'I don't believe it. I can't . . .' But the words escaped out of him as if they were spoken by another man. Weak and strangled. Something had changed. Aggie felt all the blood drain out of her face. No.

'She had a shuttle waiting. The explosion happened right after we took off,' Danny continued coldly. 'We nearly fell out of the sky in the shockwave, but the guards got it back under control just in time. We watched it all from the inner atmosphere. Even from that height we could see Adrianne burn. We saw all those people burn.'

Aggie couldn't get enough air into her lungs. She stepped back and thanked the Earth that Seb was there to hold her up.

'I thought you were gone,' Faulkner said, his voice thick. 'I thought I'd killed you.'

'You did. And Mum too. You killed us both. Then FALL

- 243 -

brought us back to life.'

Faulkner got to his feet again, supporting himself on the wall. His whole attitude was different, as if someone had deflated him. Aggie looked at Danny. That couldn't mean . . .?

Her godfather reached out a shaking hand to his son. 'Don't do this. Please.'

Danny looked back at him with a hatred that cut right into Aggie's heart. She knew that look. She knew how it felt to hate your own father. But why would Danny hate Adam?

'Daniel, please,' Faulkner muttered, reaching out.

Danny lifted an arm and landed his fist in Faulkner's face.

'No!' Aggie cried.

Faulkner staggered backwards. Something thick and black oozed from his nose and dripped down his chin. Aggie pulled at Seb's arms, but he wouldn't let her go.

'Adam!' she cried again, desperate to help him, desperate to stop Danny.

'Doesn't feel good, does it? The guilt,' Danny hissed, his grey eyes shining.

Faulkner didn't blink, but his face changed. It was a slight shift and Aggie couldn't read it. Guilt? What guilt? Aggie couldn't understand what she was hearing.

'Adrianne wasn't a mistake, was it, *Dad*? And it wasn't David Shepard's mistake either.'

Aggie pushed herself away from Seb. 'What?'

'That's a lie,' Faulkner snapped. But Danny was relentless.

'You never wanted a reactor, did you?' he said, anger tightening his jaw. 'You didn't see enough *profit* in it. You wanted to keep control over the lumite in Lunar Inc. You sabotaged the Switch On and you destroyed David Shepard's memory, so you could plough on with your precious lumite cells.'

Faulkner turned his gaze to Aggie. As he did, she felt her knees buckle under her. 'Adam?'

'YOU blew up the reactor!' Danny shouted. 'YOU killed those people. You did it all so you could get your own way.'

'Those *cells* saved us,' Faulkner shouted back. 'Without those *cells* we'd have destroyed each other years ago.'

Aggie let out a strangled cry. 'You?'

She couldn't believe what she could see in her god-father's eyes – it was as if the soul had drained out of them. They looked empty, hollow.

Aggie still didn't really understand what was happening. 'But, you told them it was his fault?'

Adam Faulkner wiped the blood from his mouth. 'The reactor was too expensive. It was as big as a town and took years to build. Understand, Aggie, if we'd gone with your father's idea, half the world would still be destitute and waiting for power. He was playing it safe. Him and the others, they wouldn't listen to reason.'

'So you decided to corrupt the reactor? To stop them?' Danny interrupted.

Faulkner looked around at them as if they were the crazy ones.

'I wanted to dull the reaction, make it too small to power even one bulb. I never intended for it to explode.'

'You didn't know what you were doing. You knew the risk!'

Adam Faulkner took a long breath. 'That reactor was costing *trillions* in wasted energy. We only had one chance. It *had* to be the cells.'

Aggie felt sick. It was Adam Faulkner who had caused the explosion, not her father? The room started to blacken at the edges. Everything she'd ever known was falling apart in front of her, collapsing into the dust just like the base.

Faulkner had tears in his eyes now. His words were coming out fast, as if he was trying to convince himself that what he'd done was right.

'The cells were the better idea, convenient, portable, easy to produce. Cells gave power to everyone, instantly. What I did saved the world!'

A grief that she'd never felt before started to grow in Aggie's chest. A big grunting sob shook her whole body. Then came another, and another, until she was shuddering like the ground itself. Despite everything, a warm and comforting thought overflowed and spilt out over her. *It wasn't his fault. It wasn't his fault.*

'How could you!' she sobbed. 'You made me ... everyone thinks that ...' She couldn't find the words. Pain, regret, elation and anger were at war inside her. She had doubted her own father. Aggie had condemned David Shepard over and over to the world, in media suites just like this one. All the while, Adam Faulkner had been whispering his poison in her ear.

Aggie was shaking now, but for the first time, it was from rage, not fear. The betrayal was so raw. How could he let her father take the blame all these years? How could he let Aggie become the spokesperson for his lies?

All the interviews, the photo shoots, all the perfectly rehearsed responses, they were all just . . . lies.

She'd believed him. She'd loved him. She felt such a fool.

Somewhere above them, a huge piece of the ceiling was dislodged and crashed to the floor. Aggie's godfather didn't even flinch. He'd taken his gaze away from Aggie.

For a moment, there was no sound except the rumble of the ground. Then –

'Come with me,' Faulkner whispered. 'Come back with me. Together, we can make changes.'

Aggie frowned. 'What?'

Her godfather's attention was on Danny, 'Father and son, together.'

Aggie gasped. Faulkner thought Aggie was lost to him now. She wasn't useful. He was trying to make a deal. This wasn't love, this was business.

'Daniel,' Faulkner continued, a smile spreading across his face, 'I can show you a different life. It couldn't have been easy, what your mother did to you. Dragging you with her, with those terrorists. I can show you the life you should have had. If it's power you want, I can give it to you. Your name can open any door. You're a Faulkner, the world is already yours.'

Aggie felt as if someone had ripped her heart out. Did her godfather care about her at all?

'Don't listen to him, man . . .' Seb began, but Danny shrugged him away. There was something unreadable about the way he looked at Faulkner, something unpredictable. It caught Aggie's breath. He wasn't really considering . . . was he?

For a long time, Danny's bright, grey eyes refused to move from her godfather's.

'Son,' Faulkner began again. 'There's nothing we can't do. My shuttle is just upstairs.' Faulkner's eyes were glassy now. Aggie had no idea if the emotion was real or not. Was anything real about the man who had brought her up as his own daughter?

'He's lying to you, man,' Seb hissed from the shadows. 'You know he's lying.'

Danny pushed Seb away.

Aggie couldn't speak, she couldn't move. She stared at Danny, terrified of what the prisoner might do. She didn't know him, really, but she felt she did. Danny wasn't rotten inside, he was good, he did what he did for what he believed in – for the Earth. He wouldn't just . . .

'Start again?' Danny growled. 'Power?' He spat. 'You think you'll still have your power when they find out why this happened?'

He lifted is arms and gestured around the room. The walls were shaking so much now that looking at them was like having double vision.

'Just another quake. The Far Side was always geologically unsafe,' Faulkner said, dismissing it with a shake of his hand. 'It's manageable.'

'Manageable?' Danny shouted. *'This*, manageable? What's wrong with you? What you've done here is unthinkable. You've lied and lied to save yourself, to save your precious company.'

Danny was now so close that Aggie could feel the heat coming off his body. 'Because Adrianne was just the warm-up act, wasn't it, Dad? Ten thousand dead, right? Well, how many have you killed on the Far Side so far? How many men and women have died for you, so you can carry on lying?'

Danny started to step towards Faulkner again, ushering him into a corner – a predator moving in on his prey.

Faulkner stepped back against the wall. 'I don't know what you're talking about.'

'No?' Danny stepped back, lifted a hand and released the clasp on his dirty old spacesuit and slid the pieces of the torso away. 'I know everything.' He lifted his sweat-soaked shirt, wincing with the effort. What he revealed underneath made every person in the room gasp.

20

Night-Cycle 01

Aggie had never seen anything like the wounds that ravaged Danny's body.

Giant welts covered every inch of his torso, making his skin a mass of mottled red. Where once he'd seemed strong and muscular under his tight-fitting overall, Aggie saw now what exposure to the Far Side had really done to him.

'An illegal mine on the Far Side of the Moon,' Danny continued, glancing between Aggie and Faulkner. 'Out of the way of the cameras. Men and women kept in conditions like animals, out on the open surface, with no protection from the radiation. The solar flares cooking them slowly inside their old suits.'

He took a breath; his eyes were on fire. 'Two full cycles. That's how long a Far Side prisoner is expected to survive. And that's if you're lucky – if the flares aren't too strong or the work too hard.'

Faulkner shook his head. 'You don't understand,' he whispered.

'Oh, I understand,' Danny snarled. 'This is murder. Mass murder on a scale the Earth has never seen. Cruelty that I thought even you weren't capable of. All so you can keep up your lumite lie.'

Danny glanced at Aggie as if he was apologizing for what he'd let her see. As if the feelings that simmered between them would suddenly die because of what he'd revealed beneath his suit. Aggie couldn't communicate how she felt in a glance. She was filled with a strange mixture of pride and sorrow. Nothing had changed. If anything, her feelings for the prisoner boy had grown stronger.

'After Adrianne we had to do something,' Faulkner said. His voice was small against the rumble of the ground. 'Lumite was almost ruined. I'd planned to take a few years, start development on the mine while we tweaked the cells, made them smaller, more efficient. The explosion meant I had to hurry; I had to ride the wave I'd created. I needed to rebuild the world's confidence, show it that lumite was good. The people needed to trust me – David would have agreed with that. We had to rush the cells into production or we'd lose decades of progress. Lumite had to succeed, no matter what the cost.'

He looked at Danny again. 'When your grandfather made the discovery, it was as if there was a light at the end of the black hole that our world had become. We were mesmerized by it, infatuated by it. Lumite's pure power, so unexpected and so ... abundant. Or so we thought. No one really expected lumite to cure the world's needs; it was a bandage to wrap around us until we developed a sustainable solution. It would take years, but we didn't have to rush when we had lumite. Only the five of us in the lab knew exactly how little there was.'

'So you always knew the lumite wouldn't last?' Danny asked calmly.

'Of course we knew. But Adrianne changed everything. There was talk of closing down the whole operation, of closing Lunar Inc. The base, the Academy – everything my father had built. The United Government were about to pull the plug. We were desperate, so we took a risk.'

Faulkner glanced back at Aggie.

'You think I'm the worst thing to happen to this planet? You should take a good long look at yourselves. We're all the same. Humans are predisposed to greed. We were a world of starving people suddenly presented with a feast. We allowed ourselves to gorge and gorge with no thought for anything else. In the blink of an eye, sustainability was forgotten. We had the lumite cells. Lumite solved everything, and we had a whole Moon's worth to use!

'I'm just the supplier. If there were no demand there'd

be no Far Side. Lumite isn't just power, it's peace. To save the many, we decided to sacrifice the few. Isn't the Earth worth that?'

Without warning, a violent tremor shook the foundations of the room.

Adam Faulkner laughed. 'Ah, but we didn't see this. When we opened the Far Side we detonated a time bomb. We faced a choice: come clean or mine the Moon until –' another rumble threatened the tiny room – 'Well, until this.'

Something clicked in Aggie's head.

'Rix didn't force you off the board, did he? It was all part of your plan.'

'Someone has to take the blame. Someone to head the company whilst it dealt with the quakes and the falling quotas. To be the new face of Lunar Inc. It couldn't be me. Rix was a puppet, just like the United Leader, just like you. I pulled your strings and you would dance for me, and oh, what a performance it was.'

Tears started to roll down Aggie's cheeks. 'I thought you loved me.'

Faulkner laughed. 'Then you're a bigger fool than your father.'

'The only fool here is you,' Danny snarled, stepping back to reveal the bank of cameras pointed directly at Faulkner.

'THAT CONCLUDES THIS SPECIAL EDITION OF THE LUNAR FORECAST,' Celeste's automated voice boomed out at full volume across the room.

Adam Faulkner stared at the cameras. Struck dumb.

As the camera whirred softly, Aggie pictured the faces of the people on Earth watching their screens. She imagined the panic in the United Government, the desperate attempts to explain it all away. She knew that they wouldn't succeed now. Celeste was right, they had had to make them see.

A weight lifted from her shoulders. The world knew now. It was over. They knew what Lunar Inc. had done.

'Stay bright, United Earth . . .' Celeste said, an edge of sadness in her voice.

21

Night-Cycle 01

Adam Faulkner leant against the wall, staring at the
blinking lights of the cameras until they faded.

Aggie could sense something creeping into him,
something desperate and unpredictable.

The ground bounced up, sending one of the great sails
crashing down from the ceiling.

Faulkner turned and ran out of the room.

'No!'

Aggie sprinted after him, as fast as she could in her old
suit.

'He's got a shuttle on the roof!' she shouted, as Danny

and Seb joined her. 'He's trying to get away!'

She sprinted after her godfather as he wove through the tumbling ruins of the Tranquillity building. Danny and Seb joined her, skidding and dodging falling masonry. The whole place shook on the brink of collapse; they didn't have much time.

As they chased Faulkner into the great Tranquillity foyer, he skidded to a stop at the edge of the broken floor and looked up at the giant orb of the Moon above him.

'It's over, dude!' Seb panted. 'It's over.'

Adam Faulkner turned, tears running down his cheeks. 'What have you done, little one? What have you done?'

Aggie padded towards him. The look on his face was almost something she recognized. She felt a hole in her chest, a hole that felt so raw that she doubted it would ever close. Adam Faulkner had ruined her life. Right from Adrianne, every pain she'd ever endured was because of him.

'The people don't want the truth,' he said now. 'They want their cars and comms pads to keep working. They want their streets lit and their hospitals running. You've given FALL their precious war.'

'They'll listen to me,' she replied shakily.

'Have you even thought about what you're going to do? Cover the globe in pathetic little windmills? Go back to Mars and see what you can squeeze out of those useless brown rocks? There's no happy ending, Aggie. The people will rebel. They'll just start killing each other all over again.'

A creak sounded high above them, echoing across the

distant ceiling.

Faulkner stepped towards her. Anger had turned his eyes into burning black holes. 'And they'll start with the Angel. Our perfect creation. Our beautiful, innocent Angel of hope, suddenly turned into the Angel of *death*—'

A great shuddering creak echoed around the rumbling foyer. The giant Moon smashed into the floor where Aggie's godfather stood.

'Adam!' Aggie cried and sprinted forwards.

The glittering projection of the base, glowing in all its industrial beauty, flickered and died.

Aggie skidded to a halt and fell to her knees. She couldn't take her eyes away from the smashed globe, lying across the broken floor of the foyer like a burst watermelon.

Her godfather was buried beneath it in his shame.

After a few minutes her heart began to settle.

It was better this way.

She was surprised at how empty she felt. Part of her wanted hysteria. Part of her wanted to scream and shout and pound at the ground; she willed those feelings to take hold, but they refused to come.

Seb pulled her towards him. 'We need to go,' he said quietly. Aggie nodded and turned back to the airlocks.

'Seb, look!' she cried and ripped herself out of his arms.

Danny was slumped on the floor, his face as pale as the suit he was wearing.

Aggie helped Seb administer the last of the blue vials in Danny's medi-kit.

Seb glanced at Aggie. Unspoken concern passed between them. It was the last dose in the box.

As soon as the blue liquid disappeared inside him, Danny's eyes opened. He looked at her sadly.

'I'm sorry,' he said as Aggie transferred her hand to his forehead. Whatever they'd thought of Adam Faulkner, they'd both lost a father today.

'Are you going to be OK?' she said thickly.

Danny smiled and embraced her. Aggie wasn't expecting it and it took the breath out of her.

'I'm OK,' Danny said into her hair. His breath was warm on her neck. He pulled back and looked at her. 'I promise.'

'I don't believe you,' Aggie said, blinking at her tears.

She glanced away, feeling her cheeks flushing. 'It makes sense, now. I always wondered how you knew.'

Danny grinned. 'I didn't see the Angel. I saw Aggie.'

Seb started loudly opening the lockers that lined one of the walls of the foyer. 'So that kind of makes you brother and sister, right?'

Aggie shot him a look.

'Seriously, though, the way this day is going, I'm gonna find out that I'm actually Celeste's great-aunt or something.' He pulled two sky-blue Tranquillity overalls out onto the seats. 'Better put these on – we're going to need exos to get out of here.'

As if in reply, the room around them started to rock more violently.

Aggie caught Danny's eye as she snapped her own collar down.

'I was right.' He smiled. 'You do look good in blue.'

Aggie blushed again, remembering the conversation they'd had a lifetime ago.

Seb rolled his eyes and stomped past them towards the airlock.

When Seb was out of earshot, Danny paused. 'You OK?'

Aggie shook her head. 'No.'

'We'll be OK.' Danny put an arm over Aggie's shoulders. 'You're stronger than you look.'

'Like graphene,' she muttered sadly.

The instant Tranquillity's huge airlock opened, Aggie felt her new overall pressurize around her – the familiar floating sensation was coupled with the tug of the exo stirring inside the fabric. She'd spent so long in the older spacesuit that the sensation sent her off-balance.

The three of them stood on the edge of Tranquillity, looking out at the broken remains of everything Lunar Incorporated had built in the name of lumite.

The larger structures on the base lay in pieces on the ground; fragments of pencil-thin Plexi littered the atmosphere like shards from a broken mirror, reflecting the warning lights from below.

Explosions went off around them sporadically, sending dust pluming into the sky; violet flames bursting and fading to a smoulder in an instant. Shuttles reflected the light of the distant sun as they flew the evacuated personnel back to Earth. The minuscule bodies of those that didn't make it floated in the sky beside them like stars, their lamps winking faintly as they drifted higher into the void.

Aggie thought of Astrid and hoped with what was left of her heart that the girl hadn't stayed.

'I think we need another plan.' Danny was staring at where the great shuttle bays should have been.

There was nothing left. A giant viewing tower had fallen across the enormous rippled roof, crushing everything in its path. Every craft visible lay wrecked and smouldering, the tiny coloured dots of desperate evacuees crawled over the remains of the shuttles, trying to get them back online before it was too late. From where they were, maybe it looked like it was worth it, but to the three people standing on the edge of Tranquillity it looked hopeless.

A fizzing sensation made her jump.

'Hey Aggie, I've calculated the safest route off the base,' Celeste buzzed in their ears.

'Nice of you to join us,' Danny mumbled.

Aggie frowned. He was right, Celeste hadn't been with them just now. Aggie could feel when the computer was present, like static in the air. Had Celeste abandoned them before? The feeling made Aggie nervous. Despite everything she'd once believed, the computer was starting to become more than just a presence or a guide to Aggie. Celeste had saved their lives more than once. She was here to protect her.

'And what would that be?' Seb said, bringing Aggie's attention back to the conversation.

'What else leaves the base on a regular basis, like the shuttles?' Celeste replied.

'Oh awesome. Quiz time. Perfect for the situation.'

'Lumite,' Danny interrupted. 'She means the lumite.'

'Oh, yeah. Let's just fling ourselves off the base like a tonne of lumite.'

'Exactly,' Celeste said. 'Please head to the Cargo Bays.'

'You can't be serious.'

Seb put his head in his hands. Aggie chewed her lip, remembering the thunderous noises echoing around the cargo tunnels when she'd used them to escape the party. She looked around them, the idea of the cargo bays was frightening, yeah, but was it any more frightening than this?

'We just need to get off the base. Quickly. I don't care how.' Aggie set off down the slope towards the centre of the base, with Danny close behind.

Seb hesitated, then started after them.

'Those things aren't designed for humans! We'll get chewed up! Hey, Aggie, wait!'

As they skimmed along, Celeste brought up a blueprint on their visor screens. 'The lumite cargo runs into the underground tunnel network as it leaves the faces. We'll access them at a central point—'

'Whole Earth,' Seb muttered as the three jumped down the broken slope of a collapsed commuter shuttle tube. 'The only bit of the base still standing.'

'Exactly.'

'So we access the tunnels, then what?' Danny butted in. Seb scowled.

The blueprint animation skimmed through the tunnel system and then brought them out to the grinding mechanisms of the cargo bays. Seb grimaced.

'The cargo bays use a magnetic catapult system to propel the capsules containing the lumite cells to a docking platform on the Lunar Inc. skyport in the European Mountains.'

'Hey, Celeste,' Seb panted, 'I didn't pay that much attention in astrophysics class, but still I can't see any human surviving those Gs. When we get back to Earth, they'll have to scrape us off the walls with a spatula or something,'

'Seb!' Aggie said with disgusted look.

Seb shrugged. 'Just speaking my mind, man.'

Celeste spun quickly, then settled. 'There is actually a forty-seven per cent chance of human survival, increasing to fifty-one per cent with the use of exo-skeletons.'

Seb's mouth dropped open. 'Oh, only forty-nine per cent chance of dying? Well, what are we waiting for?'

'We're not waiting, Seb, we're already on our way.'

Seb rolled his eyes. 'Computer's don't really get sarcasm do they?'

'No, Sebastian.' Celeste flashed.

'Well.' He sighed, turning to Danny and Aggie. 'Looks like we'll be going home with the last of the lumite. Awesome.'

22

Night-Cycle 01

They passed more than one body as they bounded through the debris. The Lunar Inc. personnel's garish overalls made them easy to pick out from the grey ground. A purple boot sticking out from beneath a collapsed tunnel, a collapsed pink helmet that had somehow lost its body, an orange human form sprawled out in the distance, its lifeless limbs sticking out at inhuman angles. Aggie was glad she hadn't seen their faces. She didn't know if she would be able take it. She focused on training her eyes to skim over any spots of colour in her path.

Soon, the dimly glowing spires of the Whole Earth grew

taller on the horizon, the only thing standing in the sea of destruction.

They found a working airlock and slipped inside.

'Follow the red markers up to the atrium,' Celeste said as they emerged into the darkness of Whole Earth's service tunnels, 'and then head to the frozen custard cart. The door that leads to the cargo tunnels is just behind it.'

Seb and Aggie exchanged a look and burst out laughing.

'Why are you laughing? Did I say something wrong?' Celeste said, sounding confused.

'Not this time, no,' Danny replied, looking totally perplexed.

Aggie smiled at Seb and stepped forwards. 'Of all the gin joints in all the world . . .'

'I don't understand,' Celeste said. 'They don't serve alcohol in Whole Earth.'

The sight of their familiar, beloved frozen custard cart torn apart brought more tears to Aggie's eyes. It was stupid, she knew, but that cart represented the good times she'd had on the base: the days when her biggest problem was cleaning up a toilet water spillage, or talking clag with Seb when they skived off their shifts. Good days, she realized now – days she'd taken for granted.

Seb placed a hand on her back. From the look in his eyes, Aggie could tell he felt the same. 'It's OK. I'll buy you a custard when we get back to Earth, I promise,' he said, with a reassuring squeeze.

They entered the black staircase the other side of the

service door and descended to the tunnels. The tunnel's gravity systems were obviously working, but as Aggie followed the boys down the stairs, her visor automatically collapsed down over her face.

'There's no air down here,' she said, her overall bleeping in agreement.

'Atmospheric systems must be down,' Seb mumbled behind his visor. 'But the ceiling's still there, so I guess we're good.'

When they finally reached the end they were hit by a sudden burst of activity.

They were standing at the edge of a great junction of thick metal conveyor belts that rose up out of the hard moon rock like the ribcages of great metal whales. Travelling along them was a constant stream of glittering raw Lumite crystal. The belts sped along their interconnecting routes, missing each other by just inches, guided by sets of mechanical connections that clicked like crickets on a summer's day.

Unlike the last time Aggie had ventured into the tunnels, these were fully active. They were lugging the day's lumite supply to the production plants, unaffected by the destruction wrought by the quake above ground.

The noise of the place permeated the thin material of their visors and rang against their ears. It was a hundred times louder than the face had ever been. For a while, Aggie wasn't sure if the vibrating of the tunnels was from the quake or just a normal side effect of walking so close to this subterranean lumite highway. She quickly decided it was a mixture of the two as she noticed the thin cracks that wove their way around its high, vaulted ceiling.

'We need to get going,'

'Good idea,' Danny replied.

'Celeste isn't here,' Aggie said. 'She should be here.' It worried Aggie – Celeste felt like a weird kind of family to her now. All this time the computer had been protecting her on her father's orders. She was a link to all the information about her father that she'd never dared ask Adam Faulkner. Her godfather had already stolen her life, she wasn't going to let him steal her father's memory too. Celeste was one of them, she mattered.

Aggie looked around the cavernous tunnel. 'Where is she?' she whispered to herself.

Danny put an arm around her shoulders, 'Celeste's trying to save the base. If there's trouble, she'll be here.'

'I'm worried she's not OK,' she replied quietly.

'Out of all of us, I'd give her the best chances, man,' said Seb, stepping up onto the walkway. 'I mean, what is she even made of, really? She's just a bunch of wires and dust and Plexi nonsense.'

'Don't talk about her like that, Seb,' Aggie snapped.

'Hey, I was trying to make you feel better.' Seb grabbed the handrail suddenly. It swung under his weight. His eyes went wide. 'OK, that's normal. I'm going to say that's normal. Nothing to be scared of. C'mon, follow me.'

Danny gave Aggie's shoulders a squeeze and gently pushed her forwards. 'Let's concentrate on getting out of here first, hey?'

Aggie nodded and stepped onto the walkway in front of him, her head turning this way and that as she scanned the chamber for signs of Ethers and Eyes.

As they ran along the thin, shaking walkway beside the speeding containers, pieces of the roof started to tumble around them like grey snowflakes. Aggie looked up and felt them rain down over her visor with a pattering noise.

'We really need to be quicker,' Danny panted, looking at the cracks in the ceiling.

Ahead, Seb stopped suddenly, his eyes wide. 'Aw, dudes, it could just work!' he said, spinning around excitedly.

'What?' Danny said,

'OK, bear with me, though, right, because this is going to sound crazy.'

Danny gestured around them, 'We're already way beyond crazy, mate.'

Seb cocked his head to the side, 'Hmm, maybe not this crazy, but hey. Right, so there's this old movie.'

Aggie rolled her eyes. 'Oh no, Seb . . .'

'Wait, wait, hear me out. There's this really old movie, I can't remember what it's called but there's a dude in a hat, he loves the hat. And he's like an adventurer in the really olden days, like a grave robber, with an awesome whip thing, that's pretty awesome, and—'

'Seb!' Aggie cried.

'OK. Yeah. So hat dude and this little Chinese dude escape from the bad guys in a cart, kinda like these things. They're like, surrounded and then they see these carts going really fast and they jump in them and they escape the bad guys.'

Danny grinned. 'So, the plan is just to jump on the conveyor?'

'Yeah, I guess that was my point.'

'Wow.' Danny laughed and slapped Seb on the back. 'Good plan. I like it.'

'Really? You feeling OK?'

Danny pulled a face. 'No, not really.'

Aggie peered over the railing at the blur of lumite that raced below them.

'They're going really fast, Seb.'

Seb looked about to implode with nerves, even though it was his idea. 'It worked out OK in the movie.'

Aggie looked back at the conveyor. They were linked together with great buzzing magnetic locks. They'd have to time the jump just right to avoid getting crushed or electrocuted or just generally ripped apart. Even with their exos, it was a risk.

Seb appeared beside her, biting his lip, 'Well, I guess it's my idea, so, I should go first.'

'Good idea,' Danny said, stepping closer to the ledge.

'Trying to get rid of me, dude?'

'Always.'

'Don't think about it too much, right?'

Danny nodded.

Seb set a shaking hand to the railings, then, without another word, leapt over the ledge and disappeared. Aggie gasped and ran forward, but when she looked over, there was no sign of her best friend.

'Seb!' she cried, searching the distance for his violet lamp.

Then, a loud crash and a rush of sound burst into her ears. 'This is cosmic!' Seb shouted, his voice only just audible over the thunder. 'I feel like it's going to rip my head off!'

Aggie looked at Danny and activated her exo with a flick of her finger, as the suit buzzed around her she jumped over the railing.

She hit the glittering mound of lumite blocks with a deep, horrible crunch. The exo moaned in protest as Aggie crumpled down into them, her limbs twisting painfully beneath her. The speed she was going was unbelievable; beyond the speeding belt; the world was a constant, sickening blur.

She turned her head and spotted another light falling onto the conveyor behind.

'Next stop, Earth!' Seb cried from the front, as the tunnel whipped and twisted and turned. Aggie screamed, terrified and thrilled in equal measures. It was like being on a roller-coaster. The lights of the narrow tunnel flew past, changing from violet to red to green to yellow, all the colours of the United Earth, blurring together above her head. The exo inside Aggie's gloves gripped the edges of the conveyor as if she'd been welded to the metal. A good thing, because the lumite blocks beneath her shifted like marbles under her surface boots. She let out a long cry as she fought to stay upright, ducking away from the pipes and debris that had fallen across the tunnel – for a few seconds all Aggie's worries were left behind on the tunnel floor.

*

Before Aggie could really enjoy it, the rush of the tunnels started to fade into a slow rumble. The tunnel began to open out into a vast, cavernous space that vibrated with noise.

'This is our stop dudes.' Seb jumped off the conveyor and punched the air. 'Oh, man! I knew that would be totally cosmic!'

Aggie rolled off the belt and staggered to her feet, her comms roaring with the sound of machines crunching and gnawing the raw crystal.

Above them, a great Plexiglas dome protected a series of clicking, whirring conveyor belts that ran like snakes along the rock floor, packing the crystal into capsules before converging at the centre. Here, they delivered their load into a huge black cannon-shaped object that pierced through the dome and spat the packed capsules out into the black void above.

The launcher. Their ride home.

'Where do we fit into this then?' Seb said, finally coming down from his conveyor-riding high and glancing worriedly around at the launcher's chewing, spinning mechanisms.

Aggie pointed to the place where the conveyors met the launcher. A stack of pebble-shaped capsules waited to be filled with their Lumite cargo. 'There, I think.'

She shook her head. Seb had been right, every part of the cargo bay looked deadly. Even getting close to the capsules through the launcher's crunching mechanisms and rushing conveyors looked impossible.

As Danny jumped down from his ride on the belt, a huge cloud of dust erupted out of the tunnel behind him.

The three of them turned and stared as a lumbering figure emerged from the mist.

23

Night-Cycle 01

'RUN!'

Celeste's voice was so loud it distorted in their helmets.

'Start running!'

The shock was enough to send all three of them racing away across the conveyors towards the empty capsules. Aggie felt terror begin to rise in her chest. She'd immediately known who the intruder was.

'It's Rix!' she shouted breathlessly. 'He's alive!'

Aggie hadn't even thought about the commander since the Forecast Suite. She glanced back just in time to see a scrambler break out of the dust cloud and catch Rix on his side, knocking him back to the ground. Instantly, the unmanned trike turned its fat wheels and rammed the Commander again. But he learnt quickly: his next move was to crawl out onto the conveyor itself – out of its reach.

When he stood upright, backlit by the dust and light of the tunnel behind him, he looked like a robot or an alien from an old movie.

His deep, desperate, ragged breathing echoed inside Aggie's helmet, as he was moved along the conveyor towards her.

She scrambled away over the lumite that littered the conveyor belt, but it was like running on ice. The ground shifted violently, sending her slamming head first into the rocks. The conveyor belt jolted and began to tear in two with a thundering groan. When the dust cleared, Aggie let out a cry. She was alone. The boys were on the other side, the side they needed to be on to get to the capsules.

Above her head, the domed ceiling shuddered, a great gap opening between its arched panels. Her overall bleeped. They were losing pressure.

'Aggie!' Danny shouted from somewhere below her.

'I'm OK. Stay there!'

Not really thinking, Aggie started to scramble up onto the tilted side of the broken conveyor. When she reached the top, she stopped.

From her new vantage point she could see the fight

between Rix and Celeste unfolding like a choreographed performance.

Ethers convulsed in the darkness as the computer used everything at her disposal to stop Rix's progress towards them. The giant Ether at the top of the conveyor system began to flicker. Then, with a deafening screech, the mechanism on the belt closest to Rix reversed and started spitting jagged chunks of crystal towards him with the force of bullets. A few met their target, but Rix's overall was doing its job too well. He stumbled, obviously dazed, but quickly regained his footing.

As Aggie watched this strange battle between man and machine, panic was rising further and further in her chest. Under her feet, the deep, steady roll of the ground was more pronounced. Somewhere nearby another building came crashing to the ground with a plume of smoke and dust.

'We need to get out of here, dudes,' Seb shouted from somewhere on the other side.

Aggie wasn't paying attention; Celeste's presence had moved to a gigantic loader truck buried in a pile of debris to the left of the tunnel. There was a low hum, then a clunk, and suddenly the loader's stack of spotlights flicked to life. Rix was blinded. He tripped, tumbled head-first into a pile of rubble and began to drag himself over the rocks on his elbows.

When Rix had crawled out of the spotlight's glare, Aggie saw the lights flicker on one of the giant robotic arms that littered the bay. The arm flexed, making it look like a massive, prehistoric reptile. Rix was on his knees now, crawling slowly towards the the broken conveyor where Aggie stood. Soon, he would be out of sight, in the deep black shadow of the machinery.

The great arm swung across the width of the bay, its bright lights leaving a blue streak in the back of Aggie's eyes. The huge metal pincer at the end of the arm met with the side of Rix's helmet with a loud crunch. The commander's cry of pain rattled out over the comms. Then, silence.

Aggie nervously watched the darkness below her. Even overalls couldn't cope with an impact like that, surely.

For a long time, the noise of the bays was replaced only by her own great gasping breaths. Every muscle in her body was tensed. But Rix didn't reappear.

'He's dead?' Danny asked quietly, as if the sound of his voice could bring Rix back to life.

'I don't know, man,' Seb replied. 'That guy's like a little angry robot.'

'We really need to go,' Aggie whispered, scanning the darkness for signs of the boys, 'Where are you?'

During the fight it had all become clear to Aggie. Celeste wasn't hurt or in danger, she was trying to keep Rix away from them. All this time, she'd been fighting him through whatever physical means she could. A slow spread of guilt started to grow in her stomach. How had she ever not trusted the computer after everything she'd done?

The lights in Aggie's comms unit suddenly lit up.

'He's down but he won't be down for long. He's very

good at fighting,' Celeste's voice said quickly. 'You need to go now. Go to the capsules.'

Aggie began to climb down from the conveyor, picking her way carefully over the shaking debris towards the launcher, where Seb and Danny's lamps winked blue and violet in the darkness beside the waiting capsules. A piece of rock skimmed past her ear, smashing into the launcher beside her. Another glanced off her temple, making the world around her shift for a second as she drunkenly found her footing. By the time she'd regained her senses, Rix was already running towards her. Half his overall had been torn apart, leaving his white ribbed exo showing through like a twisted alien skeleton. It was broken. He had no protection.

She could hear the boys shouting above her, trying to find a way to cross the debris to help her. She was on her own.

Rix slammed Aggie into the edge of the launcher like a rag doll. Her overall sang with a million warnings, pressure, oxygen, exoskeleton . . .

Aggie spotted something in the dust.

'You must go to the capsules,' Celeste repeated. 'Aggie, you're running out of time.'

'I'm trying!' Aggie shouted as she staggered to her feet. She dived through Rix's legs, skidded and grabbed the object out of the rubble. The buzzer vibrated in Aggie's grip, she pumped it up to max and raced back towards the commander with the full power of her exo.

Rix turned just in time to see the angry violet forks

spit towards him. They hit him in the legs, sending him skidding back towards the conveyors, crying out in pain.

'Aggie!' Danny and Seb cried in unison from somewhere above her.

Aggie didn't hear them. Rix was in her sights now, immobilized by the shock to his legs. He bared his teeth at her as she cornered him. There was blood on the inside of his visor.

'Stop it,' Aggie yelled as she rounded on him, 'just stop it! It's over!'

'Aggie, don't, he's not worth it. The capsules . . .'

At her feet, Rix's face was twisted in pain.

Aggie stared down at him. She suddenly wanted to hurt him, just as he'd hurt her. How much did the commander really know?

'Don't you see? You were Faulkner's little puppet too. And now you're dying for him. He didn't respect you, he didn't even *like* you.'

Rix spat blood onto his visor. 'He gave me a new life.'

'He made you murderer!'

The lighting in his helmet made Rix look like a zombie, half dead, bloodied and raging. All his charm gone.

'Adam saved me,' the commander spat. 'He trusted me. He *needed* me.'

'He *used* you.'

Rix rose up, a mixture of pain and anger on his face.

'He *made* me.'

Aggie hesitated. She'd seen something else, something

she hadn't expected. Love? Rix had loved her godfather too.

Aggie looked at the man who had orchestrated the deaths of thousands under her godfather's command. Who'd been his partner in ruining every part of her own life. Her face was stone. She powered down the buzzer. Suddenly, she knew how to hurt Rix more than the weapon ever could.

'He's dead,' she said coldly. 'He never made it back to Earth. He's just another body, lying out there in the rubble.'

Inside his visor, Aggie saw something pass over Rix's light blue eyes. 'He got the shuttle . . .'

There was a crash as Seb and Danny finally pushed away the rubble from the launcher and started to climb down towards her. Aggie pushed the dead buzzer against the Commanders neck. 'You need to come with us,' she said, registering the grief that was slowly spreading over Rix's face. He knew she was telling the truth, he just didn't want to believe it.

Danny skidded up to them 'We need to go. Now,' he panted, looking down at Rix.

Suddenly, Rix's face twisted and he started to laugh. He looked down at his own bloodied, broken body. 'Speaking of the dead. How're you feeling, 209?'

'Another word and I'll kill you.'

Rix glanced at Aggie, then chuckled evilly. 'A military man can see it. Gives the skin a certain colour, glazes the eyes . . .'

Aggie pushed Rix back. 'What are you talking about?'

Rix smiled. His teeth were red with blood. 'Tell me, Angel, what is it you think is in those little blue vials that your precious *prisoner* enjoys so much?'

Aggie looked at Danny. He stood still, staring at Rix.

'Afterlife.' Rix made the word last for a few seconds, stretching it out with a flick of his tongue.

A memory pulled softly at the back of Aggie's mind. Something she'd read, maybe? Something her father had told her?

'Military drug,' Rix continued. 'They considered it a form of torture at the time, but the gangs brought it back. Stole it, manipulated it . . .'

Aggie stared at Danny. With each word she felt weaker; Rix's voice was sapping all the strength she had left. She hadn't had much anyway.

High above them, the dome let out a long shuddering groan.

'Dudes, c'mon,' Seb shouted, pointing at the dome. 'This won't hold for long.'

Aggie wasn't listening. She looked at Danny, something dark and horrible creeping into her stomach.

'. . . FALL's little wonder drug . . .'

'Guys?' Seb shouted.

'Because Afterlife –' Rix smiled – 'gives you an afterlife. Tricks the body into using every last bit of its reserves until they're all used up. Kept our soldiers useful on the battle-field, until we didn't need them any more. See, the tricky thing with Afterlife is, once you take that first little vial . . . That's it, bye-bye, sayonara . . .'

A cold wave washed over Aggie's body. She couldn't move. Rix laughed. Danny just stared.

'So, how long was it since we last pricked your precious Danny? An hour? Maybe two? I'd say he was almost all used up.'

Aggie felt as if pins and needles were pulsing up in her fingers. Inside her head, all her thoughts washed away, replaced with only one that rang out high and wailing – *NO.*

No, it isn't true. No, Danny isn't dying. No, he isn't already dead.

She watched Rix's mouth form into a bloody smile. 'Truth hurts, doesn't it?'

'You're a DEAD MAN!' Aggie raged. She slammed him against the conveyor, but Danny was there, hands on hers, releasing her grip.

'We need to go,' he said softly and started to walk her towards the capsules, giving Seb a knowing look as they left him with Rix.

Aggie obeyed him without thinking. He pulled her up onto the launcher and into the dusty capsule. The ground was quivering so much now that she could barely hear his comms.

'Don't make this any worse, Aggs, please. Just sit down.' Tears shone in Danny's eyes.

'No,' she said, clutching on to his overall. 'No. You can't. He's lying.' She grasped at his arm, trying to pull him over the threshold and into the capsule, but she was too weak.

Danny pushed her hands away, gently this time, and

crouched down so his face was close to hers. He placed a shaking hand on the side of her helmet.

'I'm dying, Aggie,' he said softly, bringing his helmet to touch the top of hers. 'The Afterlife will wear off soon. I won't work without it.'

'No.' Aggie's whole body shook. 'No, they'll have something. Something that can fix you. Danny, they can do things on Earth, they can fix you. I know they can.'

'I'm sorry, Aggs. I've had too many doses. There's . . .' he looked up, blinking back the tears, '. . . there's nothing left to fix.'

Aggie looked at him in despair. Tears rolled down her face again, her throat closed up. She shook her head. She couldn't understand, he seemed so strong. He looked so alive.

'Just come with us, then,' she said thickly, bringing a hand up to his visor and drawing him closer. 'Die here. With us, with me. You can't be on your own, I know how that feels. I won't leave you on your own.'

'You don't need the extra weight,' he said, pulling away from her, 'You'll have a better chance if I stay here.'

Sobs erupted out of Aggie. 'No,' she cried. 'You can't leave me, I just met you. I only just met you.' She grabbed his gloved hands and twisted his fingers in hers. She wanted to rip the suit off; she wanted to feel him again, as she had in the filthy hab. She couldn't let that be the only time. She suddenly decided she didn't care – she could hold her breath, and she'd only need a second.

'Aggs what are you doing?' Danny gasped as Aggie lifted

a hand and flicked the release on her visor then reached out to his. She wrapped her hand around his neck and pulled his mouth to hers. His lips tasted like salt, she concentrated on it as she kissed him. Danny's mouth moved with hers, kissing her back as if it was the only thing he had left in the world.

As he gently pulled her closer, Aggie resigned every single detail of the moment to her memory. Every touch, every sensation, so soft and so bittersweet. For those perfect, stolen seconds, the noise and dust and devastation around them disappeared.

Much too soon, Aggie tried to breathe, but it felt like sucking in inside a plastic bag, her nose and throat closed up, choking her. Pain swept through her skull, as if the contents of her brain were pushing against the bone, expanding like a bag of popcorn in an oven.

Danny pushed her away and flicked the visor shut again. A cold flow of oxygen fed up through the vents and Aggie coughed.

'You're crazy.' Danny wheezed, smacking the side of the door. 'You could have killed yourself!'

'I don't care.' Aggie coughed, her vision blurring. 'I don't care.'

Suddenly a great crack thundered from across the base. The dome split in two, sending shards of Plexi floating down over the bays. The launcher jerked and started to tip to one side. Seb was by the conveyor, still struggling with Rix.

'Quickly,' the computer said. 'It's falling. Get Seb.'

Danny rushed and grabbed Rix's other arm, dragging

him forwards.

The platform was rocking now; the great metal struts built into the rock creaked as they were exposed like long silver tendons, the only things holding the giant platform together.

'It's going to go,' Aggie whispered.

A growl vibrated over the rumble of the ground, followed by a scream that could have come from an animal. Rix pulled away from Seb's grip and lunged towards Aggie.

In a blur, Danny leapt away from the capsule and grabbed Rix's utility belt. Rix cried out and lashed at Danny as the ground started to disintegrate around them.

Danny turned and locked eyes with Aggie for second. Then he jumped and pulled himself and Rix down over the other side of the gap, back in the direction of the collapsing dome.

'No!' Seb cried and flung an arm out in Danny's direction. 'No!'

Danny and Rix tumbled slowly back down into the rubble of the crumbling Cargo Bays, until they were just two lights dancing in the darkness. Out of reach.

'NO!' Aggie screamed and screamed, and kicked at Seb wildly as he tried to hold her back.

'Aggie, get in the capsule. Get in the capsule!' he yelled, as the tiny metal pod fought against the mechanism, keen to fly off out into space with its load. Aggie winced as Seb's grip bit into her shoulders, but she just stayed there, looking into the distance as the light of Danny's lamp vanished into the dust.

'I can't hold it much longer,' Celeste's voice vibrated. 'It's going to collapse.'

'We can't leave him!' she cried, kicking and pulling against Seb. 'Let me go!'

With one last cry, Seb hauled Aggie over the threshold and slammed her into the tiny space inside.

'Aggie, he's gone. I'm sorry, he's gone,' Seb said grabbing her waist and pulling her close. 'And we'll be gone too if we don't— I'm sorry, we need to go.'

'I'm going to secure the door now.' Celeste's voice wobbled in Aggie's helmet comms. She whipped her head around, checking inside the tiny capsule, looking for something. She didn't find it.

'Celeste!' she cried. 'There are no Ethers in here. How can you …?' The realization struck her like a shard of Plexi in her side. She would be losing two friends today.

Something like hysteria started to grip her. Danny and Celeste. Neither of them were ever planning to come home. They'd said nothing to her; they'd just waited until she was trapped. It was too much to take. Suddenly Aggie didn't care about living. She didn't want to go back to Earth without them, she wanted to stay here and die with Danny by her side, in a comforting bubble of Celeste's warmth. To keep on living was the worst option – surely they could see that?

Aggie felt the mechanisms inside the cabin begin to grind. 'Hold on tight,' Seb whispered, grabbing her and dragging her with him into the far corner of the tiny cabin.

'Aggie,' Celeste whispered softly though her helmet

comms. 'You need to be strong on the inside. You can't be strong on the outside because you're human.' The Celesteness of the words made her smile.

Aggie felt the capsule start to move slowly, further and further up the track to the launcher. Suddenly, the passing static-like warmth that indicated Celeste's presence flickered and disappeared. It left a gaping hole in Aggie's chest.

Sobbing pathetically, she dug her head into Seb's shoulder, grabbed his arm and pulled it around her, and clung to him as if he was all she had left in the world. Right now, he was.

She felt her stomach drop as the giant capsule was catapulted into the depths of space at inhuman speeds. She felt her head swim with the Gs and spots began to float before her eyes.

'What have we done?' she sobbed, as the edges of her vision started to turn black.

'What was right,' Seb replied.

Then Aggie's world went black.

Epilogue

Earth

Lunar Inc. Skyport, European Mountains

First there was light, then pain, then nothing but a vast ceiling of blue.

Sky.

Aggie took a breath. It smelt rich and green and alive.

Earth.

The smoking capsule bleeped and shuddered. Seb coughed and moaned on the ground beside her, still holding Aggie's hand so tightly he nearly snapped her fingers.

Footsteps beat against the tarmac. Unfamiliar voices drifted back and forth. Bee stings in her arms. Pressure on her wrists.

The Moon hung like a ghost above them. A great black scar stretched across its pale grey face. Tiny specks of shuttles buzzed around it like flies.

A tear fell away down Aggie's cheek.

They were alive.

A spinning, crunching sound rattled over the skyport, followed by a guttural roar. The medics were pushed back, buffeted by the wind.

Aggie watched a large, grey wedge hover over the tarmac, then land, badly, with a screech of metal. A red cross was painted on its hull. A rescue shuttle.

The fans stopped.

The medics ran, not to Aggie, but to the people emerging from the shuttle's battered doors. A girl in yellow – wearing the red cross badge of the ERMs – held a man. As they staggered down the ramp she shouted for the medics to run faster – the man didn't have much time.

His overall was the colour of the sky.

Acknowledgements

Firstly, to my wonderful family, for always being the best, most encouraging and slightly loopy people: Mum, Dad, Smell, Nan, Grandpa, Gran, Granddad and all the crazy Cross Clan. To my friends, the Uni Crew and the Mansfield girls, for giving me SO many stories over the years and, more recently, for putting up with my constant moaning about 'that book' – I'm mainly looking at you Jo, Lorne and Neds.

To my Stevie, for all the tough love, and for making me believe I could do it when I insisted that I couldn't. I promise to buy you that jet ski one day.

To Sandra, my awesome agent, for seeing the potential in the Frankenstein's monster of a manuscript (I apologize AGAIN for my grammar), and to Barry and all the other chickens in the coop, for taking it under their wing. In particular, to Rachel L, my very own Celeste IRL, who pretty much deserves to have her name on the front cover too.

To Dr Dave Clements at Imperial College, for all the advice about living on the Moon that I mostly ignored (sorry Dave!). To Luke Speed, and Andy, Bradley and the gang at Altitude Films, for their support and feedback. And last but by no means least, to the staff at Starbucks Hornchurch, for keeping me cabin-fever free and appropriately caffeinated.

Thank you all to the Moon and back, you're all totally cosmic!

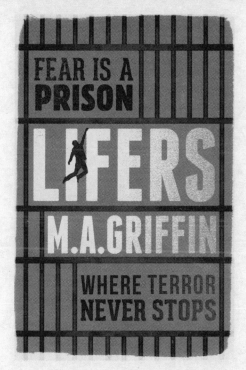

LIFERS by M. A. GRIFFIN

Fear haunts the streets of Manchester: a schoolgirl has disappeared.

Preston is drawn to investigate, exploring the city in the hunt for his missing friend. Deep in the bowels of a secret scientific institute, he discovers a sinister machine, used to banish criminal teenagers for their offences. Captured and condemned to the cavernous dimension, Preston is determined to escape – but this is no ordinary jail.

Friendships are forged and lives lost in a reckless battle for freedom, revenge – and revolution.

Paperback, ISBN 978-1-910002-25-4, £7.99 • ebook, ISBN 978-1-910002-26-1, £7.99

TRY ANOTHER GREAT BOOK FROM CHICKEN HOUSE

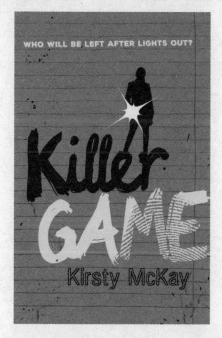

KILLER GAME by KIRSTY MCKAY

This is Killer, and you have all been invited to play. And you should play like your life depends on it.

At Cate's isolated boarding school, Killer Game is a tradition. Only a select few are invited to play. They must avoid being 'killed' by a series of thrilling pranks, and identify the 'murderer'.

But this time it's different: the game stops feeling fake and starts getting dangerous – and Cate's the next target. Can they find the culprit . . . before it's too late?

> 'There are plenty of twists and dark humorous turns in this thriller . . .'
> THE TELEGRAPH ONLINE

> '. . . will keep readers on edge . . .'
> THE GUARDIAN CHILDREN'S BOOKS

Paperback, ISBN 978-1-909489-11-0, £6.99 • ebook, ISBN 978-1-910002-82-7, £6.99

TRY ANOTHER GREAT BOOK FROM CHICKEN HOUSE

THE ROAR by EMMA CLAYTON

Twins Mika and Ellie live behind a wall, safe from the plague animals that live beyond.

Or so they've been told.

But when one of them disappears and the other is recruited into a weird game, they begin to discover that their concrete world is built on lies.

Determined to find each other again, they go in search of the truth.

'Fresh and exciting . . .'
EOIN COLFER

perback, ISBN: 978-1-910002-03-2, £6.99 • ebook, ISBN 978-1-910002-04-9, £6.99